The Further Adventures of

Beowulf

The Further Adventures of

BEOWULF

Champion of Middle Earth

Edited by Brian M. Thomsen

Including the prose translation of the Beowulf epic
THE DEEDS OF BEOWULF
&
All-New Tales of His Heroic Exploits by
Jeff Grubb • Lynn Abbey • Wolfgang Baur • Ed Greenwood

CARROLL & GRAF PUBLISHERS
NEW YORK

THE FURTHER ADVENTURES OF BEOWULF
Champion of Middle Earth

Carroll & Graf Publishers
An Imprint of Avalon Publishing Group, Inc.
245 West 17th Street, 11th Floor
New York, NY 10011

AVALON
publishing group incorporated

Copyright © 2006 by Brian M. Thomsen

"Beowulf and the City of the Dark Elves" © 2006 by Jeff Grubb
"Beowulf and the Titan" © 2006 by Lynn Abbey
"Beowulf and the Attack of the Trolls" © 2006 by Wolfgang Baur
"Beowulf and the Wraith" © 2006 Ed Greenwood

First Carroll & Graf edition 2006

Library of Congress Cataloging-in-Publication Data is available.

ISBN-13: 978-0-78671-847-4
ISBN-10: 0-7867-1847-1

9 8 7 6 5 4 3 2 1

Interior design by *Ivelisse Robles Marrero*

Printed in the United States of America
Distributed by Publishers Group West

For the original fanticists
And those to whom they have passed the mantle
of storyteller

TABLE OF CONTENTS

Beowulf and the Master of His Critics

Beowulf and the Wraith

Beowulf and the Master of His Critics

. . . But first, a few words of introduction

⚜

When we think of heroes of the old world, what are some of the names that come to mind?

Hercules.

Perseus.

Odysseus.

Aeneas.

All larger than life fellows of Latin and Greek literature.

But what of our native tongue and literary lineage?

Only one name comes to mind.

The first hero of English literature.

The warrior Beowulf.

BEOWULF THE EPIC—
ITS HISTORY

Beowulf is one of the oldest surviving epic poems in what we have come to recognize as an early form of the English language.

In the poem, the eponymous Beowulf, a hero of a Germanic tribe from southern Sweden (called the Geats), travels to Denmark to help defeat a terrible monster that has been cannibalistically reeking havoc on the locals. The English people are descendants of Germanic tribes called the Angles, Saxons, and Jutes. Jutes and northern Saxon tribes came from what is now southern Denmark and northern Germany.

But why was a poem about Danish and Swedish kings and heroes preserved in what is now Great Britain?

The same reason Virgil drew from Homer, as evidenced by the overlapping of archetypal stories, plots, and characters in the *Aeniad*.

It's a literary embrace of an ancestral tradition.

Thus, the Beowulf author tells a story about the old days in their homeland, the acts of heroism that are part of their lineage.

The poem is obviously a work of fiction, "fantasticly" embellished but nonetheless based in the historic canon of known events. It makes mention of actual historic moments, such as the raid by King Hygelac into Frisia (ca. 516 AD), and several of the characters featured in *Beowulf* (e.g., Hrothgar, Hrothulf, and Ohthere) and some of the events also appear in early Scandinavian sources, such as the *Prose Edda, Gesta Danorum*, the *fornaldarsagas*, etc. (In these sources, especially the Hrólf Kraki, the tales deal with the same tribes of people in Denmark and Sweden.) As a result, it is reasonable to conclude that many of the credible people and events depicted in the epic were probably real, dating from between 450 AD and 600 AD in Denmark and southern Sweden (Geats and Swedes). As far as Sweden is concerned, this dating has been confirmed by archaeological excavations of the barrows indicated by Snorri Sturluson and by Swedish tradition as the graves of Eadgils and Ohthere in Uppland. Like the Finnsburg Fragment and several shorter surviving poems, *Beowulf* has consequently been used as a source of information about Scandinavian personalities such as Eadgils and Hygelac, and about continental Germanic personalities such as Offa, king of the continental Angles.

The precise date of the manuscript is debated, but most estimates place it close to 1000. Traditionally the poem's date of composition has been estimated, on linguistic and other grounds, as approximately 650–800. More recently, doubt has been raised about the linguistic criteria for dating, with some scholars suggesting a date as late as the eleventh century, near the time of the manuscript's copying, probably by a Christian scribe who may or may not have further influenced the text. The poem appears in what is today called the *Beowulf* manuscript or Nowell Codex (British Library MS Cotton Vitellius A.xv).

BEOWULF AND MIDDLE EARTH

It is in *Beowulf* that Middle Earth first makes its appearance in literature.

J. R. Tolkien was a wonk for ancient variations of English and also one of the world's foremost experts in this area of linguistics.

In Tolkien wonk-speak:

"Middle Earth came from Midgard which was the common English transliteration of Old Norse Miogzror, Midjungards (Gothic), Middangeard (Old English), and Mittilagart (Old High German), from Proto-Germanic *medja-garda* (*meddila-*, *medjan-*, projected PIE *medhyo-gharto*), and as a result, is an old Germanic name for our world, the places inhabited by men, with the literal meaning 'middle enclosure.'"

In Middle English, the name became Middel-erde and resulted in the modern name Middle Earth.

Or more simply:

Middle Earth is another name for Midgard, which is the domain where men dwell in ancient Norse mythology, which was the source for the original Beowulf tale. It is located somewhere between the realm of the gods and the realm of the underworld (more simply in Judeo-Christian terms—heaven and hell).

Or in the quasi-scholarly parlance of Wikipedia:

"Midgard is the realm of the humans in Norse mythology. Pictured as placed somewhere in the middle of Yggdrasil, Midgard is surrounded by a world of water or ocean, which is impassable. The ocean is inhabited by the great sea serpent Jormungand, who is so huge that he encircles the world entirely, grasping his own tail. In Norse mythology, *Miogzror* became applied to a fortress in the middle of the world, and *Mannheim* 'the home of men' was used to refer to the entire world (there is no direct relation to the German city of Mannheim, which is attested from the 8th century, named after an early settler called *Manno*). The association with *earth* (OE *eor_e*) in Middle English *Middel-erde* is by popular etymology; the continuation of *geard* 'enclosure' is *yard*.

"It is depicted as an intermediate world between heaven (Asgard) and hell (Nifelheim or Hel). Thus it is part of a triad of upper (Heaven), middle (Earth), and lower (Underworld). It was said to have been formed from the flesh and blood of the frost giant Ymir, his flesh constituting the land and his blood the oceans, and was connected to Asgard by the Bifrost Bridge, guarded by Heimdall.

"According to legend, Midgard will be destroyed in Ragnarok, the battle at the end of the world. Jormungand will arise from the ocean, poisoning the land and sea with his venom and causing the sea to rear up and lash against the land. The final battle will take place on the plain of Vigrond, following which Midgard and almost all life on it will be destroyed, with the earth sinking into the sea.

"The concept of Midgard occurs many times in Middle English (as *Middel-erde*). The name was popularized in the form Middle-earth by J. R. R. Tolkien, a noted Old English scholar. He drew heavily upon Middle Earth and other Germanic concepts in his fictional works. Consider this fragment in the Crist poem of

Cynewulf, which references *Middangeard* and someone named *Éarendel* (The connection with Tolkien's character Eärendil is not accidental):

Éala Éarendel / Engla Beorhtast
Ofer Middangeard / Monnum sended
Hail Earendel / Brightest of angels
Above the Middle Earth / Sent unto men

"The name *middangeard* occurs half a dozen times in the Anglo-Saxon epic poem Beowulf, and is the same word as Midgard in Old Norse. The term is equivalent in meaning to the Greek term Oikoumene, as referring to the known and inhabited world. It is consistently misspelled as 'Middle Earth' by journalists."

Whew!

Ergo, Midgard/Middle Earth is also the setting for *Beowulf* (as mentioned specifically in the text no less than six times), a manuscript that Tolkien spent many hours studying, and, as it turns out, being inspired by, specifically in terms of his own creative fictional output.

BEOWULF AND TOLKIEN

Indeed, of Tolkien's academic publications, the 1936 lecture "Beowulf: the monsters and the critics" is credited with having had a lasting influence on *Beowulf* research, in fact changing the course of criticism on this epic work, and generally elevating it from the status of an incidental vestige of early literature to a work deemed worthy of the label of literature in and of itself. Tolkien utilizes an extended metaphor of a partially destroyed tower that has been primarily examined in terms of its contents, construction, the land it has been built on, its degree of degradation, etc., everything except an examination of it as a tower. Up until that time, the examination of the *Beowulf* poem had been in terms of linguistic evolution, poetic syntax, and possible hints to a better understanding of the anthropological/cultural milieu that produced it.

In essence, prior to Tolkien, no one seriously looked at *Beowulf* in terms of what it really was—an epic poem of mythological heroism.

Indeed many of the archetypes and creatures that later would dwell in the pages of *The Lord of the Rings* also had their antecedents in the lines of *Beowulf*.

Beowulf, like other classical period works of storytelling (like the works of Homer in Greek and Virgil in Latin), purports to be history as much as invented narrative. They are all tales of a previous age where men came to prominance and in many ways replaced the gods and other fantastic beings as the lords of this dominion.

Tolkien, as evidenced by references in his correspondences, felt the same for the setting of *The Lord of the Rings*. Indeed, Middle Earth is only a single part of the world of Arda (Earth), and the chronological setting of his epic tale is actually many years ago in our own past, thus casting it in the same pseudohistorical mode as the *Odyssey*, *Aeniad*, and, indeed, *Beowulf*.

It is quite fair to say that no one has done a better job of embroidering this midlevel world between good and evil, gods and demons, than the old Oxford don J. R. R. Tolkien, and though he has every right to claim ownership to all of his characters and the adventures they partook in . . . the actual world of Middle Earth is as preexistent and as much a part of the public domain as the Garden of Eden, and probably a much more exciting and fertile place for adventure storytelling to boot.

WHICH BRINGS US TO THESE NEW ADVENTURES

But the Beowulf story as it exists is quite incomplete.

Like the legendary labors of Hercules, we the readers are

only treated to a few chosen excerpts of his heroic career, and one can easily assume that Grendel was not his first feat of monstrous interventionism, nor do we really believe that life became boring betwixt the slaying of the mother and the meeting with the dragon.

Such things are not possible for heroes of legend.

Indeed there were still many other of "that woeful breed" left to slay, as related in the following passage (from the Gummere translation):

Grendel this monster grim was called,
march-riever mighty, in moorland living,
in fen and fastness; fief of the giants
the hapless wight a while had kept
since the Creator his exile doomed.
On kin of Cain was the killing avenged
by sovran God for slaughtered Abel.
Ill fared his feud, and far was he driven,
for the slaughter's sake, from sight of men.
Of Cain awoke all that woeful breed,
Etins and elves and evil-spirits,
as well as the giants that warred with God
weary while: but their wage was paid them!

This passage raises numerous possibilities for both the hero and his legacy.

On the one hand it sets the mythos within a Judeo-Christian legacy with references to Genesis and the sin of Cain, a canon of beliefs that was probably not conveniently contemporaneous in situational locale with the events of the heroic tale (once again raising the possibility of a later "modernization" of the work by a Christian scribe saving civilization as it was known in the British Isles).

And on the other hand it incorporates into this mythos the pagan and heathen myths and creatures of Northern folklore and magic, many of which managed to survive the purging of these soon-to-be outlawed beliefs by firmly taking root in alternate forms of cultural expression (alternate meaning something other than religion), and indeed remained around to provide the foundation for the rich canon of fantasy literature that was brought into full and brightest bloom during the age of Tolkien and further forward in all forms of media including not just novels and poems, but role-playing games, comic books, movies, etc.

So what of these other dark foes, the etins (trolls), elves, evil spirits, and giants?

Did Beowulf slay them, too?

Of course he did, and probably many others as well.

And where these exploits might have been told around a fire late at night after a particular celebration (or perhaps just as an excuse to bring everyone in closer on a cold winter's night) during the days of yore before the coming of the great gods of radio, TV, and DVD, now they are related via the printed page for you, gentle reader, to enjoy.

It is impossible to imagine a dull moment in the life of a hero such as Beowulf.

That is why he is really the first true champion of Middle Earth.

Brian M. Thomsen
April 2006

The Deeds of Beowulf
An English Epic of the Eighth Century

Translated into prose by John Earle

A NOTE ON THE TEXT

This is a slightly modernized/regularized version of John Earle's 1892 prose translation The Deeds of Beowulf: An English Epic of the Eighth Century. *Though it was not the first prose version of the Beowulf text, it was indeed one of the first intended for a general audience of readers outside of the ranks of scholars and poetry aficionados.*

The original manuscript becomes fragmentary about two-thirds of the way through–missing sections are either noted or synopsized.

The First Part

Prologue. The chivalry of the Danish Empire. The coming of Scyld and his glorious career. The birth of Beowulf and the exemplary pursuits of his youth. The passing of Scyld.

What ho! We have heard tell the grandeur of the imperial kings of the spear-bearing Danes in former days, how those Athelings promoted bravery. Often did Scyld of the Sheaf wrest from harrying bands, from many tribes, their convivial seats: dread of him fell upon warriors, whereas at birth a lonely foundling: —of all that humble a beginning he lived to experience solace: he waxed great under the heavens, he flourished with trophies, till that everyone of the neighboring people over the sea were constrained to obey him, and pay tribute as was expected to a good king.

To him was born a son to succeed him, a young prince in the palace, to who god sent for the people's comfort. God knew the hard calamity, what these people had already endured when they were without a king for a long while: and in consideration thereof the Lord of Life, the ruler of Glory accorded to them a time of prosperity.

Beowulf was renowned, his fame sprang wide: the heir of Scyld in the Scedelands. So ought a young chief to work with his wealth, with gracious largesse, while in his father's nurture so that in his riper age willing comrades may in return stand by him at the coming of war, and that men may do his bidding.

Eminence must, in every nation, be attained by deeds worthy of PRAISE.

† † †

As for Scyld, he departed, the destined hour, full of exploit, to go into the Master's keeping. They then carried him forth to the shore of the sea, his faithful comrades, as he himself had requested, while he with his words held sway as lord of the Scyld- ings: dear chief of the land he had long tenure of power.

There at harbor stood the ship with ringed prow, glistening fresh, and outward bound: convoy for a prince. Down laid they there the loved chief, dispenser of jewels, on the lap of the ship, the illustrious deceased by the mast. There as store of precious things, ornaments from remote parts, brought together: never heard I of craft comelier fitted with slaughter weapons and campaigning harness, with bills and breast-mail: —in his keeping lay a multi- tude of treasures, which were to pass with him far away into the watery realm. Not at all with less gifts, less stately opulence, did they outfit him than those had done, who at the first had sent him forth, lone over the wave, when he was an infant. Furthermore they set up by him a gold-wrought banner, high over his head: they let the helm bear him, gave him over to ocean; sad was their soul, mourning their mood.

Men do not know what to say of a sooth, not heads of Halls, men of mark under heaven, who received that burden!

1.

King Hrothgar, his popularity. The building of Heorot and the happy life of the court. Grendel.

Then was in the stronghold Beowulf of the Scyldings, the dear king of his people, for many years famous among the nations—his father was gone otherwhere, patriarch from family sat—till in succession to him was born the lofty Healfdene: he governed while he lived, old and warlike, contented Scyldings. To him four children, one after another, awoke in the world: Heorogar commander of armies and Hrothgar and Halga the good (I heard that Elan queen of Ongentheow was consort of the warlike Scylfing).

To Hrothgar was given martial spirit, warlike ambition: insomuch that his cousins gladly took him for leader, until the younger generation grew up, a mighty regiment of new clansmen. It occurred to him that he would give orders for men to construct a hall-building, a great mead-house, greater than the children of men had ever heard tell of; and that there within he would freely deal out to young and old what God should give him, tend to people's land and the lives of men.

Thus I heard of work widely proclaimed to many a tribe throughout this world, to make a fair gathering place of people. The plan was in good time accomplished, with a quickness surprising to most men: thus it was soon all ready, the greatest of hall-buildings. He gave it the name of Heorot, he who with his word had wide dominion. He belied not his announcement: —towered aloft, high and with pinnacles spanning the air: awaited the scathing blasts of destructive flame. No appearance was there as yet of knife-hatred starting between son-in-law and father-in-law in revenge of blood.

Then the outcast creature, he who dwelt in darkness with torture for time endured, heard joyance day by day, loud sounding in hall: there was the swough of the harp, the ringing song of the minstrel.

Said one who was skilled to narrate from remote time the primeval condition of men: quoth he—

"The almighty made the earth, the country radiant
with beauty, all the water surrounded, delighting in
Magnificence. He ordained Sun and Moon, luminaries for light to the dwellers on earth and adorned the rustic regions with branches and leaves: life also he created for all the kinds that live and move." Thus they, the warrior-band, in joyance lived in full delight: —Until that one began to work atrocity, a fiend in the hall. The grim visitant was called Grendel, the dread mark-ranger, he who haunted moors, fen, and fastness: —The unblessed man had long time kept the abode of monsters, ever since the creator had proscribed them. On Cain's posterity did the eternal Lord wreak that slaughter, for that Abel. He profited not by that violence: but he banished him far away, the Maker for that crime banished him from mankind. From that origin all strange broods awoke, etins and elves and ogres, as well as giants who warred against God long time: —All he paid them due retribution.

11.

*Grendel, his successful raid. The dejection of Hrothgar
and his court.*

He set out then as soon as night was come, to explore the lofty house: how the mailed Danes had after carousal bestowed themselves in it.

So he found therein a princely troop sleeping after feast: they knew not of sorrow, or desolation of men. The baleful wight, grim and greedy, was ready straight fierce and furious, and in their sleep he seized thirty of the thanes: thence hurried him back, yelling over his prey, to go to his home with the war-spoils and reach his habitation. Then was in the dawning and with early day the war-craft of Grendel plain to the grooms: then was upraised in lieu of the previous festivity the voice of weeping, a great cry in the morning. The illustrious ruler, the honored prince, sat woebegone: majestic rage he held, he endured sorrow for his thanes:— since they had surveyed the track of the monster, of the accursed goblin; —that contest was too severe, horrible, and prolonged.

It was not a longer space, but the interval of one night that he again perpetrated a huger carnage: and he thought not of it—outrage and atrocity: he was too fixed in those things.

Then was it not hard to find some who sought a resting-place elsewhere more at large, a bed among the castle-bowers, when to them was manifested and plainly declared by conspicuous proof the malice of the hell-thane; —whoever had once escaped the fiend did from thenceforward hold himself farther aloof and closer. So domineered and nefariously warred he single foe against them all, until that best of houses stood empty.

The time was long: twelve winters space did the friend of the Scyldings suffer indignity, woes of every kind, unbounded sorrows: and so in process of time it became openly known to the sons of men through ballads in lamentable wise, that Grendel warred continually against Hrothgar: he waged malignant hostilities, violence and feud, many seasons, unremitting strife: he would not have peace with any man of the Danish power, or remove the lifebale, or compound for tribute; nor were any of the thanes worthy compensation at the hands of the destroyer; the foul ruffian, a dark shadow of death, was pursuing the venerable and the youthful alike. He prowled about and lay in wait; at nights he continually held the misty moors; —men do not know in what direction hell's agents move in their rounds.

Many were the atrocities which the foe of mankind, the grisly prowler, oft accomplished, hard indignities, —Heorot he occupied, the richly decorated hall, in dark nights—yet was he by no means able to come near the throne, scared God, nor did he share the sentiment thereof.

That was a huge affliction for the friend of the Scyldings, heartbreaking. Many a time and oft did the realm sit in conclave; they mediated on a remedy, what course it were best for them, soul-burdened men, to take against these awful horrors. Sometimes they vowed at idol fanes, honors of sacrifice; with words they prayed that the Goblin-vanquisher would afford them relief against huge oppressions. Such was their custom, heathens' religion; they thought of hell in their imagination; they were not aware of the maker, the judge of actions, they knew not God the Governor, nor did they at all understand how to glorify the Crowned Head of the heavens, the Ruler of glory. It is woe for him who is impelled by headlong perversity to plunge his soul into the gulf of fire; not to believe in consolation nor in any way turn: —well is it for him who is permitted, after death-day, to visit the Lord, and claim sanctuary in the Father's arms.

III.

The voyage of the hero. A parley.

Thus was the son of Healfdene perpetually tossed with the trouble of the time; the sapient man was unable to avert the woe. Too heavy, horrible, and protracted was the struggle which had overtaken that people; tribulation cruel, hugest of nocturnal pests.

That in his distant home learnt a thane of Hygelac's a brave man among the Goths; he learnt the deeds of Grendel; he was of mankind strongest in might in the day of this life; he was of noble birth and of robust growth. He ordered a wave traveler, a good one, to be prepared for him; said he would pass over the swan road and visit the gallant king, the illustrious ruler, inasmuch as he was in need of men. That adventure was little grudged him by sagacious men, though he was dear to them; they egged on the direful spirit, they observed auguries. The brave man had selected champions of the Leeds of the Goths, the keenest who he could find; with fourteen in company he took to ship;—a swain for pilot, a water-skilled man, pointed out the landmarks.

Time went on; the floater was on the waves, the boat under the cliff. Warriors ready mounted on the prow; currents eddied, surf against the beach; lads bore into the ship's lap bright apparel, gallant harness of war; the men, the brave men of adventure, shoved off the tight-timbered craft. So the foamy-necked floater went forth over the swelling ocean urged by the wind, most like to a bird; till that in due time, on the next day, the curly-stemmed cruiser had made such way that the voyagers saw land, sea-cliffs gleaming, hills towering, headlands stretching out to sea; then was the voyage accomplished, the water-passage ended. Then lightly up the Weder Leeds and sprang shore, they made fast the sea-wood, they shook out their sarks, their war-weeds, they thanked God that their seafaring had been easy.

Then from his rampart did the Scyldings' warden, he bulwark bright shields, accoutrements ready for action; curiosity urged him with impassioned thoughts to learn who those men were. Off he set then to the shore, riding on horseback, thane of Hrothgar; powerfully he brandished a huge lance in his hands, and he demanded with authoritative words—"who are ye arm-bearing men with mail-coats, who have come thus with proud ship over the watery high-way, hither over the billows? Long time have I been in fort, stationed on the extremity of the country; I have kept the coast guard, that on the land of the Danes no enemy with ship-harrying might not be able to do hurt: —never have shield-bearing men more openly attempted to land here; nor do ye know beforehand the password of our warriors, the confidential token of kinsmen. I never saw, of earls upon ground, a finer figure in harness than is one of yourselves. He is no mere good man bedizened with armor, unless his look belies him, his unique aspect. Bow I am bound to know your nationality, before ye on your way hence as explorers at large proceed any further into the land of the Danes. Now ye foreigners, mariners of the sea, ye hear my plain meaning; haste is best to let me know whence your comings are."

IV.

Beowulf explains their visit to the Warden's satisfaction. Thereupon he guides their march to Heorot. The Warden returns.

To him the chiefest gave answer; the captain of the band unlocked the treasure of words: "We are people of Gothic race, and hearth-fellow of Hygelac. My father was celebrated among the nations, a noble commander by the name of Ecgtheow; he lived to see many years, before he departed an aged man out of his mansion; he is quickly remembered by every worshipful man all over the world. We with friendly intent have come to visit thy lord, the son of Healfdene, the guardian of his people; be thou good to us with instructions! We have for the illustrious prince of the Danes a great message; there is no need to be dark about the matter, as I suppose. Thou knows if it is so as we have heard say for a truth, that among the Scyldings some strange depredator, a mysterious author of deeds, in the darkness of night inflicts in horrible wise monstrous atrocity, indignity, and havoc. Of this I can, in all sincerity of heart, teach Hrothgar a remedy; how he, so wise and good, shall overpower the enemy; if for him the fight of afflictions was ever destined to take a turn, better times to come again, and the seethings of anguish grow calmer; or else for ever here-after tolleth a time of tribulation, sore distress, so long as the best of houses reset there upon her eminence."

The Warden addressed them, where he sat on his horse, an officer undaunted: "Of every particular must a sharp esquire know the certainty as to words and works—anyone who hath sense of duty. I gather from what I hear that this friendly band to the lord of the Scyldings. March ye forward bearing weapons and weeds, I will guide you: likewise I will command my kinsmen thanes honorably to keep against every foe your vessel, the newly dight, the boat on the beach: until the neck-laced craft shall bear back again over the water-streams her dear lord to Wedermark. To such a benign adventurer is it given that he passed unscathed through the encounter of battle."

They proceeded then on their march; the vessel remained still, rode on her cable, the wide-bosomed ship, at anchor fast; the boar-figures shone, over the cheek-guards; bedecked with gold, ornate and hard-welded; the farrow kept guard. In fighting mood they raged along, the men pushed forward; downhill they ran together, until they could see the hall structure, gallant and god-adorned; that was to dwellers on earth the most celebrated of all mansions under the sky, that in which the Ruler dwelt; the gleam of it shot over many lands. Then did the warrior point out to them the court of the valiant, which was now conspicuous; —that they could go straight to it. Like a man of war, he wheeled about his horse, and spoke a parting word; "It is time for me to go; may the all wielding Father graciously keep you safe in adventures! I will to the sea, to keep guard against hostile force."

V.

Arrival and accost. Beowulf sends in his name.

The street was stone-paved; the path guided the banded men. The war-corset shone, hard, hand-locked; the polished ring-iron sang in its meshes, when they in grim harness now came marching to the Hall. The sea-weary men set down their broad shields, bucklers mortal hard, against the terrace of that mansion. Then they seated themselves on the bench; their mailcoats rang harness of warriors; —the spears stood, sea-men's artillery, stacked together, ash-timber with tip of grey; the iron troop was equipped worthily.

Then a proud officer there questioned the martial crew as to their kindred: —"Whence bring ye pile of war shafts? I am Hrothgar's herald and esquire. Never saw I foreigners, so many men, loftier looking. I think that ye for daring, not at all of desperate fortune, but for courageous enterprise, have come to visit Hrothgar."

To him then with gallant bearing answered the proud leader of the Wederas; words spoke back, firm under helmet: —"We are Hygelac's table-fellows; my name is Beowulf. I will expound mine errand to the son of Healfdene, to the illustrious prince, to thy lord, if he will deign us that we may approach him so good."

Wulfgar addressed them—that was a lead of the Wendlas; his courage had been witnessed by man, his valor and wisdom: — "There now will I ask the Friend of the Dane, the Scyldings' lord, the ring-dispenser, according as thou dost petition, the illustrious chief will I ask concerning thy visit; and to thee promptly declare the answer, which the brave prince is please to give me."

Thereupon he returned briskly to where Hrothgar sat, old and hoary, with his guard of warriors: he went with gallant bearing till he stood before the shoulders of the Danish prince; he knew the custom of nobility. Wulfgar addressed himself to his liege lord: "Here are arrived, come from far, over the circuit of ocean, men of the Goths: the companions name their chief Beowulf. They make petition that they, my prince, may be permitted to exchange discourse with thee: do not thou award them a refusal of thy conversation, benignant Hrothgar! They by their war-harness appear worthy of the reverence of earls; certainly the chief is a valiant man, he who has conducted those martial comrades hither."

VI.

The old king knows a lot about him, and orders him to be admitted. Beowulf explains his visit and enterprizeth the battle to fight the foe. He will remove the scourge, or die in the attempt.

Hrothgar, crown of Scyldings, uttered speech; "I knew him when he was a page. His good old father was Ecgtheow by name; to whose home Hrthel of the Goths gave over his only daughter; it is his offspring surely, his grown-up son, that is hither come, come to visit a loyal friend. Sure enough they did say that—the sailors who carried thither for compliment the presents to the Goths—that he hath thirty men's strength in his handgrip, valiant campaigner. Him hath holy God of high grace sent to us, sent to the western Danes, as I hope, against Grendel's terror; I must proffer the brave man treasures for his great heartedness. Be thou full of alacrity, request the banded friends to enter, one and all, into my presence. Say to them moreover expressly with words, that they are welcome visitors to the Danish leads." Then to the door of the hall Wulfgar went he announced his message:—"To you I am commanded to say by my chieftain the lord of the eastern Danes, that he knoweth your noble ancestry, and ye to him are, over the sea-waves, men of hardihood, welcome hither. Now ye can go, in your warlike equipage, with helm on head, to the presence of Hrothgar; leave the war-boards, here to abide, and the wooden battle-shifts till the parley is over."

Up then arose the prince: about him many a trooper, a splendid band of thanes; some remained there, they kept the armor, as their brave captain bade. They formed all together, as Wulfgar showed the way, under the roof under his helmet, till he took his stand in the royal chamber. Beowulf uttered a speech— on him his byrnie shone, a curious network linked by cunning device of the artificer—"To Hrothgar hail! I am Hygelac's kinsman and cousin-thane; I have undertaken many exploits in youngsterhood. To me on my native soil the affair of Grendel became openly known; seafaring men say that this hall does stand, fabric superb, of every trooper empty and useless, as soon as the light of evening under the cope of heaven is hidden from view. Then did my people, the best of them, sagacious fellows, O royal Hrothgar, incense me that I should visit thee; because they knew the strength of my might; they had themselves been spectators when I came off my campaign battered by foes, where I bound five monsters, humbled the troll brood; and in the waves I slew sea demons in the nighttime, I ran narrow risks, avenged the grievance of the Wederas—they had been acquainted with grief—a grinding I gave the spoilers; —and now against Grendel I am bound, against that formidable one, single-handed, to champion the quarrel against the giant, wherefore I will now petition thee, prince of the glorious Danes, thou roof-tree of the Scyldings, one petition; that thou refuse me not, oh thou shelter of warriors, thou imperial lord of nations, now I have come from such a distance, that I may have the task alone—I and my band of earls, this knot of hardly men—to purge Heorot. I have learnt, too, that the terrible one out of bravado despises weapons; I therefore will forgo the same—as I hope that Hygelac my prince may be to me of mood benign, —that I bear not sword or broad shield, or yellow buckler, to the contest; but with handgrip I undertake to encounter the enemy, and contend for life, foe to foe; there shall he whom death take resign himself to the doom of the Lord.

"I supposed that he will, if he can have his way, in the hall of battle devour fearlessly the men of the Goths, just as he often did the power of the Hreth-men thou wilt not need to cover my head with a mound, but he will have me al blood-besprent, if death take me; he will bear away the gory corpse with intent to feast upon it, the solitary ranger will eat it remorselessly, will stain the moor-swamps; no need wilt thou have to care any longer for the disposal of my body. Send to Hygelac, if Hild take me, the matchless armor that protects my breast, bravest of jackets;—that is, relic of Hrethlas's a work of Weland's. would goeth ever as she is bound.

VII.

Hrothgar embraces his visitor's offer, and pours out the take of his misery. The newcomers are feasted in the hall.

Hrothgar, king of Scylydings, uttered speech: "For pledged rescue thou, Beowulf my friend, and at honor's call, hast come to visit us. Thy father did fight out mighty feud; he was the banesman of healthlaf among the Wylfings: then the nation could not keep him for dread of invasion. There from he went over the yeasty waves to visit the Southern folk of the Danes, of the honorable Scyldings, at the time when I had just then become king over the Danish folk, and in my prime swayed the jewel-stored treasure-city of heroes: when Heregar my elder brother was dead, no longer living, Halfdene's son. He was better than I! Afterward I composed the feud for money; I sent to the Wylfings over the water's ridge ancient treasures; he swore oaths of fealty to me.

"It is sorrow for me and my soul to tell any mortal man what humiliation, what horrors, Grendel hath brought upon me in Heorot with his malignant stratagems. My hall-troop, my warrior band, is reduced to nothing; wyrd hath swept them away in the hideous visitation of Grendel. God unquestionably can arrest the fell destroyer in his doings. Full oft they boasted when refreshed with beer-hall would receive Grendel's onset with clash of swords. Then was this mead-hall at morning-tide, this royal saloon bespattered with gore, at blush of dawn, all the bench-timber was reeking with blood, the hall with deadly gore; so much the less owned I of trusty lieges, of dear nobility, when death had taken those away.

"Sit now to banquet, and merrily share the feast, brave captain, with thy fellows, as thy mind moves thee."

Then, was there for the Goth-men all together, in the beer-hall, a table cleared; there the resolute men went to sit in the pride of their strength. A thane attended to the service; one who bore in his hand a decorated ale-can; he poured forth the sheer nectar. At times a minstrel sang, clear-voiced in Heorot; there was social merriment, a brave company of Danes and Wederas.

VIII.

Unferth the king's orator is jealous. He baits the young adven-turer, and in a scoffing speech dares him to a might-watch for Grendel. Beowulf is angered, and thus he is drawn out to boast of his youthful feats.

Unferth made speech, Ecglf's son; he was not content at the feet of Scydings' lord, broached a quarrel some theme the adventure of Beowulf the high-souled voyager was great despite to him, because he grudged that any other man should ever in the world achieve more exploits under heaven than he himself;—"Art thou that Beowulf, he who strove with Breca on open sea in swimming-match, where ye twain out of bravado explored the floods, and foolhardily in deep water jeopardized your lives? Nor could any man, friend or foe, turn the pair of your arms the awful stream, meted the sea-streets, buffeted with hands, shot over ocean; the deep boiled with waves, a wintry surge. Ye twain in the realm of waters toiled a se 'night; he at swimming outvied thee, had greater force. Then in morning hour the swell cast him ashore on the Heathoram people, whence he made for his own patrimony, dear to his Leeds he made for the land of the Brondings, a fair strong-hold, where he was lord of folk, of city, and of rings. His entire boast to thee-ward, Beanstan's son smoothly fulfilled. Wherefore I anticipate for thee worse luck—though thou wert everywhere doughty in battle-shocks, in grim war-tug—if thou dare bide in Grendel's way a night-long space."

Beowulf son of Ecgtheow uttered speech: "Lo, big things hast thou said, my friend Unferth, beer-exalted, spoken about Breca; hast talked of his adventure! Rightly I claim, that I have proved more sea-power, more buffetings in waves, than any other man. He and I used to talk when we were pages, and we used to brag of this—we were both of us at that time in youngsterhood—how that we two would out on the main and put our lives in jeopardy; and that we matched so. Drawn sword we had, as we at swimming plied, firm in hand: we meant to guard us against the whale-fishes. Not a whit from me could he further fleet on sea-waves, swifter on holm; not from him would I. So we twain kept together in the sea for the space of five nights, till the flood parted us, the seething billows, coldest weather, darkening night, and a fierce wind from the north came dead against us; rough were the waves. The sea-fishes temper was stirred; and then it was that my body-sark, firm, hand-locked, gave me help against the spiteful ones; the plaited war jacket lay about my breast, gold-plated. Me to the bottom dragged a spotty monster, tight the grim thing had me in grip; nevertheless 'twas given me that I got at the vermin with point, with handbill; combat dispatched the might sea-brute by my hand.

IX.

Beowulf continues his story; and tells how he made havoc of the sea-monsters. He waves warm, and flouts the orator. He vows to face Grendel. Restoration of social harmony, whereof the queen is the centre. Hrothgar solemnly commits to Beowulf the night-ward of Heorot.

"As repeatedly as the spiteful assailants shrewdly pressed me, I served them liberally with precious sword as was meet. They did not have their slaughterous revel, the foul brigands, that they should eat me up sitting around their supper, by the floor of the sea; but on the contrary next morning, wounded with weapons along the wreck of the wave, they lay high and dry; by swords they had their quietus, so that never afterwards about the swelling highway should they let seafaring men of their destine course.

"Light came from the East, the bright signal of God; the waves grew calm, so that I was able to see the forelands, the windy walls. Fortune often rescues the warrior, if he is not fated to die; provided that his courage is sound! Anyhow 'twas my good luck, that I slew with the sword nine sea demons. Never did I hear of a harder fight under the heaven's roof in the night time, nor of a man more distressed in ocean streams: howbeit I escaped the clutch of foes with my life, though worn and spent. Me the sea upcast, the swirling flood, upon the land of the Fins, the heaving billow. I never heard say aught by thee of such deadly fightings, sword-clashings; Breca never yet, at war play, not he nor you, deed achieved so valorously with flashing swords—of that I brag not much—though was banesman to thy brother, thy next of kin; for which thou shall in hell damnation deed, though doughty be thy wit. I say to thee of the sooth, thou son of Ecglaf, that never had Grendel the foul ruffian made such a tale of horrors for thy prince, such disgrace in Heorot, if thy courage were, if thy spirit were, so formidable as thou thyself claims. But he hath found out that he need not greatly fear reprisals, grisly edge—clash, from your people, the mighty Scyldings he taketh blackmail, respect no one of the people of the Danes, but make a sport of war, slaughtereth and feasteth: —thought hath he of a fight with the spear-Danes. But no shall the Goth show him erelong puissance and emprize in the way of war. After that, he who can shall go proud into the mead-hall, when over the sons of men the morning light of another day, the sun, with radiance clothed, shall shine from the south."

Then was in bliss the dispenser of wealth, grey-haired and militant; he believed in help; the prince of the glorious Danes, the shepherd of the people, perceived in Beowulf a resolute purpose. There was laughter of mighty men; music sounded; and the words of song were jovial.

Wealhtheow moved forward, Hrothgar's queen, mindful of ceremonies; she greeted in her gold array the men in Hall; and then the noble lady presented the beaker first to the sovereign of the east-Danes, wished him blithe at the banquet, and dear to his Leeds; —he merrily enjoyed the feast and the Hall-cup, valiant king.

Then the Helming princess went the round, to elder and to younger, every part; handed the jeweled cup till the moment came, that she, the diademed queen, with dignity befitting, brought the mead-cup nigh to Beowulf; she greeted the head of the Goths, she thanked God with wise choice of words, for that her desire was come to pass, that she in any warrior believed for remedy of woes. He, the death-doing warrior, accepted the beaker at Wealtheow's hand, and then he descanted, elate for battle; —Beowulf son of Ecgtheow uttered speech: "I undertook that, when I went on board and set out on the sea-boat, with the company of my fellows, that I once for all would work out the will of your Leeds, or fall in the death-struggle, in the grip of the fiend. I am bound as an earl to fulfill the emprize, or in this mead-hall to meet my death-day."

Then was again as was within the hall the lofty word outspoken, the company was happy, the sound was that of a mighty people; until that sudden the son of Healfdene was minded to retire to his nightly rest; he knew that against the high Hall war was determined by the monster, from the time when they could not see the sun's light or shrouding night came over all, and the creatures of darkness came stalking abroad; he warred in obscurity.

All the company arose.

Then did man greet man, Hrothgar greeted Beowulf, bespake him luck, mastery in the house of hospitality; and delivered this speech: "Never before, since I could heave hand and shield, did I trust the guard-house of the Danes to any man, but only to thee now this occasion. Have now and hold the best if houses; resolve on success: show valor a man; be vigilant against the foe! Thou shall not have any desire unfulfilled, if thou that mighty work with life achievest."

X.

Beowulf doffs his armor, and watches unarmed. A point of honor.
His companions sleep.

So Hrothgar, chief of Scyldings, took his departure with retinue of men, out of hall; he was eager to join Wealhtheow his queen and consort. The Glory of kings had—so men told one another—set up a hall-service about the patriarch of the Danes, offered watch against the monster; —assuredly the Gothic Leed with joyous men trusted in valorous might and the smile of Providence.

Then took off him his iron byrnie, helmet from head; delivered to his esquire the richly-dight sword, choicest steel; and charged him with the care of his war-harness. Then did the valiant man Beowulf the Goth utter some vaunting words ere he mounted on bed: "I reckon myself to be in the fury of battle, in warlike feats, no wise below the pretensions of Grendel; for that reason I will not with sword give him his quietus, deprive him of life, although I very well may. Naught knoweth he of those gentle practices, to give and take sword-cuts, to hew the shield; dread though he be in feats of horror: —but we twain shall in the nighttime supersede the blade, if he dare to court war without weapon: and thereafter may the All wise God, the holy Lord, adjudge success on which side so ever may to him appear meet!"

Then the daring warrior laid him down; the pillow received the noggin of the Earl; and round about him many a smart sea-warrior couched to his hall-rest. Not one of them thought that from that place he would ever again visit his own estate, his folk and castle, where he was brought up; but they had been informed that before now a bloody death had to all too much reduced them, the Danish people, in that festive hall. But to them, the Leeds of Wedermark, did the lord grant webs of war-speed, strength and support, that they by the force of one, by his single prowess, should all be victorious over their foe. For a truth it is shown, that the mighty God has governed mankind in every age!

He came in dim night, marching along, ranger of the dark. The defenders slept, they whose duty it was to guard that gabled mansion.

Indeed, all slept but one!

It was very well known to all men that the ruthless destroyer might not be against the will of God and whirl them under darkness; but all the same he, valiant in defiance of the foe, awaited in full-fraught mood the arbitrage of battle.

XI.

Grendel's last meal. The battle begins.

Then came Grendel marching from the moor under the misty brows; he bore the wrath of god. The assassin meant to catch some one of human-kind in that lofty hall; he tore along under heaven in the direction where he knew the hospitable building, the gold-hall of men, metal-spangled, ever ready for his entertainment; — that was not the first time he had visited Hrothgar's homestead. Never had he in his life-days, earlier or later, met so tough a warrior, among the hall-guards!

Came then journeying to the hall the felon mirth-bereft; suddenly the door fastened with the bars of wrought iron, sprang open as soon as he touched it with his hands; thus bale-minded and big with rage he wrecked the vestibule of the hall quickly. After that the fiend was treading on the paved floor; he went ravening; out of his there stood likest to flame an eerie light. He perceived in the hall many warriors, a troop of kinsmen, grouped together, a band of cousins, asleep. Then was his mood exalted to laughter; he counted, the fell ruffian, that he should sever, before day came, the life of each one of them from his body, seeing that luck had favored him to gratify his slaughterous appetite. That was not however so destined, that he should be permitted to eat any more of mankind after that night.

Mighty rage the kinsman of Hygelac curbed, considering how the assassin meant to proceed in the course of his ravenings. Nor was the marauder minded to delay it; but he seized promptly at his first move a sleeping warrior, tore him in a movement, crunched the bony frame, drank blood of veins, swallowed huge morsels; in a trice he had devoured the lifeless body, feet, hands, and all. He stepped up and neared forward; he was then taking with his hand the great-hearted warrior on his bed. The fiend reached towards him with his fang; —he promptly seized with shrewd design and grappled his arm.

Quickly did the boss of horrors discover that, never in all the world, all the quarters of the earth, had he met a man more strange with bigger hand-grip. He in the mood became alarmed in spirit; but never the quicker could he get away. His mind was to be going; he wanted to flee into darkness; rejoin the devils' pack; his entertainment there was not such as he before had met with in bygone days. Then did the brave kinsman of Hygelac remember his discourse of the evening; up he stood full length, grappled with him amain; his fingers cracked as they would burst. The monster was making off, the earl followed him up. The oaf was minded, if so be he might, to fling himself loose, and away there from to flee into swamplands; he knew that the control of his fingers was in the grip of a terrible foe; that was a rash expedition which the devastator had made to Heorot!

The Guard-hall roared; —upon all the Danes upon the inhabiters of the castle, upon every brave man, upon the earls, came mortal panic. Furious were both the maddened champions, the building resounded; it was a great wonder that the genital saloon endured the combatants, that it did not fall to ground, that fair ornament of the country; only that it was inwardly and outwardly so firmly besmithied with iron stanchions of mastery skill! There, from the sill started—as my story tells—many a mead-bench adorned with gold where the terrible ones contended. There anent had he Scylding senators weaned at the first, that never would any man by mortal force be able to wreck it, the beautiful and ivoried house, or by craft to disjoint it; —leastwise fire's embrace should swallow it up in vapory reek.

The noise rose high, with renewed violence; the north-Danes were stricken with eldritch horror every one, whosoever heard even out on the wall the doleful cry, the adversary of God yelling a dismal lay, a song unvictorious; —the thrall of hell howling for his wound. He held him too fast, he who was in main the strongest of men in the day of this life.

XII.

Grendel's flight. His arm remains with Beowulf, and is set up as a trophy. Heorot is purged.

The shelter or earls was not by any means minded to let the murderous visitant escape alive; he did not reckon his life-days useful to any one of the leeds. There did many earl of Beowulf's unsheathe his old heirloom; —would rescue the life of their master, their great captain; if so be they might. They knew it not, —when they plunged into the flight, the stouthearted companions, and thought to hack him on every side, reach his life, —that no choicest blade upon earth, no war-bill would touch that destroyer, but he had by enchantment secured himself against victorious weapons, edges of all kinds. His life-parting in the day of this life was destined to be woeful, and the outcast spirit must travel far off into the realm of fiends. Then discovered he that, he who erst in wanton mood had wrought huge atrocity upon mankind—he was out of God's peace—that his body was not at his command, but the valiant kinsman of Hygelac had got a of hold of him by the hand; to either was the other's life loathsome. A deadly wound the foul warlock got; on his shoulder the fatal crack appeared; the sinews sprang wide, the bone-coverings burst. To Beowulf was victory given; Grendel must flee life-sick from there to the coverts of the fen, must make for a cheerless habitation; — full well he knew that the end of his life was reached, the number of his days. All the Danes had in the issue of that dire struggle the fulfillment of their desire.

He had then purged, he who but now came from far, sagacious and resolute, Hrothgar's hall; he had rescued it from danger; had succeeded in his night-task with brilliant achievement. The Leed of the Gothic companions had made good his vaunt to the east-Danes; likewise he had entirely remedied the horror, the harrowing sorrow, which they were enduring before, and of dire necessity were forced to suffer; —huge indignity. That was a token conspicuous, when the hero of battle he affixed the hand, arm, and shoulder—that was the whole affair of Grendel's fang—under the gabled roof.

XIII.

Horseman upon Grendel's track. Riding, racing, and tale-telling. Beowulf's adventure a minstrel's theme; —his fame coupled with Sigemund's contrasted with Heremond's.

Then was in the morning—so goes my story—about the gift-hall many a warrior; the chiefs of the folk came from far and near, through divers ways, to survey the prodigy, the traces of the loathed one. His life-ending was no grief whatever to any of those who surveyed the track of the vanquished, how he in doleful mood away from that place, in mortal terror to the sea demons. There was the face of the lake swirling with blood, the gruesome splash of waves all turbid with reeking gore, with sword-spilt; —the death-doomed Grendel had discolored it; —presently he, devoid of joyance, in fenny covert yielded up his life, his heathen soul; there did Hela receive him.

Thence back home went the old Companions along with many a

bachelor from the pleasure-trip; from the Mere in high spirits riding on horses, barons on jennets. There was Beowulf's achievement rehearsed; many a one often said that south nor north between the seas all the wide world over, other none of shield-bearing warriors under the compass of the firmament preferable were or worthier of sovereignty. They did not however at all disparage their natural lord, gracious Hrothgar; but he was a good king!

Now and then the gallant warriors loosened their russet nags for a gallop, to run a match, where the turfways looked fair, or were favorably known. Other whiles a thane of the king's, bombastic groom, his mind full of ballads, the man who remembered good store of old-world tales—began immediately to rehearse, cunningly to compose, the adventure of Beowulf, and fluently to pursue the story in its order, with interlacing words. At large he detailed, what he had heard say of Sigemund's exploits, much that was strange, the battle-toil of the Waelsing, distant expeditions, things the sons of men quite knew not of, feud and atrocity; —none but Fitela by his side, when he would say aught of such matter, uncle to nephew, as they had ever stood by one another in every struggle: they had with swords laid low many of monster brood. To Sigemund there sprang up after his death-day no little fame; forasmuch as he, hardy in fight, had quelled the Dragon, the keeper of treasure; he, the son of a prince, in under the hoary rock, single-handed enterprized the perilous deed; —Fitela was not with him. Nevertheless he succeeded so well that the sword sped though the stupendous worm, till it stuck in the bank, noble iron! The dragon died the death. The champion had by valor attained that he might enjoy the jewel-hoard at his own discretion; he laded the sea-boat, the son of Waels bore to the bosom of the ship the bright ornaments; the worm dissolved with heat. He was by daring exploits the most famous of adventurers far and wide over the world, shelter of warriors; such eminence he won.

When Heremond's warfare had slackened, his puissance and emprise, he among the Eotens was decoyed forth into the power of enemies, promptly sent out of the way. Him did billows of sorrow disable to long; he to his Leeds, to all his princes, became a loyal anxiety. Moreover, in his earlier times, many wise countrymen had often deplored the adventurous life of ardent soul, such a one as had trusted to him for remedy of grievances, that the royal child might grow powerful, succeed to the state of his fathers, protect the people, the treasure and the castle, realm of heroes, patrimony of the Scyldings. There was he, Hygelac's kinsman, to all mankind, and to his friends, more acceptable; the other was seized with fury.

At intervals racing they with their horses measured the fallow streets. Then was the light of morning launched and advanced; there was many varlet going eager-minded to the lofty Hall to see the strange prodigy; —likewise the king himself from his domestic lodge, keeper of jeweled hoards, trod with glorious mien, gorgeously distinguished in the midst of a great retinue; —and his queen with him, measured the path to the mead-hall with a bevy of ladies.

XIV.

A patriarchal thanksgiving. Beowulf's account of the fray. Effect upon Unferth.

Hrothgar uttered speech—he was going to the Hall; he stood on the Staple; he beheld the steep roof gold-glittering, and the arm of Grendel.

"For this spectacle a thanksgiving to the Almighty be done without delay! Much despite I endured, capturings by Grendel; always can God work wonder after wonder, the Lord of Glory! It was but now that I thought I should never see a remedy for any of my woes, while the best of houses stood blood-stained, soaked in slaughter; the woe had scattered all my senators, as men who weaned not that they ever should rescue the national edifice of my Leeds from the hateful ones, the demos and boggles.

"Now hath a lad, through might of God, achieved the deed which we all meanwhile were unable to wait our wisdom to compass. Lo! That may she say, what lady so ever mothered that child by human generation, if yet she lived, that to her was the Ancient Master favorable in her child-bearing!

"Now I will heartily love thee, Beowulf, youth most excellent, as if thou were my son; from this time forth keep thou up the new relation. There shall be no lack to thee of any desires in the world, so far as I have power. Full oft have I less service decreed recompense, honor from the treasury, to less distinguished hero, less prompt to fight.

"Thou thyself hast by deeds achieved, that thy fame will live ever and always. May the Almighty reward thee with good, as he hath just now done!"

Beowulf uttered speech, Ecgtheows's son: "We discharged that high task, fighting with right good heart; shrewdly we enterprized the terror of the unknown. I'd a' liked it vastly better, that thou dost a' seen his very self, the fiend in full gear, ready to drop. I thought quickly to fix him on a bloody bed with hard grapplings, that he for my hand-grip should lie death—struggling, unless his body vanished; I could not, as the Ancient would not, baulk his passage; I did not stick close enough to him, the man-vanquisher; the fiend was too over-mighty in his life and mark his track—his arm and shoulder: not thereby however has the wretched being bought reprieve; none the longer will he live, he loathsome pest burdened with crimes; but the wound hath him, in deadly grip close pinioned, in baleful bands; in that condition must he, crime-stained wretch, abide the great doom, according as the Ancient One may will the assign his portion."

A silenter man was then the son of Ecglaf in the brag of martial exploits; since it was by the hero's valor the athelings beheld the hand, the fiendish fingers, over the high roof, every one straight before him. Each one of the nail-places was likest to steel, hand-spur of the heathenish marauder, horrible spikes; every one declared there as nothing so hard would graze them, no sword of old celebrity that would take off the monster's bloody war-fist.

XV.

Heorot restored. Rejoicings and giving of gifts.

Then was order promptly given that the interior of Heorot should be decorated; many they were, of men and of women, who garnished that genial palace, hospitable hall. Gold-glistering shone the brocaded tapes-tries along the walls, pictures many for the wonder of all people who have an eye for such. That bright building was terribly wrecked in its whole interior, though it had been strengthened with iron fastenings; the hinges were wrenched away; the roof alone had escaped altogether unhurt, when the destroyer, stained with atrocities, took to flight in desperation of life.

It is not easy to elude death, try it who will; but every living soul of the sons of men, dwellers upon ground, must of necessity approach the destined spot, where his body, bedded in fast repose, shall sleep after supper.

Then was the time and the moment, that Healfdene's son should go to the Hall; the king was minded himself to share the feast. Never that I heard of did that nation in stronger force about their bounty-giver more bravely muster. They went to bench in merry guise—while their kinsmen enjoyed the copious feast, and with fair courtesy quaffed many a mead-bowl—mighty men in the lofty hall, Hrothgar and Hrohulf. The interior of Heorot was wholly filled with friends; no treachery had imperial Scyldings at that early date attempted.

Then did the son of Healfdene present to Beowulf a golden ensign in reward of victory, decorated staff-banner, helmet and mail-coat; many beheld when they brought the grand treasure-sword before the hero. Beowulf tasted the beaker on the hall-floor; no need had he to be ashamed of that bounty-giving before the hero. Beowulf tasted the beaker on the hall-floor; no need had he to be ashamed of that bounty-giving before the archers. I heard not many instances of men giving to other at ale-bench four treasures gold-bedight in friendlier wise. About the helmet's roof the crest was fastened with wire-bound fencing for the head, in order that file-wrought war-scoured blades might not cruelly scathe it, when the shielded fighter had to go against angry foes.

Then did the Shelter of earls command to bring eight horses gold cheeked into the court within the palings; on one of them stood the saddle gaily caparisoned and decorated with silver, which was the war-seat of the high king, when the son of Healf-dene was minded to exercise the play of swords; —never failed in the front the charger of the famous king when the slain were falling. And then did the chief of the Ingwines deliver unto Beowulf possession of both at once, both horses and arms; —bade him enjoy them well. So manfully did the illustrious chieftain, with horses and treasures, so as to never cause any to mispraise them who is minded to speak sooth according to right.

XVI.

Gifts to Beowulf's comrades. Music and Song. The Lay of Hnaef,
relating the consequences of Finn's treachery.

Moreover, to each one of those who had made the voyage with

Beowulf, did the Captain of warriors give a precious gift at the mead-bench and old heir-loom; and gave orders to compensate with gold for that missing one, that one whom Grendel had atrociously killed, as he would have killed more of them, had not the providence of God, had not Wyrd, stood in his way; —and, the courage of that man. The Ancient One ruled then, as he now and always doth, over all persons of human race; there fore is prudence each—where best, fore-cast of soul. Much experience of pleasant and of painful must he make, who long here in these struggling days brooks the world.

Then was song and instrumental music together blended, concerning Healfdene's war-chief, —the harp was struck, a ballad often recited, what time the hall-joy along the mead-bench was invoked by Hrothgar's minstrel—concerning the sons of Finn, when the alarm overtook them: "A mighty man if the half—Danes, Hneaf the Scylding, was doomed to fall in the Frisian conflict.

"Hildeburh however had no cause to extol the fidelity of the Eotens; without her fault she was in the clash of shields bereft of those dear to her, sons and brother; they fell one after another wounded with the spear; —that was a doleful princess. Not without cause did the daughter of Hoc bewail the sad event when morning came, and she in full daylight could see the carnage of her kin, where she had till now enjoyed the world's best happiness.

"Battle had destroyed all Finn's thanes, save a few only, so that he could not, on the place of debate, against Hengest at all contend, nor rescue the sad remnant of his men from the hostility of the king's thane; but the Frisians proffered Hengest conditions of peace, that they would wholly yield to him the possession of another mansion, hall, and high seat, so that the Danes might share equal possession of it with the sons of the Eotens, and at money-givings the son of Folcwalda should day by day honor the Danes, should gratify with rings the troop of Hengest, with metallic wealth of beaten gold, in exactly the same measure as he purposed in the festive hall to encourage the Frisians born. Thereupon they ratified on the two sides a fast treaty of peace; Finn engaged loyally and unreservedly, with oaths to Hengest, that he would govern that sad remnant by constituted law in all honor; so that not any man of them, by word or work, should break the treaty; nor with guileful intent ever mention make, though they had followed their patron's banesman, when bereaved of a lord, seeing that they were by necessity driven to it. If on the other hand any of the Frisians with aggressive speech were recalling the blood-feud, it should be atoned by the edge of the sword. The oath it was sworn, and massive gold was hoisted out of the treasury.

"Of the warlike Scyldings the best campaigner was on the fire-heap—ready; at the pyre was conspicuous the blood-stained sark, the swine all gilded, the boar of hard iron, many a noble wounded to death; —several had fallen in the struggle. Orders were given by Hildeburh, that at Hnaef's pyre her own son should be committed to flame, that the body should be burnt and placed on the bale-fire. The poor lady wailed on his shoulder, she uttered her grief in lamentations; the war-hero passed up in flame, soared to the clouds. Hugest of corpse-fires, it roared on its eminence; heads wasted away, wound- gates did burst; then sprang blood from the place where the body had been cruelly assaulted. The fire devoured them all—greediest of demos—all of those whom war had there destroyed, of both peoples; their bloom was departed."

XVII.

The remainder of the Lay of Hnaef. A picture of social pleasure.
Speech of the queen to the king.

"The warriors departed to visit their dwellings, bereft of friends to re-visit Friesland, their homesteads and head-borough.

Hengest however during that blood-stained winter tarried with Finn, loyally and without cavil; his home he thought of, though he was not able to drive over the sea his ring-prowed ship; the helm surged with storm, battled with wind; winter locked the wave with icy barrier; until that the next year came to town, as even now it continues to do; and those punctual time-keepers, the days of glorious weather. Then was winter gone, the bosom of the earth was fair; the adventurer was astir, the guest forward to quit hospitable courts.

"He however thought more on revenge than on sea-voyaging, if he could bring about collision, that he might therein remember the sons of the Eotons. So the better to hide his thought he did not decline military brotherhood, when Hun laid upon his breast the sword Lafing, luminary of battle, best of blades; the edges of that sword were famous among the Eotens. Consequently the savage-minded Finn was by and by overtaken by glib sword-bale at his own manor; when once Guthlaf and Oslaf, off their sea-voyage, made sore mention of the grim assault, brought up a deal of wrongs; he could not refrain his wild rage in his breast. Then was the hall bedight with embattled corpses; —likewise, Finn was slain, the king in the midst of his guard, and the queen taken. The archers of the Syldings conveyed to their ships the whole establishment of the king of the country, whatsoever they at Finn's Ham could find of jewels and curious gems. On the sea-path they conveyed the courtly ladies to the Danes, brought them to their Leeds." The lay was sung to its end, the minstrel's descant.

Enjoyment rose high as before, bright was the sound of revelry; the drawers served wine out of curious flagons. Then came Wealhtheow forward, moving under her golden diadem, to where the two brave men sat, uncle and nephew; up to that time was their natural affection undisturbed, either to other true. Likewise there Unferth the speaker sat at the feet of the Scyldings' lord; every man of them trusted his spirit that he had great courage, though he had not been loyal to his kindred at sword-play.

Spake then the lady of the Scydings;—"receive this beaker, sovereign mine, wealth-dispenser! Be thou merry, a munificent friend of men, and speak to the Goths with comfortable words. So it behooves one to do! Near and far, thou now hast peace! To me it hath been said, that thou would have the hero for thy son. Heorot is purged, the bright ring-hall; dispense wiliest thou mayest many bounties; —and to thy children leave folk and realm, when thou must away to see Eternity. I know my gracious Hrothulf that he will honorably govern the younger ones, if thou earlier than he, O friend of the Scyldings, quitest the world. I think that he will repay out children with good, if he that fully remembers, what gracious attentions thou and I bestowed for his comfort and advantage in the time past when he was an infant."

She turned then toward the bench where her boys were, Hrethric and Hrothmund, and the sons of mighty men, the youth all together; there the brave man sat, Beowulf of the Goths, by the two brothers.

XVIII.

Gifts of the queen to the hero, and her speech to him. The hall is
arranged as a dormitory.

To him the cup was borne; and friendly invitation to drink was offered with words; and twisted gold rings; the grandest of celebrations that I have heard of on Earth. None superior among the treasures of men heard I ever of under heaven, since Hama bore away to the bright fortress the necklace of the Brisings—jewel and casket; he fled the toils of Eormanric; chose eternal counsel.

That collar had Hygelac of the Goths, grandson or nephew of sweating, on his latest expedition, when under his flag he defended his prize, guarded the spoil; he, took off, when for him wantonness challenged woe, feud with the Frisians; he carried that decoration the costly stones over the wave-bowl, the mighty chieftain; he fell shield in hand; so then came into the power of the Franks the corpse of the king, the breast apparel, and the collar along with the rest; inferior combatants stripped the slain by the fortune of war; the people of the Goths tenanted the bed of death. The Hall echoed with the sound of music.

Wealhtheow uttered speech; she spake before that company; "Brook this collar, Beowulf, beloved youth, with luck, and make use of this mantle; stately possessions; and prosper well; make thyself famous by valor, and to these boys be thou a kind adviser! I will reward thee for it. Thou hast attained, that far and near, got all future time, men will celebrate thee, even as widely as the sea encircled windy walls. Be thou, whilst thou live, a happy prince! With good will I accord thee precious possessions. Be thou to my son loyal to their chief; the thanes are obedient, the people all ready! Retainers be merry, do as I bid you."

She went then to her chair. There was high festivity; men drank wine, Wyrd they knew not, the cruel destiny, as it had gone forth, for many a noble. By and by the evening came, and Hrothgar betook him to his lodge, the prince to his repose.

Countless nobles guarded the Hall, as they often did in earlier time; they cleared away the bench-boards; it was strewn throughout with beds and bolsters. One of the revelers, whose end was near, lay down to rest in hall a doomed man. At their heads they set the shields, the bright bucklers; there on the bench was over each etheling, plain to be seen, the towering war helmet, the ringed mail-cost, the shaft of awful power. Their custom was that they were constantly ready for war, whether at home or in the field, in both cases alike, whatever the occasion on which their liege lord had need of their services; —it was a good people.

The Second Part

XIX.

*In the night the old water-hag comes, seizes one of the sleepers, and
fetches away Grendel's arm. Beowulf is hastily summoned to the
king at early dawn.*

So they sank down to sleep.

One who was there sorely paid for that night's rest, in the
manner that had very often happened to them, since Grendel had
occupied the gold-hall, perpetrated violence, until his end
arrived, death after crimes. That became manifest, widely known
to men, that an avenger still lived after the slain foe; long to
remember the disaster; Grendel's mother, beldam's troll-wife,
thought of her desolation, a creature that had to dwell in the drea-
riness of water, cold streams ever since Cain was the knife-bane of
his only brother, his father's son; he then went forth an outlaw,
marked with murder, shunning human society; he kept the
wilderness. Thence grew a number of branded creatures; —one
of those was Grendel, horrible ban-wolf who at Heorot found a
vigilant man waiting for battle. There did the monster grapple with
him; he however remembered the strength of his might, the marvelous gift which God had given to him, and he trusted to the
Supreme for grace, courage, and support; therefore he overcame
the fiend, subdued the hellish demon; so he departed crest-fallen,
void of joyance, to see his death-place, foe of man. And yet his
mother, nevertheless, bloodthirsty and gallows-minded was going
to enter upon a sorrow-fraught way to wreak the death of her son.

So the hag came to Heorot, where the jeweled Danes slept
throughout the Hall. Then was it for the earls a sudden upset, when
Grendel's mother burst into their midst. The terror was less than
the terror of Grendel just in the same proportion as female

strength, woman's war-terror, is of less account with an armed man; when the well-hafted steel, hammer-toughened, the bloodstained sword, with edge effective, sheareth resisting boar on helmet. Then was the hard-edged sword drawn throughout the niches, many a wide buckler raised firm in hand; many one thought not of helmet, nor spacious byrnie, when the alarm surprised him.

The hag was in a hurry; it wanted to get out from there with life, because it was discovered; promptly it had seized one of the athelings tight, and then it left. That man was to Hrothgar, in quality of comrade, dearest of warriors between the seas, mighty shield-combatant; —him the hag crushed in his sleep, illustrious baron. Beowulf was not there; but another lodging had been assigned, after the gift-giving to the distinguished Goth. A cry was heard in Heorot; the blood-sprent hag took away the well-known hand; anxiety was not good, which they on both sides were compelled to pay for with lives of friends.

Then was the venerable king, the hoary man of war, in embittered mood, when he knew that his chiefest thane no longer lived, that the man most dear to him was dead. Hastily to the king's bower was Beowulf fetched, the victorious stripling. At early dawn, he went with his warriors, the noble champion, he and his comrades, where the sapient king was waiting to be resolved, whether the Almighty will ever, after the spell of woe, bring about a change. He accosted with words the wise lord of the Ingwines, and enquired if, according to his sincere wish, he had had a restful night.

X X .

Hrothgar's answer to Beowulf's morning salutation; he deplores the fate of Æschere; and describes the haunt of the water-demons.
Hrothgar, king of Scyldings, uttered speech: "Ask not thou after welfare! Grief is renewed for the Danish Leeds. Æschere is dead,

Yrmenlaf's elder brother, my secretary and my counselor; my body-squire, when we in battle defended our heads, what time foot-fighters closed, boar-crests clashed; —such should a warrior be, a long tried etheling, such as Æschere was. In Heorot hath he met his death at the hands of the raging destroyer; I know not in what direction the gruesome corpse-exulting thing took its return-way leaving tracks of its forage. She hath wreaked the feud, for that thou yester night didst quell Grendel in masterful wise with stern grapplings; for that he too long had wasted and destroyed my people. He in fight succumbed with forfeiture of life; and now hath come the other, a mighty ravager, would avenge her kin; —yea hath further aggravated the feud, as may well appear to many a thane, who along with his sovereign groans in spirit, in cruel heart-grief; now the hand of him who was the promoter of all your desires lies still in death.

"That I did hear say by land-owners. Leeds of mine, heads of Halls, that they saw a pair of such, huge mark-stalkers, keeping the moors, creatures of strange fashion; one of them was, according to the clearest they could make out, a bedlam's likeness, the other miscreant thing trod lonely tracks in a man's figure; only he was huger than any other man; him in old times the country folk used to call Grendel: they know not about any father, whether they had any in pedigree before them of mysterious goblins. They inhabit unvisited land, wolf-crags, windy bluffs, the dread fen-track where the mountain waterfall amid precipitous gloom vanished beneath, flood under earth; not far hence it is, reckoning by miles, that the Mere standeth, and over it hang rimy groves; a wood with clenched roots over shrouds the water. There may every night a fearful portent be seen, fire on the flood; none so wise liveth of the children of men as to know the depth. Though the heath-roamer, when exhausted by hounds, the heart strong in his horns, make for the wood-coverts, driven from afar; sooner will he resign his breath, his life on the bank, sooner than he will there in plunge his head. That is no comfortable place. There from mount up the raging waves, murky to the clouds, when wind stirred foul weather, till the air thickens, the skies crack. Now is it again to thee alone that we look for counsel! The haunt as yet thou knowest no, the dreadful place, where thou mayest find the guilty felon; go for it if thou dare! I will recompense thee for that warfare with treasure, with old stored wealth, as I did before, with coiled gold, if thou comest away."

XXI.

Beowulf soothes the king, and gaily undertakes the new adventure. The cavalcade to the Mere. The look of it. Beowulf arms; his sword is described.

Beowulf son of Ecgtheow uttered speech: "Sorrow not, experienced Sire! Better is it for every man that he should avenge his friend, then that he should greatly mourn. Every one of us must look for the end of worldly life; he who has the chance should achieve renown before death; that is for a mighty man, when life is past, the best memorial. Rouse thee, guardian of the kingdom! Let us promptly set forth to explore the route of Grendel's kin. I vow it to thee; he shall by no means escape to covert; neither in the bowels of the earth, nor in the haunted wood, nor in oceans depth—go where he will! This day have thou patience of all thy woes, as I have high confidence in thy behalf."

Up sprang then the aged king. He thanked God, the mighty Lord, for what that man had spoken. Then Hrothgar's horse was bridled, the cruel-maned charger. The wise monarch rose forth stately; the foot-force marched, of shield-bearing men.

Traces there were broadly visible along the slopes of the weald, the track of the hag over the grounds; right forward she had gone, over the murky moor, it had carried off, lifeless, the most beloved of kindred thanes, of those who kept home with Hrothgar.

Then did the Scion of Athelings pass lightly over steep stone-banks, narrow gullies, strait lonesome paths, an untraveled route, sheer bluffs, many habitations of sea demons. He with few companions, practiced men, went forward to explore the ground, until that he of sudden perceived the gloomy trees overhanging the grisly rock, a joyless wood; beneath it was a standing water, dreary and troubled; all the Danes, all the friends of the Scyldings, had a shock of feeling, many a thane had to suffer; horror seized each warrior, when on that lake-cliff they came across the head of Æschere. The pool seethed with blood—the folk beheld it—with hot gore.

The horn sounded from time to time a spirited bugle-blast. The troop all sat them down; there saw they along the water many things of serpent kind, monstrous sea-snakes at their swimming gambols; and likewise on the jutting slopes sea demons lying, those that in the early hours of the morning often procure disastrous going on the sail road; dragons and strange beasts: —they tumbled away, spited and rage-blown; they had caught sound of the racket, the clarion's clang. The Leed of the Goths with an arrow out of his bow detached one of them from life, and from all future swimming matches; insomuch that in his vitals stood fixed the inexorable war-shaft; he in the element was the slacker at swimming, from the circumstance that death had caught him. Promptly was he on the waves with boar-poles harpoon-armed, tightly nipped—barred of his tricks—and landed on the point the prodigious wave-tosser; —the men beheld the grisly goblin.

Beowulf geared himself in the knightly armor; in no wise was he anxious for his life; now must the war-byrnie, hand-woven, spacious and decorated, make trial of swimming; the byrnie which knew to protect the body, that his breast, his life, might not be scathed by the grip of battle, the spiteful clutch of the furious one. Moreover the white helmet guarded his head, the helmet that was to plunge into the depths of the pool, to face buffeting waters, with all its decoration of silver, encircled with princely wreathings, as a weapon-smith in ancient days wrought it, wonderfully executed it, set it round with boar figures, so that never might brand nor war-blades make any impression upon it.

That moreover was not the least important of help to his valor, which Hrothgar's orator lent to him at his need; —the name of that hafted blade was Hrunting, it was preeminently one of old heirlooms; —the edge was iron, mottled with poison-twigs, hardened with battle-gore; never had it in conflict proved false to any man who brandished it with hands, such man was durst adventure on paths of terror, where nations meet as foes; that was not the first occasion that it had been required to discharge heroic work. Manifestly Ecglaf's son, of doughty puissance, remembered not what he had recently uttered when flushed with wine, seeing now he made loan of that weapon to the rater sword-gallant; — for himself he durst not adventure his life among the turmoil of waves, to fulfill mastery; —there he feel short of glory, of high achievement. It was not so with the other, when he had harnessed him for combat.

XXII.

Beowulf's impromptu will. He plunges into the abyss and meets the troll-wife. The battle beings.

Beowulf son of Ectheow uttered speech; "Bethink thee now, great son of Healfdene, sapient monarch, now I am ready to start, oh thou gold-friends of men, what we two lately talked of; —if I in thy service had to quit life, that thou to me wouldst ever be, after my departure, in the place of a father; —be thou protector to my kindred thanes, my familiar comrades, if Hild should take me; in such a case do thou, beloved Hrothgar, forward the presents which thou hast given me, to Hygelac. So will the master of the Goths be able to understand by that gold, Hrethel's son will be able to see for himself when he gazed upon that treasure, that I had found a bountifully good distributor of jewels, and was in luck while my fortune lasted. And do thou let Unferth have the ancient heir-loom, the curious damasked sword; let the far-famed man have Hardedge; I will with Hrunting achieve for myself renown, or death shall take me."

After these words the leed of the Weder-Goths dashed bravely off, would await no answer; —the eddying flood engulfed the warrior. It was then a main while of the day ere he could reach the country at the bottom.

Soon it was that perceived by the blood-thirsty creature, grim and greedy, which for a hundred seasons had kept the watery region, that one of the children of men was exploring from above the habitation of goblins. It made a grab then towards him; it caught the brave man with grisly talons; nevertheless it pierced not to wound the wholeness of his body; ring-mail outside fenced him about, insomuch that the hag could not get through the jacket of service, well-knit limb-sark with its loathsome fingers. Then did the she-wolf of the lake, when she came to the bottom, bear the jeweled prince to her mansion, so that he had no power at all—courage enough he had—to wield his weapons; but so many monsters harassed him in swimming, many a water-beast with hostile tusks battered his war-sark the brigands were in pursuit.

Then did the earl perceive that he was in some strange abysmal hall, where no water molested him, nor could the violence of the flood touch him, being kept off by the roofed hall; firelight he saw, an eerie luster, shining bright. Then the hero knew it was the she-wolf of the abyss, the mighty carline of the Mere; —onset he delivered with slaughter-bill, his hand delayed not the stroke, so that about her head the costly blade resounded a greedy war-song. Then did the visitor discover that the battle-gleamed would not bite, not scathe life, but the edge failed the master at need; it had in times past supported many encounters, had often cleft helmet, war-harness of the doomed; —that was the first time for the honored treasure, that its fame broke down. Again he was for action, in courage never faltering, mindful of exploits, Hygelac's kinsman. Away did the wrathful combatant then fling the dama-scened blade cunningly bedizened, insomuch that it lay along on the earth, stark and steel-edged; he trusted to his strength, the hand-grip of his might.

So it behooves a man to act, when he in battle thinks to attain enduring PRAISE; —he will not be caring about his life.

Then did the Leed of the warlike Goths—naught racked he of deadly peril—seize Grendel's dam by the shoulder; then did the man valiant in fight, as he was full of rage, sway his deadly adver-sary so that she sank on the pavement. The hag swiftly paid him back reprisal with fell grapplings, and closed in upon him: —then staggered he with spirits exhausted, he the strongest of warriors, the champion-soldier, insomuch that he fell prostrate. Then did the hag sit upon the visitant of her hall, and drew her knife, broad and brown-edged; would revenge her bairn, her only offspring. About his shoulder lay the breast-net interlaced; that fenced his life; against point and against edge it barred the entrance.

Then had the son of Ecgtheow, the champion of the Goths, mis-carried under the vast profound, had not his campaigning byrnie, his hard war-net, afforded help; —and holy God controlled the victory, the Lord of providence, the heavenly Ruler, he deter-mined it aright, and that with ease; —presently he again stood erect on his feet.

XXIII.

Beowulf finishes the business. The king's party give him up, and go home. Beowulf's comrades remain on the cliff. Fidelity rewarded. An after-dinner surprise.

Then saw he among the armor a monumental cutlass, an old etenish sword, of edge effective, a trophy of warriors; —that was the very pride of weapons, only then it was huger than any other man could bear to the battle-game; it was good and gallant, handiwork of giants. Then did he, the champion of the fight draw the jeweled arm; despairing of his life, he smote in his fury; insomuch that the hard steel caught her by the neck, broke through the bone-rings, the bill sped all through the doomed flesh-jacket; — she dropped on the pavement; the sword was gory; the lad was fain of his work.

The glimmer flashed up, light filled the place, even as when from heaven serenely shined the candle of the firmament. He scanned the apartment with his eye, then took his way along by the wall; stubborn the thane of Hygelac swung his weapon aloft by the hilt, fierce and aggressive. That blade was not flung away by the hero, but he was forthwith minded to repay Grendel the many fatal assaults he had wrought on the west Danes oftener far than a single once, when he slew Hrothgar's hearth-comrades in their slumber; sleeping men of the Danish folk he devoured fifteen, and an equal number he conveyed away hideous spoil. He had paid him his recompense for that, the furious champion had; insomuch that he now beheld him at rest, weary of war, even Grendel he saw lying, bereft of life, so deadly for him had erst the conflict at Heorot been. The carcass gaped wide, when it after death received the blow, the hard sword-slash; then did he cut the head from off him.

Forthwith was that perceived by the observant men who with

Hrothgar were watching over the water, that the wave-splash was all turbid, the surf was tinged with blood: the men of grizzled locks, the old men, spake together about the brave man, how that they expected not the etheling back again, did not expect that he would come radiant with victory to seek the illustrious prince; inasmuch as the more part were of opinion, that the she-wolf of the Mere had torn him in pieces.

Then came the ninth hour of the day. The impetuous Scyldings quitted the bluff; the gold-friend of men took his departure homeward thence. The foreigners sat fast, sick at heart, and upon the pool gazed; they wished and did not expect, that they might ever get sight of their lord and captain in the body.

Then did that sword begin—under spilith of blood in fearful clots—the war-bill began to waste away; —that was a marvelous thing that it melted all away, likest to ice when the father dissolved the rigor of frost and untwined the ropes of the torrent, he who had control of times and seasons; that is the true Governor.

The leader of the Weder-Goths took not of rare possessions in those halls—though he saw many there—aught more than the head, and with it the hilt that was metal-spangled; the sword had already melted away, the decorated weapon had burnt up; —so fiercely hot was that blood, and so venomous the strange goblin which had perished there in that habitation.

Soon was he swimming, he who previously had struggling encountered the worst of furious beasts; up through the water he dived; the wave-depths were all purified spacious haunts; now that the gobbling had quitted life, and this transitory scene.

Then came he to land, the crown of the men from over the sea, bravely swimming; —he exulted in his lake-spoil, in the mighty burthen that he had with him. Then went they to meet him, they thanked God, the valiant band of thanes, they rejoiced over their captain, for that they had been so happy as to get sight of him whole and sound. Then was from the ardent hero his helmet and byrnie promptly slackened: —sullenly the Mere subsided, water under welkin, duck with battle-gore.

Forth thence they fared upon the tracks of their former march, fain in their souls, they passed over the country, and along the public highways: men of kingly courage bore the head-piece away from the Mere-cliff, toilsomely for every one of them: of the lusty and stalwart fellows four were required to convey with much ado on the gory pole the head of Grendel to the gold-hall; and so they went till unexpectedly to Hall the brave adventurers arrived, fourteen of Goths marching; their captain withal, glorious in their midst, trod the grounds of the mead-hall. Then did the commander of the thanes proceed to enter, deed-keen man, adorned with glory, warlike hero, to accost Hrothgar: then was Grendel's head borne by the hair into the hall where men drank; —startling for the nobles and the lady withal; visage indescribable did men behold.

XXIV.

Beowulf reports his experience to Hrothgar, and gives him the wondrous hilt, which is examined and described. Hrothgar's paternal discourse.

Beowulf son of if Ectheow uttered speech: "Lo and behold! We unto thee, oh son of Healfdene, Leed of the Scyldings, have joyfully brought these Mere-spoils which thou here lookest on, in token of achievement! Not easily did I fight it though with life: in battle under water I had hardly faced out the task, well-nigh had the struggle failed, only that God shielded me. I could not in conflict accomplish aught with Hrunting, though that be a good weapon; but the Ruler of men vouchsafed to me that I on the wall saw smilingly hanging an old sword of huge size—oftenest hath

He guided men when they have no other friend—insomuch that I grasped at the weapon. Then smote I in that campaign—occasion favoring me—the keepers of the house. Then did that battle-bill consume away, that twisted piece, by reason of that blood which gushed forth, hottest of battle-gore; I brought away from the enemy that hilt as a trophy; I avenged the atrocities, the death-agony of Danes, as it was meet. Accordingly I promise it to thee that thou in Heorot mayest sleep free from care with the regiment of thy troopers; and so may every thane of thy troopers; and so may every then of thy Leeds, of the seniority and of the juniority, for that thou needest not on their account apprehend danger, O chief of Scyldings, in that quarter, life-bale to warriors; as erewhile thou didst."

Then was the gilded hilt given to the veteran soldier, the hoary leader in battle, given into his hand, ancient workmanship of giants; it passed, after the demon were quelled, into the possession of the prince of the Danes, a work of mystic smiths; and so when the atrocious creature, God's enemy, murder-criminous, left this world, and his mother too, it went into the possession of the best of worldly kings between the seas, of all that ever in Scania distributed wealth.

Hrothgar uttered speech; —he surveyed the hilt of the old relic; upon it was written the origin of the primeval quarrel, what time the flood, the rushing ocean, destroyed the giants' brood; they got for themselves a bitter fate; that was a tribe estranged from the Eternal Captain, to them did the Ruler assign final retribution with whelming water. Likewise on the mounting of sheer gold there was with rune-staves rightly inscribed, set down, and said, for whom that sword had erst been wrought, best of steely fabrics, with wreathen hilt, and dragon ornament.

Then did the wise son of Healfdene utter speech—all held their peace: —"That, lo! May a man say, a man who promoteth truth and right among folk, —he remembereth all long ago, the old housemaster—that this earl was born superior! The fame is spread through distant parts, my friend Beowulf, the fame of thee over every nation. Withal thou lost carry it modestly, thy prowess with discretion of mind. I shall make good to thee my plighted love, according as was before said betwixt us two; thou art destined to: prove a comfort sure and lasting to thy Leeds, a help to mankind.

"Heremond did not prove so to the descendants of Ecgwela, to the honorable Scyldings; he waxed great not for their pleasure. But for mortal fray and for death-blows to the Danish Leeds; he in his ungoverned mood crushed his boon companions, the squires of his body; until that at last he wandered forth alone, the illustrious monarch, away from human society; notwithstanding that the might God had with the attractions of strength, with puissance, exalted him, promoted him, above all men. Nevertheless in his soul there grew a blood-thirsty passion; —far was he from giving rings to the Danes according to merit; he continued estranged from social joy, so that he suffered the penalty of that outrage in the settled disaffection of his people.

"Do thou take warning by that; understand the ornament of man! It is about thee that you being old in years and experience have told this tale.

"Wonderful it is to tell, how the mighty God with large intelligence dispenses understanding to mankind, dispenses position and prowess—he holds the disposition of all things. Sometimes he lets the purpose of a man of noble race turn towards possession, he giveth to him early joy on his estate, to hold the citadel of men, he assigns to him regions of the world so extensive, a realm so wide, that he in his unwisdom is not able to carry his thought to the end of it; he dwelleth in prosperity, not anything annoys him, not sickness nor age carking care darkens his spirits, no quarrel on any side, no feud appears; but all the world moves to his mind, he knows not reverse."

XXV.

The conclusion of Hrothgar's discourse. More feasting; —and then came bed —time for which the hero had huge desire. Beowulf slept till the voice of the bird proclaimed sunrise. Preparing to return home, he restores Hrunting to Unferth courteously.

"Until at length within the man himself something of arrogance grows and develops; then slept the guardian, the soul's keeper; it is too fast that sleep, awfully profound, the assassin is very nigh, he who from his arrow-bow malignantly shooteth. Then is he, helmeted man, smitten in the breast with a bitter shaft: he cannot defend himself from the crooked exorbitant counsels of the damned sprite; he fancies that it is too little, all that he has so long enjoyed; he is covetous, and malignant; gloried not in the pomp of bestowing gilded decorations; and he forgetteth the ulterior consequences; he too lightly considers how that God the Dispenser of glory had erewhile given him the post of dignity. Then at the end of the chapter it returns to this, that the body shrunken falls away, the outgoing life drops;— another fills his room, one who ungrudgingly distributes treasure, the earl's old accumulations;—timed prudence he despises.

Guard thee against the foul grudge, beloved Beowulf, youth most excellent, and choose for thee the better course, enduring counsels! Incline not to arrogance, thou mighty champion! Now is thy strength in full bloom for one while; soon it will happen that sickness or sword will bereave thee of puissance; —either clutch of fire or whelm of flood, either assault of knife or flight of javelin, either wretched eld or glance of eyes, will mat and darken all; without more ado it will come to pass that death will subdue thee, thou Captain of men!

"For example I myself during fifty years ruled beneath the heavens over the jeweled Danes, and I by valor made them secure against many a nation throughout this world with spears and swords, insomuch that I had no apprehension of any rival under the circuit of the sky. When lo! in my ancestral seat there came a change over all that; distress where mirth was before, as soon as Grendel, the old adversary, became an inmate of mine; because of that visitation I continually carried great anxiety at heart. Thanks therefore be to Governor, the Eternal Captain, for that which I have lived to see, that I, the old tribulation past, upon that severed, that bloody headpiece, with mine eyes do gaze!

"Go now to settle, share the festive joy, crowned with honors of war! Thou and I must have dealings together in many many treasures, when to-morrow comes."

The Goth was glad of mood; he moved promptly off, drawing to settle, as the sapient king ordained him. Then was again as before, to the gallant warriors, to the company in hall, fair banquet served afresh.

Night's covering grew dim, dark over the banded men. Up rose all the seniors: —it was that the gray haired king, the venerable Scylding, was minded to draw to his bed. Vastly well did the Goth, the illustrious warrior, like the thought of repose; promptly was he, now weary of adventure, the man of far country, marshaled forth by the chamberlain, one who with meet ceremony supplied all the wants of a gentleman, such things as in that day the lords of the main required to have.

So the great-hearted hero rested him; —high in the air loomed the edifice, wide spanning and gold-gleaming:—the stranger slept within, until the black raven announced heaven's glory with a blithe heart. Then came bright light striding over shadow; fiends scampered off. The ethelings were ready dight to fare back to their Leeds; —the magnanimous visitor was minded to take ship, for a voyage far away.

And when the departing warriors were equipped in harness,

the etheling honored by the Danes went up to the dais, where the other warlike hero was; —he greeted Hrothgar.

XXVI.

Beowulf's parting interview with Hrothgar, who is moved to tears.
Beowulf son of Ecgtheow uttered speech:

"Now we sea-voyagers with to say, we who have come from far, that we are purposing to go to Hygelac. Here we have been well entertained to our satisfaction; thou hast been to us very generous. If I therefore may by any means upon earth undertake for thy further gratification, O Captain of men, labors of war beyond what I have yet done, I shall be ready promptly. If they bring me word over the circuit of the floods that neighbors press thee with alarm as while some of thy haters did, I will bring thee a thousand thanes, warriors to help thee. I undertake for Hygelac, captain of Goths, young though he be, shepherd of people, that he will forward me by words and by works, so that I may do high service to thee, and for thy support bring a forest of spears, a mighty subsidy, when thou shalt have need of men: —if moreover Hrethric, princely child, is in treaty for admission at the courts of the Goths, he may there find many friends; foreign countries are best visited by him who is of high worth in himself."

Hrothgar bespake him in answer, "These considerate words hath the All-wise Lord put into thy mind; never heard I a man so young in life speak more to purpose; thou art strong in might and ripe in understanding; wise in discourse of speech. I count it likely, if it cometh to pass that the spear, the grim dispatch of battle, taketh away Hrethel's offspring, if ailing or iron taketh thy chieftain, the shepherd of the people, and thou hast thy life, that the sea-faring Goths have not any thy better to choose for king, for treasurer of warriors, if thou art willing to hold the realm of thy kinsfolk. To me thy disposition is well-liking more and more, beloved Beowulf; thou hast achieved, that the nations—Gothic leeds and spear-bearing Danes—shall have mutual friendship, and strife shall cease, the hostile surprise whence they suffered erewhile; —there shall be, while I rule the wide realm a community of treasure: many friends shall greet one another with gifts across the bath of the gannet; the ringed ship shall bring over ocean presents and tokens of love. I know the people to be equally as towards foe so towards friend constant in mind, either way irreproachable, in olden wise."

Then did the Shelter of warriors, the son of Halfdene, further give into his possession twelve hoarded jewels; he bade him go with the presents visit his own people in comfort, and soon come back again. Then did the king of noble ancestry, the chief of the Scyldings, kiss the incomparable thane and clasp him by the neck; tears from him fell, the grey-haired man; forecast was both ways to the man of old experience, but one way stronger than the other, namely, that they might never meet again, proud men in the assembly. To him the man was so dear, that he could not restrain the passion of his breast, but deep in the affections of his soul a secret longing after the beloved man stemmed the current of his blood.

Beowulf departing thence, a warrior gold-bedight, trod the grassy earth conscious of wealth: —the sea-goer, which was riding at anchor, awaited his owner and lord. Then upon the march was the liberality of Hrothgar often praised; that was a king, every way without reproach; until old age had bereft him of the vantage of his prowess, —him who had often been a terror to many.

XXVII.

The warden of the port, his respectful demeanor. How Beowulf repays the care of the boat-warden. The home-bound voyage. Beowulf's progress to Hygelac's mansion. Talk by the way: the domestic felicity of that young king: his consort Hygd. Offa and his son Eomaer.

So the troop of gallant bachelors came to the water; they wore ring-armor, netted limb-sarks. The land-warden observed the return-march of the earls, just as he had done before; —not with suspicion from the peak of the cliff did he greet the visitors, but instead he rode towards them; he said to the Leaders of the Wed-eras that the bright-mailed explorers came welcome to their ships. Then the roomy sea-boat laden with war-harness was on the beach, the ring-prowed ship with horses and treasures; the mast rising high over the wealth from Hrothgar's hoard.

He presented to the boat-warden a gold-bound sword, insomuch that ever after he was on the mead-bench the more worshipful by reason of that decoration, that sword of pedigree. The Gothic cap-tain with his band of warriors took him to ship, plowing deep water. The Danes' land he departed by the mast a manner of sea-garment, a sail with sheet made fast; the sea-timber hummed. There did the wind over the billows not baffle the wave floater of her course; the sea-goer marched, scudded with foamy throat forward over the swell, with gorgeous prow over the briny currents, till they were able to spy the familiar headlands of the Gothic cliffs. The keel grated up ashore, with way on her from the wind; she stood on land.

Quickly was the harbor-warden ready at the strand, he who already for a long time expectant at the water's edge had eyed the craft of the beloved men; he bound to the shore the wide-bosomed ship with anchor-cables fast, lest the violence of the waves might snatch the winsome craft away from them. Then did he give orders to carry ashore the pricey riches, jewels and wrought gold; not are thence had he to go find the dispenser of wealth: Hygelac the son of Hrethel dwelleth there at court, himself with his peers, nigh unto the "sea-wall"; —the building was magnificent, the king was majestic, high in his hall; Hygd was very young, wise, of good discretion, though she had experienced a few winters in the castle, the daughter of Haereth; she was howsoever not mean-spirited, not too grudging of gifts, of stored possessions, to the Leeds of the Goths.

Thrytho displayed a moody pride, the haughty queen of the people, terrible savagery; no brave man dared venture on that, not even one of the favorite courtiers (save her own consort), that he openly gazed at her with his eyes; but he might reckon on bands of destruction being prepared for him, woven by hand; in quick succession after arrest was the knife engaged, that the instrument of outrage might settle it, making assassination famous. Such is not a queenly guise, for a lady to practice, although she be without peer; that a peace-weaver should upon a false pretense of injury, assail the life of a liege man.

However, that was checked by the kinsman of Heming; —those who drink at the ale told an altered story, namely that she did less of leed-quelling, of personal revenges, from the moment when she was given gold-adorned to the young champion, the noble and the brave; as soon as she had by her father's counsel voyaged over the fallow flood to seek Offa's hall; ever since, she had, as long as she lived in her royal state, been famed for kindness, and had well used life's opportunities; had held high love to the commander of men, who was of all mankind, my story tells, the most excellent between the seas the wide world over; forasmuch as Offa was, the spear-keen man, for graces and war-feats widely celebrated; with wisdom he ruled his ancestral home; whence Eomaer was born for people's aid, kinsman of Heming grandson of Garmund, and a skilful campaigner.

XXVIII.

The meeting of Beowulf and Hygelac. Hygelac's enquiries.
Beowulf's report.

So marched the valiant man, with his band of comrades.

He went along the strand treading the sea-laved floor, the spacious foreshores. The world's candle shone, the sun in his course shone from the South; —they pursued their journey, with mighty pace they covered the ground, to where report said that the Shelter of warriors, the banesman of Ongentheow, the war-king young and brave, was in his towers distributing rings.

Beowulf's arrival was promptly announced to Hygelac, how that there in the precincts the Shelter of fighters, his shield-companion, was coming alive, sound from battle-play, and marching to court. Quickly was cleared as the ruler commanded, for the travelers, the interior of the hall.

He sat down then by the king himself, he who had escaped the struggle, kinsman by kinsman, soon as his liege lord with loud accost had greeted his loyal man with generous words. With bombards of mead moved about that hall, Haereth's daughter loved the folk, she bore the soothing bowl to the hands of the warriors.

Then began Hygelac graciously to question his bench fellow in that lofty hall—curiosity urged him—what were the adventures of the Goths at sea: —"How befell you on your voyage, beloved Beowulf, when thou suddenly resolves to seek combat far away over salt water, battle at Heorot? But didst thou for Hrothgar, for the mighty tribute, at all mend the wide-known woe? I seethed with anxiety therefore, with gushings of sorrow; I mistrusted the adventure for a man so dear; I long besought thee, that thou wouldst have no dealings with the destructive monster, that thou wouldst let the Southern Danes themselves dispose their quarrel with Grendel. To God I offer thanks, for that I have been permitted to behold thee safe and sound."

Then did Beowulf son of Ecgtheow utter speech; "That is no secret, Hygrlac my liege, the grand meeting (is known) to numbers of men, what manner of match I and Grendel had upon that field where he many a time had wrought sorrow for the conquering Scyldings, desperate ignominy; —I avenged it all, so that not any kin of Grendel upon earth hath cause to brag of that twilight crash, not he of the detested race that longest liveth among the fens.

"At my first arrival there, I went to the ring-hall to greet Hrogthar; promptly did the mighty successor of Healfdene, when he knew my purpose, assign me a place by the side of his own son. The company was joyous; —never in my life did I see under heaven's vault guests in hall more social over mead. At one time the lofty queen, bond of peace to the nations, passed down the length of the hall, kept the young lads to their duty; —often would she bestow on some guest a laurel decoration before she went to settle. At another time before the seniors did Hrothgar's daughter bear the ale-flagon from end to end of the nobles; her I heard the hall-guests name Freaware, while she presented to the heroes the silver-studded vessel; she, the young, the gold-dight, was promised to the gay son of Froda; so hath it pleased the Friend of the Scyldings, that he through that woman should compose great contentions, sanguinary feuds. Often and not seldom anywhere, after Leed-slaughter, it is but a little while the baneful spear reposes, good though the bride may be!"

[XXIX missing from fragment]

XXX.

Continuation of Beowulf's Report to Hygelac. [partial]

† † †

"Well may it dislike the ruler of the Heathbards and every thane of that nobility, when he with the lady goeth into Hall, a prince of the Danes amidst the high company upon him do glisten heirloom of their ancestors, hard and ringed harness, Heathobardic treasure, so long as they could retain the mastery of those weapons, until they in an unlucky hour led to that buckler-play their dear comrades, and their own lives. Then sayeth one at the beer, one who observes them both, an old lance-fighter, one who fully remembers the spear-quelling of the men-bitter is the spirit within him; —sore at heart he begin to practice upon a young champion's feelings through the passions of his breast, to awaken war-fury; and that word he sayeth: —

"Canst thou, my friend, recognize the blade, the precious steel, which thy father carried into battle wearing his helmet for the last time where the Danes slew him, —when the indemnity fell through after the carnage of men, —and the masters of the battlefield were the fiery Scyldings? Now here a boy of one or other of those banesmen, proud of the spoils, walketh our hall, boasteth of the slaughter, and he weareth the treasure, of which thou by right should be the master!"

So urges he and eggs him on at every turn with galling words, until the moment comes, that for his father's deeds the lady's thane slept blood-spattered after the falcon's bite, life-doomed; —the other gets him thence away alive; knows his way well enough over land. By and by the sworn oaths of the warriors on either side will be broken; when in ingeld's mind rankle warlike purposes, and his domestic affections grow cooler amidst agitations of care. Therefore I esteem not the loyalty of the Heathbards, nor the matter of the high alliance towards the Danes sincere, the friendship firm.

"I must resume and tell about Grendel again, that thou mayest fully know, O Wealth-distributor, how far was carried the grapple of combatants. After that heaven's jewel had passed over the lands away, the monster came in fury, grisly with nocturnal raving, to visit us, where we in good heart were guarding the hall; there was the battle fatal to Hondscio, life-bale to the death-doomed; he was the first to fall, a belted champion; Grendel killed him, my brave cousin and thane, with his jaw; the beloved man's body he entirely devoured.

"But for all that, now the readier was he to depart from the gold-hall empty handed, the bloody-toothed assassin of murderous mind; but confident in strength he made trial of me, grasped with ready hand. The glove hanged, huge, and of foul aspect, strengthened with intricate bands, it was mysteriously geared with devilish machinations and dragon's fells; therein was he minded to have put in offensive me—the ferocious ruffian—with many others; he could not so manage it, when I in rage had stood upright. Too long it is to relate, how I repaid the leed-vanquisher for every evil requital due; —there did I, my prince, honor thy leeds by my works. He escaped and got away; little while did he enjoy the delights of life; —at any rate, his right hand remained behind in Heorot as a mark of his track, and he in abject plight, in woeful mood, tottered from that place down to the bottom of the sea.

"The friend of the Scyldings largely rewarded me for that encounter with beaten gold and many treasures, when the morrow had come and we had taken our seats at the banquet. There was song and glee; the venerable Scylding, a large enquirer, told tales of long ago; now a gallant warrior would waken the charm of the harp, striking the game-wood; now would one tell a tale true and piteous; now a strange story circumstantially related by the magnanimous king. At another time, by and by one in the fetters of eld, an aged veteran, would begin regretting the time of youth, of vigor for battle; his breast within him swelled, as the old man revived many memories. So we there in that place the live-long day took out delight, until that another night arrived to men.

Soon after there was one eager for vengeance, Grendel's mother; she journeyed woeful; her son by death was taken off, by the hostility of the Wederas. The awful Mere-wife revenged her bairn, quelled a baron furiously; there was an Æschere, the experienced councilor, bereaved of life; nothing could they do for him when morning came; the Danish people could not consume the lifeless man with fire, could not lay the beloved man on the funeral pile; she had borne away the body in fiendish clutches, under the mountain waterfall. Of those griefs, which had long harassed the sovereign, that was the bitterest to Hrothgar. Then did the chieftain in despairing mood entreat me—with thy leave—that I in the rush of waters would exert valor, hazard life, achieve renown; he promised me mead. I then, as it is widely known, found the grim and grisly keeper of the whirl-pool's abyss. There we two for a while had equal battle. The water gurgled with blood, and I in that abysmal dwelling shore off the head of Grendel's mother with sword of might; not easily came I thence away my life; I was not then fated to die yet, but upon me did the Shelter of heroes, the son of Healfdene, gratefully bestow bounty of treasures.

XXXI.

Beowulf concludes his report; and then he renders up to Hygelac, and to the queen, his gifts and rewards. Beowulf is promoted. Ultimately he reigned.

"So the imperial king lived in good customs; —by no means had I missed the rewards, the mead of my achievement but he gave me precious things, did Healfdene's son, into my own disposal; them will I render unto thee, noble king, as a grateful presentation. Surely all my satisfactions are along of thee; I have hardly any kinsman in chief, save thee, O Hygelac."

Then he ordered to bring in a boar head-crest, a battle-towering helmet, a gray mail-coat, a gallant cutlass; and he thereafter descanted: —"This battle-suit did Hrothgar, sapient prince, give to me, and with express word he bade, that I the pedigree thereof should report to thee; —he said that king Hiorogar, lord of the Scyldings, had it for a long while; nevertheless he would not give to his own son, the keen Heoroward, though he was loyal to him, this breast-apparel. Enjoy all well!"

I heard that upon those ornaments four horses exactly alike, followed close, apple-fallow; he to him made grateful presentation of horses and of treasures. So should a kinsman do, and not by any means spread the deceitful net for his fellow, with hidden artifice contrive death, his nephew was thoroughly loyal, and either to other studious of kindnesses.

I heard that he presented the jeweled collar to Hygd, the curiously wrought wonderful jewel, the one that Wealhtheow, daughter of a prince, had given to him; and therewithal three palfreys elegancy and saddle-dight; —from that time was her breast decorated upon collar-bestowing occasions.

So Ecgtheow's son increased in confidence, a man known in wars, in valiant deeds; he conducted himself with discretion; never did he smite his hearth fellows in their cups; his was no ruffian soul, but he of all mankind most prudently controlled the mighty talent that God had given him, like a brave soldier. Little esteemed he had been for a long time, as the children of the Goths had not counted him good for anything, nor had the Captain o hosts been pleased to make him of much dignity at the mead-bench; very often they said that he was slack, an unpromising prince; —reversal of every indignity came to the man when he was radiant with glory.

Then commanded the Shelter of warriors, the battle-famed king, to fetch in Hrethel's heir-loom, mounted with gold; there was not among the Goths at that time a treasure of more distinction in the way of a sword; that he laid upon Beowulf's bosom, and conferred upon him seven thousands, mansion, and seat of authority.

Both of them alike possessed in that community hereditary land, a family estate; but the dominion was rather to the other, who in that respect had the preeminence. By and bye that accrued, in process of days, through violence of way, when Hygelac had fallen, and instruments of war despite shield and buckler had proved fatal to Heardred; what time the tough war-wolves, the bellicose Scyldings, had come to look him in the face among his battalions, and had humbled from his raids the nephew of Hereric.

Consequently the broad realm came to the hand of Beowulf; he governed well fifty winters—that was a venerable king, an old ethel-warden—until one began in dark nights, even a dragon, to have mastery; one that is a high heath kept a hoard, a steep stone-castle; a path lay beneath, unfrequented by people. There within had gone some man or other, deftly he took of the heathen hoard, took a thing glistening with precious metal; —that he afterwards [rued], that he had tricked the horrid keeper while sleeping, with thievish dexterity . . . . . *[missing]* . . . . that he was infuriate.

The Third Part

XXXII.

How it happened that the man robbed the Dragon's hoard. That treasure was the accumulated store of ancient and forgotten warriors. The Dragon prepares revenge. The beginning of the fatal war.

Not of set purpose nor by his own free choice had he visited the dragon's hoard, he who brought sore trouble on himself; but for dire necessity had he, the slave of some one or other of the sons of men, fled from outrageous stripes a houseless wretch, and into that place had blundered like a man in guilty terror.

[Here four (or five) mutilated lines seem to say that the fugitive, though quickly horror-struck at his new danger, still by the impetus of despair borne forward had espied a cup of precious metal.]

There was a quantity of such things in that earth-cavern, ancient acquisitions; just as some unknown man in days of yore had in pensive thought hidden them there, the prodigious legacy of a noble race, treasures of worth. Death had carried them all off previously, and that solitary one then of the proud company who had there longest kept afoot, a possessor mourning lost friends, would fain survive, if only he might for a little space enjoy the long-accumulated wealth.

A barrow already existed on the down, nigh by the waves, sheer over the cliff, cunningly secured; therein did the owner of rings carry a ponderous quantity of beaten gold: a few words he spake: "Hold thou now O earth, now that the heroes could not, the possessions of mighty men. Lo! In thee at first the brave men found it; a violent death carried them away, a fearful slaughter carried off every one of the men, my peers surrendered this life; they attained the joy of the hall. Not one have I to wear a sword, or furbish the bossy tankard, the precious drink-stoup; the valiant are departed other-where. Now must the hard helmet, dama-scened with gold, shed its detailed foliations; the furbishers sleep. They whose task it was to keep the masks of war; likewise the war-coat which in battle and through the crash of shields was proof against the bite of swords, shall molder like the warrior. No longer can the ringed mail along with the war-chief widely travel by the hero's side; —no delight of harp, no joy of glee-wood, no good hawk swinging through the hall, no swift horse tramping in the castle-court. Destructive death hath sent many generations far away." Thus did he with sorrowful heart lament his unhappiness sole survivor of all he sadly wept, by day and by night, until that death's ripple touched at his heart.

The dazzling hoard was found open standing by the old pest of twilight, the flaming one that haunted barrows, the scaly spiteful dragon, the flyer by night, surrounded with fire, who country-folk hold in awful dread. His portion is to resort to the hoard under gold: he will be no whit the better for it. So had that wide-ravager for three hundred winters held in the earth an enormous treasure-house, until that one angered him, a man angered his mood; —to his chieftain the man bore a tankard bossed with gold, and prayed his lord for a covenant of peace. Then was the hoard rifled, quantity of jewels carried; the friendless man had his petition granted. The lord contemplated men's ancient work for the first time.

When the Wyrm woke, the quarrel was begun: forthwith he sniffed the scent along the rock; the marble-hearted one found the enemy's track; —he had stepped forth abroad with undetected craft, hard by the dragon's head. So may that man, who retains the fealty of the Supreme, elude death and freely escape both harm and pursuit. The hoard-keeper sought diligently over the ground, he wanted to find the man, the man who had wrought him mischief in his sleep; fiery and in raging mood he often swung around the tumulus, all out round about; there was not any man there in that desert waste. Nevertheless he exulted in purpose of battle, of bloody work, at intervals he would dash back into the barrow, would seek the costly vessel; presently he had satisfied him self of that, that some one of the man folk had invaded the gold, the mighty treasures. The hoard-keeper waited with difficulty until evening came; so enraged was the master of the barrow, the malignant one designed with the fire to revenge the loss of the precious tankard. Presently the day was gone, the

Wyrm had his will; no longer would he bide in fenced wall, but he issued forth with burning, equipped with fire. The commencement of it was frightful to the people in the country, likewise it speedily had sore ending upon their Benefactor.

XXXIII.

The Dragon's devastations. The King's mansion burned.
Beowulf's proud resolve to fight the dragon single handed.
Retrospect of the hero's former achievements, and how he
had become king.

The monster began to spurt gouts of fire, to burn the cheerful farmsteads; the hostile air-flyer would leave nothing there alive.

The war-craft of the Wyrm was manifest in all parts; the rage of the deadly foe was seen far and near; how the ravaging invader hated and ruined the Gothic people; to his hoard he shot back again, to his dark mansion, before the hour of the day. He had encompassed the land folk with flame, with fire and conflagration; he trusted in his mountain, his war-craft and his rampart; the confidence deceived him. Then was the crushing news reported to Beowulf with swiftness and certainty, that his own mansion best of buildings, was melting away in fiery eddies, even the gift-seat of the Goths. That was to the goodman a rude experience in his breast, hugest of heart-griefs the wise man felt as he should, in despite of venerable law, break out against Providence, against the Eternal Lord, with bitter outrage; his breast within him surged with murky thoughts, in a manner unwonted with him. The fire-drake had desolated the stronghold of the nobles, the sea-board front, that enclosed pale, with fiery missiles. For him therefore the war-king, the lord of the Storm-folk, studied revenge. He gave orders, that they should make for him, the shelter of warriors, the captain of knights, wholly of iron, a war-shield, a master-piece; he knew assuredly, that forest-timber would not serve him, linden-wood against flame! Destined he was, the prince of proved valor, to meet the end of the allotted days, of his worldly life; —and the Wyrm was to die at the same time, long though he had held the hoarded wealth.

Then did he, of rings the patron, think it scorn that he should go seek the wide-flyer with a band, with a large host; he had no fear of the encounter for himself, nor did the Wyrm's war-craft at all subdue his puissance and enterprise; for as much as he, in shrewd jeopardy, had carried him safe through many a contest, many a battle-crash, since the time that he, a victorious boy, had purged Hrothgar's hall, and with battailous grip had done for Grendel's kinsfolk, a loath-some brood. Not by any means littlest of hand-to-hand encounters was that, where Hygelac was slain, what time the Gothic king in the clash of battle, the liege-lord of nations, in the Frieslands, the son of Hrethel, died by the thirsty sword, felled with bill. Thence Beowulf came off by his own peculiar strength, he went through a labor of swimming; he had upon his arm thirty sets of war-harnesses when he all alone went down into the deep. The Hetware, who had confronted him bearing the linden, had no cause to be jubilant over the affray; few arrived back again from that battle-wolf to visit their home. He over swam the circuit of the fore-shore. Waters, Echtheow's son, woebegone and solitary, and got back to his people, where Hygd proffered him treasure and realm, jewels and royal throne; —she had not confidence in the Child, that he against foreigners would be able to vindicate the ancestral seats, now that Hygelac was dead. None the more readily could the bereaved people prevail with the etheling on any conditions whatever, that he should become Headred's lord, or should consent to accept the kingdom; nevertheless he held to him in the public assembly with friendly guidance, respectfully with honor, up to the time that he became of full age and reigned over the Storm-Goths.

He (Heardred) was visited from over sea by outlawed companions, other's sons; they had renounced allegiance to the crowned head of the Scyldings, the most excellent of the sea-kings that dispensed bounty in the Swedish realm, illustrious potentate. That was the limit of his (Heardred's) career; he there for his hospitality got a deadly wound with dent of sword, did Hygelac's son; and Ongentheow's (grand)son returned to draw to his home, when Heardred had fallen; he let Beowulf possess the royal throne and reign over the Goths; —that was a good king.

XXXIV.

When Beowulf had come to the throne by the king's death, he had remembered Heardred's banesman with vengeance. Preparing now for his last battle, he is filled with retrospective thoughts, and reviews his life from Childhood.

For that national disaster he meditated retribution in later days; he became a friend to Eadgils in his desolation. With force of men he supported the son of Ohthere over the wide sea, with warriors and weapons; he had his revenge at length by means of cold and painful marches; he deprived the king of life.

Thus had he, Ecgtheow's son, come well off out of all his contests, his perilous encounters, his daring adventures, up to that particular day when he had to engage with the Dragon. He had by that time learnt what was the origin of the feud, the quarrel at first; captive, rueful, he was compelled submissively to show the way to the spot; he went against his will, to where he knew of a lonely earthen dome, a tumulus topped with mould, near the sea-breakers, the clash of billows; it was inwardly full of curiosities and filigrees; the portentous keeper, aggressive war-demon, defended the golden treasures, old subterranean inhabitant; no easy bargain to go in for was that, be the man who he may. Then did the resolute king sit him down on the headland, and from that point he bade farewell. The Gothic lord, to his hearth-fellows; he had a sorrowful soul, agitated and boding, Wyrd awfully nigh, which was to greet the aged man, visit the soul's recess, divide asunder life from body; not long then was the etheling's soul encircled with flesh.

Beowulf, Ecgtheow's son, uttered speech: "Many a fierce fight have I lived through in my youth, many an hour of contest; all that I now remember. I was seven winters old when the master of riches, the liege-lord of peoples, received me from my father; king Hrethel held me as his own, gave me pocket-money and sustenance, remembered kinship; I was not at all less pleasing to him as a varlet in the castle, than any one of his own boys, Herebeald and Haethcyn, or my own lord Hygelac. For the eldest a bloody bed was unnaturally strewn by the doings of a brother, inasmuch as Haetheyn by arrow from horn-bow brought him down, his high kinsman; he missed the target and shot his brother; one brother killed the other with bloody dart; that was an assault past compensation, dastardly perpetrated, heart-paralyzing; —any way and every way it was unavoidable that the etheling must quit life unavenged.

"In like manner it is a rueful thing for an aged husbandman to experience, that his son should ride young on the gallows-tree, and he wail a dirge, a sorrowful song, while his son hangs for the raven's benefit, and he, old and of ripe experience, cannot bring him any help. Continually he is reminded, every morning, of his son's absence; he cares not to look forward to another heir in the family seat, when the one hath through violent death received for his deeds.

Sorrow-worn he beholds in his son's bower a deserted guest-hall, a lodging for the wind, bereft of hilarity; the riders sleep, the men are in the grave; there is no sound of harp, no revels in the courts, as there were once."

XXXV.

Beowulf continues the story of Hrethel, who died of a broken heart.
Further discourses Beowulf. He gives a great shout, and the
dragon comes forth. The fight begins; Beowulf in distress.

He takes to his bed; chained by a lay of sorrow, the solitary one
in memory of one (departed); to him all seemed too open, both
country and town-place.

So did the crowned head of the Storm-folk, in memory of Here-
breald, carry about a tumult of heart-sorrow; he could not possibly
requite the feud upon the man-slayer; nevermore could he pursue
the warrior with that wound had stricken him, resigned the enjoyment of human life, chose the light of God; to his children he left,
as a wealthy man doth, land and castle, when he went out of life.

Then was there provocation and reprisal between Swedes and
Goths over wide water, claims reciprocal, obstinate hard struggle,
after Hrethel was dead, and Ongentheow's sons were impetuous,
keen for adventure, and would not keep peace across the lakes; but
about Hreosnabeorh they often contrived a truculent ambuscade.
That did my cousins (i.e., Haetheyn and Hygelac) revenge, the
outrage and the wrong, as it was notorious, though one of them
paid for it with his life, a hard bargain: —to Haethcyn, the Gothic
monarch, the war was fatal. Then in the morning, so runs the tale,
brother avenged brother with sharp sword upon the smiter, where
Ongentheow engaged with Eofer; the war-helmet was split, the
aged Scylding fell blanched in death; the smiting hand made reckoning for feuds enough, Skrank not from the deadly swoop. "The
treasures which he had bestowed upon me I paid him in war, as
opportunity was given me, with flashing sword; he gave me land,
a dwelling-place, the joy of proprietorship. No need had he, that
he among the Gepidae, or the Spear-Danes, or in the Swedish
realm, should have to seek inferior champions, hire them with

pay; ever would I be to the fore in his marching ranks, single in the van; and so shall I lifelong practice warfare, while this sword holdeth out, which hath often done me good service early and late, since the time when of my prowess I did with (unarmed) hand kill Daeghrefn, the champion of the Hugas; he might not (as he had expected) bring the rich spoils [viz. of the slain Hygelac?], the breast-decoration, to the Frisian king; but in the battle-field he crouched, the standard-keeper, prince in chivalry. No weapon was his bane, but the war-grapple checked his heart-currents broke his bone-house. Now (on the contrary) must the weapon's edge, the hand and the hard sword, contend for the treasure."

Beowulf uttered speech, with boastful words he spake, for the last time: "I hazarded many wars in youth; yet again will I, the aged keeper of the folk, seek strife, and do famously; if the fell ravager out of his earthen dome will come forth to meet me." Then did he address a word of greeting to each of his men, the keen helm-wearers, for the last time, his own familiar comrades. "I would not bear sword or weapon to meet the Worm, if I knew how I might otherwise maintain my vaunt against the monster, as I formerly did against Grendel. But there I expect fire deadly scorching, blast and venom; for that reason I have upon me shield and byrnie. I will not flee away from the keeper of the mountain, no not a foot space; but it shall be decided between us two on this rampart, as Wyrd allots us, (and) the Governor of every man. I am in spirit so eager for action, that I cut short bragging against the wingy warrior. Await ye on the mountain, with your byrnies about you, men-at-arms, to see which of us twain may after deadly tussle best be able to survive his hurt. That is not your mission, nor any man's task save mine alone, that he try strength against the monster, achieve heroism. I must with daring conquer gold, or else war carrieth. Pitiless life-bale carrieth away your lord!"

Up rose then by the brink the resolute warrior, stern under his helmet, he wore battle-sark among rugged cliffs, he trusted the strength of his single manhood; such is not the way of a craven. Then he beheld near the rampart—he who, excellent in accomplishments, had survived a great number of wars, of battle-clashes, when armed men close—beheld where stood a rocky arch, and out of it a stream breaking from the barrow, the surface of that burn was steaming hot with cruel fire; nigh to the hoard could not the hero unscorched any while survive for the flame of the dragon.

Then did the prince of the Storm-Goths, being elate with rage, let forth word out of his breast, the strong-hearted stormed; the shout penetrated within (the cavern), vibrating clear as a battle-cry, under the hoary rock. Fury was stirred; the hoard-warder recognized speech of man; opportunity was there no more, to stickle for terms of peace. In advance first of all there came the reeking breath of the monster, out from the rock, a hot jet of defiance; the ground trembled. The warrior under the barrow side, the Gothic captain, swung his mighty shield against the hideous customer; therewithal was the heart of the ringy wyrm incited to seek battle. Already the brave war-king had drawn sword, ancient heirloom of speedy edge; each of the belligerents had a dread of the other. Resolute in mind the Prince of friends took stand well up to his hoisted shield, while the Worm buckled suddenly in a bow; —he stood to his weapons.

Then did the flaming foe, curved like an arch, advance upon him with headlong shuffle. The shield effectually protected life and limb less while for the glorious chieftain than his sanguine hope expected, supposing he, that time, early in the morning, was to achieve glory in the strife; —so had Wyrd not ordained it. Up swung he his hand, the Gothic captain, he smote the spotted horror with the mighty heirloom that its brown edge turned upon the bony crust; less effectually bit than was required by the king's need, who was sorely pressed. Then was the keeper of the barrow after that shrewd assault furious with rage, cast forth devouring fire, the deadly sparks sprang every way: the gold-friend of the Goths plumed him not on strokes of vantage; the war-bill had failed him with its bared edge on the foe, as it had not been expected to do, metal of old renown. That was no light experience, inducing the mighty son of Ecgtheow to relinquish that emprize; he must consent to inhabit a dwelling otherwhere; —so must every man resign allotted days.

Then was it not long until the combatants closed again. The hoard-warder rallied his courage, out of his breast shot steam, as beginning again; direly suffering encompassed with fire, was he who erewhile had ruled men. Not (alas!) in a band did his life-guardsmen, sons of ethelings, stand about him with war-custom of comrades; no, to the wood they slunk, to shelter life. In one only of them did his soul surge in a tumult of grief; —kindred may never be diverted from duty, for the man who is rightly minded.

XXXVI.

Beowulf has one faithful follower in the desperate struggle. His fatal wound.

Wiglaf was his name, Weohstan's son, a beloved warrior, a Lord of the Scyldinges, a kinsman of Ælfhere: he beheld his liege-lord under helmet, distressed by the heat. Then did he remember the (territorial) Honor which he (Beowulf) had formerly given him, the well-stocked homestead of the Waemundings, every political prerogative which his father had enjoyed; then could he not refrain; hand grasped shield, yellow linden, drew the old sword, known among men as the relic of Hammond, son of Ohthere, whom, when a lordless exile, Weohstan had slain, in fair fight, with weapon's edge; and from his kindred had carried off the brown-mottled helmet, ringed byrnie, old mysterious sword; which Onela yielded to him, his nephew's war-harness, accoutrement complete; not a word spake he (Onela) about the feud, although he (Weohstan) retained the spoils many years, bill and byrnie, until when his boy was able to claim warrior's rank, like his father before him; then gave he to him before the Goths armor untold of every sort; after which he departed out of life, ripe for the parting journey.

Now this was the first adventure for the young champion wherein he had with his liege lord to enterprise the risk of war; his courage did not melt in him, not did his kinsman's heirloom prove weak in the conflict; a fact which the Worm experienced, as soon as they had come to close quarters.

Wiglaf discoursed much that was fitting; he said to his comrades that his soul was sad: —"I recall the time, when we enjoyed the mead, then did we promise our lord in the festive hall, to him who gave us rings, that we would repay him the war-harness, if any need of this kind should befall him, would repay him for helmets and tempered swords. That is why he chose us of his host for this adventure by his own preference, reminded us of glory and promised rewards, because he counted us brave warriors, keen helm-wearers; although our lord had designed single-handed to accomplish this mighty work, the shepherd of his people, forasmuch as he of all men had achieved most of famous exploits, of desperate deeds. Now is the day come, that our liege lord behooves the strength of brave warriors; let us go to him, help our war-chief, while the scorching heat is on him, the grim fiery terror! God knows of me, that I had much believed the flame should swallow my body with my gold-giver. Me thinketh it indecent, that we bear our shields back to our home, unless we can first quell the foe, and rescue that life of the Storm-folk's ruler. I know well those were not the old habits of service, that he alone of the Gothic nobles should bear the brunt, should sink in fight; our sovereign must be requited for sword and helm, byrnie and stately uniform, and so he shall by me, though a common death take us both."

After these words were spoken, the Worm came on in fury, the fell malignant monster came on for the second time, with fire-jets flashing, to engage his enemies, hated men; with the waves of flame the shield was consumed all up to the boss; that mail-coat could not render . . . . *[obscured text]* . . . . assistance to the young warrior; but the young stripling valorously went forward under his kinsman's shield when his own reduced to ashes by the flames. Then once more the warlike king remembered glory, remembered his forceful strength, so smote with battle-bill that it stood in the monster's head, desperately impelled. Naegling flew in splinters, Beowulf's sword betrayed him in battle, through old and monumental gray. To him was it not granted that edges of iron should help him in fight; too strong was the hand of the man who with his stroke overtaxed (as I have heard say) all swords whatsoever; so that when he carried to conflict a weapon preter-naturally hard, he was none the better for it. Then the third time was the monstrous ravager, the infuriated fire-drake, roused to vengeance; he rushed on the heroic man, and he had yielded ground, fiery and destructive, his entire neck he enclosed with lacerating teeth; he was bloodied over with the vital stream; gore surged forth in waves.

XXXVII.

The Dragon slain. Beowulf in mortal agony.

Then I heard tell how, in the glorious king's extremity, the young noble put forth exemplary prowess of force and daring, as was his nature to; he regarded not that (formidable) head, but the valiant man's hand was scorched, while he helped his kinsman, insomuch that he smote the fell creature a little lower down, the man-at-arms did, with such effect that the sword penetrated, the chased and gilded sword, yea with such effect that the fire began to subside from that moment.

Then once more the beloved king recovered his senses, drew the war-knife, biting and battle-sharp, which he wore on his mail-coat; the crowned head of the Storm-folk gashed the Worm in the middle. They had quelled the foe, death-daring prowess had executed revenge, and they two together, cousin ethelings, had destroyed him;— such should a fellow be, a thane at need. To the chieftain that was the supreme triumphal hour of his career by his own deeds of his life's completed work.

Then began the wound that the earth-dragon had just now inflicted on him, to inflame and swell. That he soon discovered, that in his breast fatal mischief was working, venom in the inward parts. Then the etheling went until he sate him on a stone by the mound, thoughtfully pondering; he looked upon cunning work of dwarfs, how there the world-old-earth-dome do contain within it stone arches firmly set upon piers. Upon him then, gory from conflict, illustrious monarch, the thane immeasurably good, ladled water with hand upon his natural chieftain, battle-worn; — and unloosened his helmet. Beowulf discoursed in spite of his hurt he spake, his deadly exhausting wound; he knew well that he had spent hours, his enjoyment of earth; surely all was gone of the tale of his days, death immediately near. "Now I would have given heir had been given to come after me, born of my body. I have ruled this people fifty winters; —there was not the king, not any king of those neighboring peoples, who dared to greet me with war-mates, to menace with terror. I in my habitation observed social obligations, I held my own with justice, I have not sought insidious quarrels, nor have I sworn many false oaths. Considering all this, I am able, though sick with deadly wounds, to have comfort; forasmuch as the Ruler of men cannot charge me with murder-bale of kinsmen, when my life quitteth the body.

Now quickly go thou, to examine the treasure, under the hoary rock, beloved Wiglaf, now the Wyrm lieth dead, sleepeth sore wounded, of riches bereaved. Be now on the alert, that I may ascertain the ancient wealth, the golden property, may fully survey the brilliant, the curious gems; that I may be able the more contentedly, after (seeing) the treasured store, to resign my life, and the lordship which I long to have held.

XXXVIII.

Beowulf is gratified with seeing the treasure; he demises the crown, and dies.

Then I heard tell how the son of Wihstan after the injunction promptly obeyed his wounded death-sick lord; bore his ring-mail, linked war-sark, under the roof of the barrow. Then the victorious youth, as he went along but the stony bench, the true and courageous thane, beheld many jewels of value, gold glistening, indenting the ground, wondrous things in the barrow; —and the lair of the Wyrm, the old dawn-flyer vases standing, choice vessels of men of old, with none to burnish them, —their incrustations fallen away. There was many a helmet, old and rusty, many a bracelet, with appendage of trinkets. Treasure may easily, gold in the earth, may easily make a fool of any man; heed it who will! Likewise he saw looming above the hoard a banner all golden, greatest marvel of handiwork, woven with arts of incantation; out of it there stood forth a gleam of light, insomuch that he was able to discern the surface of the floor, and survey the strange curiosities. Of the Wyrm there was not any appearance, but the knife had put him out if the way.

Then I heard how in the chambered mound the old work of dwarfs was spoiled by a single man, how he gathered into his lap cups and platters at his own discretion; the banner also he took, the most brilliant of ensigns the sword with its iron edge had even now dispatched the old proprietor, the one who had been the possessor of these treasures for a long while; a hot and flaming terror he had waged for the hoard, gushing with destruction at midnights; until he died the death.

The messenger was in haste, eager to return, fraught with spoils; painfully he wondered in his brace soul whether he should find alive the prince of the Storm-folk, on the open ground where he left him erst, chivalrously dying. He then bearing the treasures, found the illustrious king, his captain, bleeding from his wounds, at the extremity of life; he began again to sprinkle him with water, until the point of speech forced open the treasures of his breast. Beowulf discoursed, the old man in pain, he contemplated the gold: "I do utter a thanksgiving to the Lord of all, to the king of glory, to the eternal captain, for those spoils upon which I here do gaze; to think that I have been permitted to acquire such for my Leeds before the day of my death. Now I have sold my expiring life-term for a hoard of treasure; you now shall provide for the requirements of the Leeds; I cannot be any longer here. Order my brave warriors to erect a lofty cairn after the bale-fire, at the headland over the sea; it shall tower aloft on Hronesness for a memorial to my Leeds, that sea-faring men in time to come may call it Beowulf's Barrow, those who on distant voyages drive their foamy barks over the scowling floods."

The brave-hearted monarch took off from his neck the golden collar and gave it to the thane, to the young spear-fighter, his gold-hued helmet, coronet, and byrnie; bade him brook them well: "Thou art the last remnant of our stock, of the Waegmundings; Fate has swept all my kinsmen away into eternity, princes in chivalry; I must go after him."

That was the aged man's latest word, from the meditations of his breast, before he chose the bale-fire, the hot consuming flames; —out of his bosom the soul departed, to enter into the lot of the Just.

XXXIX.

A brief review of the situation. Wiglaf upbraids the recreant guards. He pronounces upon them and their kin a sentence of degradation.

Thus had a hard experience overtaken the inexperienced youth, that he saw upon the ground the man who was dearest to him at his life's end in a helpless condition. His destroyer likewise lay dead, the horrible earth-dragon, bereft of life, rushed in ruin; no longer was the coiled Wyrm to be lord of the jewel-treasures, but they had been wrested from him with weapons of iron, hard battle-sharp relics of hammers, insomuch that the wide-flyer tamed by wounds had fallen on earth night to the hoard-chamber; no more through the regions of air did he sportively whirl at midnights, and elate over his treasured property display his presence; but on earth he collapsed, through mighty hand of warrior-prince.

Howbeit that had rarely in the world prospered with men, even men of fame, —by my information, —daring though a man might be in all deeds whatsoever; that he should rush against the breath of the poisonous destroyer, or with hands molest the ring-hall, if he found the keeper waking, at home in the barrow. Beowulf had purchased the gain of princely treasures with his death; he had howsoever reached the end of transitory life.

Then was it not long until the war-laggards quitted the wood, the faint-hearted traitors, ten all together, those who while there dared not sport their lances in the great need of their liege lord; but they in shame bore their shields, their war-weeds, to the place where the aged warrior lay dead; —they looked upon Wiglaf!

He sat wearied out, the active champion, near his lord's shoulder; was refreshing him with water; his care availed nothing; he could not retain upon earth, well as he would have wished it, that chieftain's life; nor turn the Almighty's will; the dispensation of God would take effect upon men of all conditions, just as it does at present. Then had the young man a grim answer promptly ready for such as erst had failed in courage. Wiglaf discoursed, Weohstan's son; the youth with sorrowful heart looked upon men whom he no longer loved; —

"That, look you, may a man say, a man who is minded to speak the truth, that the chieftain who gave you those decorations, military apparel, which ye there stand upright in, —when he at ale-bench often presented to inmates of his hall helmet and byrnie, as a prince to thanes, of such make as he far or near could procure most trusty? that he utterly threw away those war-weeds miserably. When stress of battle overtook him, the folk-king had no means cause to boast of his companions-in-arms; nevertheless it was accorded to him by God the ordainer of victories, that he avenged himself single-handed with his weapon, when his valor was put to the proof. Little protection could I afford him in the conflict, and I attempted nevertheless what was beyond my ability, to help my kinsman; —ever was he (the dragon) the feebler, when I with sword smote the destroyer, the fire less violently gushed from his inwards. Defenders too few pressed round their prince, when the dire moment overtook him. Now must (all) sharing of treasure, and presentation of swords, all patrimonial wealth and estate, escheat from your kin; every man of that family may roam destitute of land-right as soon as ethelings at a distance are informed of your desertion, your ignominious conduct, death is preferable, for every warrior, rather than a life of infamy."

XL.

Announcement of the event to the armed host. The envoy adds a discourse, reviewing the situation.

Order gave he then to announce the issue of the conflict to the camp up over the sea cliff, where the host of earls, from morning all day long, had with anxious hearts sate by their shields, in divided anticipation between a fatal day and the return of the beloved man. Little reticent was he of the latest tidings, he who rode up the bluff; he truthfully spake out in the hearing of all; Now is the bounteous chief of the Leeds of the Stormfolk, the captain of the Goths, motionless on bed of death, he dwells in war-like repose by the deeds of the Wyrm! With him in even case lieth his mortal antagonist, smitten with dirk-wounds: —with sword he could not upon the monster by any means effect a wound. Over Beowulf sitteth Wiglaf, Wihstan's boy, a living earl over a dead; over his unconscious head he holdeth guard against friend and foe.

Now the Leeds may expect a time of war, as soon as the king's fall is published abroad Franks and Frisians. The obstinate quarrel with the Hugas was set up when Hygelac came with embarked army vanquished him; resolutely they struck with over-whelming force, insomuch that the mailed warrior was compelled to bow his head; he fell among the fighting men; far was he from giving spoils as chieftain the fighting veterans; —to us ever since that time has the favor of the Merwing been unaccorded;

"Nor do I anywise count upon peace or good understanding on the side of Sweden; —indeed it was a far-famed story, how that Ongentheow slew Haethcyn the son of Hrethel by Ravenswood, when as the warlike Scyldings had been the first to invade for sheer insolence the people the Goths. Promptly did the veteran, the father of Ohthere, old and awful, deliver his onslaught, demolished the sea-king (Haethcyn), rescued his consort, the aged man rescued the wife of his youth, though plundered of her jewels, the mother of Onela and of Ohthere, and then pursued his deadly foes, until they got away, with great difficulty, into Ravensholt, bereaved of their lord. Then did he, with host drawn out, surround those whom the sword had left, men exhausted with wounds, he repeatedly threatened woe to the poor band all the livelong night: he said that in the morning he would reach them with the edge of the sword, and (hang) some on gallows-trees to please the birds.

"Courage at length returned to the dejected men with dawn of day, when they heard Hygelac's horn, and the sound of his trumpet; presently the brave (prince) came marching upon their track with the best of his Lords."

XLI.

Conclusion of the envoy's discourse. The battalion visits the scene of the supreme conflict.

"Then was the gory track of Swedes and Goths, the deadly strife of men, widely conspicuous, how the folk on either side revived the feud. Then did the valiant man proceed with his comrades, the solemn veteran, to seek a place of strength; the warrior Ongentheow turned towards the hill; he had heard tell of the warfare of Hygelac, the war-craft of the valiant; he trusted not in resistance, that he could defy the seaman, the travelers of the deep, could protect his treasure, his children, and his wife; so he retired back there-from, the old king retired behind the earth-wall.

Then was chase given to the Swedish Leeds; the banners of Hygelac moved forward over that peaceful plain, and presently the Hrethkings massed themselves upon the garrison. Then was Ongentheow, the grey-haired, driven to bay with sword-edges, insomuch that the mighty king was constrained to put up with one-handed decision of Eofor. Him (Ongentheow) had Wulf son

of Wonred fiercely attacked with weapon, so effectually, that with
the stroke his blood flew from his veins out from under his hair.
He was not daunted however, the aged Scylding; but he quickly
repaid that deadly assault with worse barter, as soon as the mighty
king had collected himself. The brisk son of Wonred failed to give
counter-blow to the old veteran, but he (Ongentheow) had first
shorn he was forced to bow, he fell on the ground: —he was not
at the time death-doomed as yet, but he recovered from it, though
the wound had touched him close. Then did Hygelac's valiant
thane [i.e., Eofor] let his broad blade, gigantesque old sword, his
dwarf-wrought helmet, break over the shield-wall; then crouched
the king, the people's shepherd, he was fatally smitten. Then were
there, many who bound up his brother's wounds (of Wulf the
brother of Eofor), who quickly raised him up, when they had got
the ground cleared, so that warrior stripped warrior; he (Eofor)
captured on Ongentheow the iron breast-mail, his hard sword
with hilt, and his helmet likewise, the grey-beard's accoutrements;
—to Hygelac he bare them. He accepted the spoils, and made him
a fair promise of rewards before his Leeds, and he kept his word;
he the lord of the Goths, the son of Hrethel, when he arrived at
his mansion, repaid Jofor and Wulf for that war-brunt, with
treasure extraordinary; he gave to each of them a hundred thousand of land and collars of filigree; none could jeer at them for
those rewards, not a man in the world, since they had achieved
those exploits; —and moreover he bestowed upon Jofor his only
daughter, to make his home honorable, and for a pledge of loyalty.

Such is the feud and the enmity and the deadly grudge of the
men, even the Swedish Leeds, who, as I apprehend, will attack
us, as soon as they shall learn that our prince is dead, he who
whilere hath upheld against hostilities, our treasure and our
realm, was master of public counsel, or won ever-increasing glory
in war. Now is quickness best, that we should there look upon the

mighty king, and bring him who gave us bracelets, on the funeral-pile. It is not meet that some trifling matter be consumed with the high-souled man; but yonder is a hoard of precious . . .
. . . . . . [*obscured*] . . . . Things, gold uncounted, frightfully bargained for, and now at last jewels purchased with the hero's own life; those must fire devour, the flame must enfold them; never a warrior wear ornament for memorial. Nor maiden sheen have on her neck the decorated collar, but on the contrary must in dejected mood and stripped of gold ornaments tread often and often the land of the stranger, not the army leader hath laid aside laughter, game hoisted in the hand; no swough of harp shall waken the warriors: but the bleak raven fluttering over carnage shall chatter abundantly, recount to the eagle of his luck at the spread, while alongside of the wolf he stripped the slain."

Thus was the ardent youth discoursing of painful themes; he erred not widely of events or words. All the troop arose, they went unjoyous, under the Eagle's Crag, with gushing tears, to behold the tremendous sight. They found there, on the sand, bereft of life, and keeping his helpless bed, the man who had given them rings in times bygone; there had the final day come to the valiant, in the warlike king, the prince of the Wederas, had perished with a death heroic.

. . . . . never saw they frightfuller object? The dragon on the ground there right before their face, the loathsome beast lying dead; all scorched with flames was the fire-drake, the grisly gruesome pest; it was forty foot measurements long where it lay; in the pride of the air he had been supreme during the hours of night, and then down would he return back again to reconnoiter his lair: —now he was there stock dead, had made his last use of earthly caverns. By the side of it stood pots and bowls; there dishes lay about, and swords of price, rusty and corroded, as if they in earth's lap a thousand winters there had sojourned;

forasmuch as that patrimony, huge and vast, that gold of ancient men, had been closed about with enchantment; and therefore that treasure-chamber might not be touched by any one of mankind, save in so far as God himself, the true king of achievements, should grant to the man of his choice to open the hoard the sorcerers' hold: —even to such one of mankind whom so he deemed to be meet.

XLII.

Reflections upon the great event. Wiglaf publishes Beowulf's dying orders. Preparations for the bale-fire. The cavern is rifled, and the treasures are piled on a wagon to follow the bier. The last of the dragon.

Then was it manifest, that good luck attended not upon the course of them who by unlawful means had closely safe-guarded valuables under the mound. At first the keeper slew one here and there; at length the feud had grown to be expiated furiously, by a heroic death therefore in some manner should a brave warrior accomplish the end of life's record, seeing that he cannot much longer as a man in the midst of his kinsfolk inhabit the mead-hall. Such was Beowulf's lot, when he went forth to seek the Keeper of the barrow, went to seek deadly strife, he himself knew not by what means his severance from the world was destined to happen, according as the mighty captains, when they that deposited there, had uttered a deep spell to hold till doomsday, that the man who invaded that ground should be criminally guilty, cabined in heathen fanes, fast bound with hell-bands, penally doomed; yet never did he at any previous time more effectually experience the gold bestowing favor of god.

Wiglaf son of Wihstan lifted up his voice: "Often must many a brave man, by the will of one, endure tribulation, as it hath happened to us. We were not able to convince our beloved master, the shepherd of the kingdom, by any reasoning, that he should not challenge you gold-warden, but should leave him to lie where he had long been. And to dwell in his haunts till the end of the world, fulfill high destiny. The hoard is laid open to our view, fearfully purchased; too overpowering was that boon which attracted our prince thither. I was in the interior of the place, and I explored the whole of it, the stores of the chamber, inasmuch as the way had been opened for me and that by no gentle means, passage was permitted in under the earthen dome. Hurriedly I grappled with my hands a huge mighty burden of hoarded treasures; out hither I bore them to the feet of my king. He was still alive then, wise and sensible; freely did he talk, the aged one in death-pang; and he commanded me to give you his greeting, he bade that you should construct, in memory of your chieftain's deeds, upon the scene of the bale-fire, a barrow of the highest, mighty and magnificent, according as he was of all men the warrior most famous, through the wide earth, so long as he might enjoy the wealth of his castle.

"Go to, let us now hasten, a second time, to see and to visit the ruck of jewels, the spectacle beneath the earthwork. I will be your guide, so that ye shall have your fill of seeing close at hand, collars and bullion gold.

"Let the bier be ready, promptly equipped, attending us as we go forth of this place, and so let us convey our master, the beloved man. To the place where he shall tarry longing the safe keeping of the Almighty."

Then did the son of Wihstan order his brave warriors that they should issue commands to many homestead-owners, for them to haul pyre-timber from far to meet the occasion of the Ruler of men: —"Now must fire devour, the scowling flame must wash, the Pillar of warriors, him who often stood the shock of the iron shower, what time the storm of missiles, urged by bow-strings, hurtled over the shield-wall, the shaft did its duty, with feather-fittings eager it backed up the arrow's point."

Thereupon the prudent son of Wihstan called out of the squadron some thanes of the king, seven of them together, the choicest; he made the eighth, and when with them under the dangerous roof; a warrior bore in hand a flaming torch, and he walked in front. It was not staked upon lot who should have the looting of that hoard, when the warriors had partly taken a view of it in its keeperless state occupying the chamber, lying helpless. Little did any man scruple that they should with all dispatch convey abroad the valuable treasure; the Dragon moreover they haled, they shoved the Wyrm over the precipitous cliff, they let the waves take him, the flood engulf him, that warder of precious spoils. There was coiled gold laden upon wagon, countless in quantity of every kind; —the etheling was borne on a bier, the hoary warrior, to Hronesness.

XLIII.

The Funeral and the Epitaph.

For him then did the Leeds of the Goths construct a pyre upon the earth, one of no mean dimensions, hung about with helmets, with battle-boards, with bright byrnies, as he had requested; then did they, heaving deep sighs, lay in the midst of it the illustrious chieftain, the hero, the beloved lord. Then began the warriors to kindle upon the hill the hugest of bale-fires; the wood-smoke mounted up black over the combustive mass, the roaring blaze shot aloft, mingled with the howling of the wind-currents; until the sweltering element had demolished the bone-house. With hearts distressed and care-laden minds they mourned their liege lord's death; likewise a dirge of sorrow was sung in honor of Beowulf by the aged dame, her hair bound up, her soul sorrowing; she said repeatedly, that she sorely dreaded for herself evil days, much bloodshed, the warrior's horror, shame and captivity. Heaven swallowed the smoke.

Then did the people of the Wederas construct a tumulus on the hill; it was high and broad, to sea-voyagers widely conspicuous; and during of the war-hero's beacon: they surrounded the ashes of the conflagration with an embankment in such wise as men of eminent skill could contrive it with noblest effect. They deposited in the barrow collars and brilliants, the whole . . . *[Here are six mutilated lines]* . . . . of such trappings as war-breathing men had recently captured in the Hoard; they abandoned the accumulated wealth of earls for the earth to retain it, gold in marl, where it now still continues to be as useless to mankind as it ever was.

Then there rode around the tumulus war-chiefs, sons of ethelings, twelve in all; they would bewail their loss, bemoan the king, recite an elegy, and celebrate his name. They admired his manhood, and they loftily appraised his daring work; as it is fitting that a man should with words extol his liege lord, should cherish him in his affections, when he must take his departure from the oh-so-temporary body.

Thus did Leeds of the Goths, the companions of his hearth, lament the fall of their lord; —they said that he was of all kings in the world, the mildest and most affable to his men; most genial to his Leeds; and most desirous of PRAISE.

BEOWULF AND THE
MASTER OF HIS CRITICS
Interlude 1

°‡°

Oxford—the late summer/early fall of 1936

The former student from Cambridge felt quite at home on the outstretches of the university that was Oxford even though he was sober, a state almost entirely unfamiliar to him during his tenure as a student. The short walk from where the bus had left him to 20 Northmoor Road was more than enough to clear his head.

His foreign contacts were beginning to get a little impatient with him, and he hoped that either this excursion didn't turn out to be another fruitless wild goose chase or that perhaps the BBC would get back to him about the producing position that he had interviewed for.

Not for anything he was actually looking forward to meeting this fellow. He had seen a transcript of the Monster speech he gave, and liked the passion and objectivity of his approach.

Just because it was a monster tale was no reason not to take it seriously, he concurred. *Indeed, some of my most recent acquaintances have turned out to be monsters, and they will probably be joined by many more of my comrades before the revolution is over.*

And the fact that he had expressed to a mutual acquaintance a certain admiration for the virtues and patriotism of the Germanic people had to be a plus. (The fact that the real project at hand, pardoning the pun, would no doubt be a scholar's delight, particularly an underpaid one who might be in search of some recognition outside of the classroom.)

"Are you the fellow who sent me those stories?" a tweedy fellow in his midforties harrumphed from the front garden at 20 Northmoor.

"Indeed," the man from Cambridge answered to the Oxford master, "as well as the bank draft to cover your time."

"Why anyone would pay me to read these . . . It's just the silliest of riddles."

"May I come in?"

The Oxford Master opened the gate, and allowed him to pass into the humble home.

"The time has been paid for so I have no reason to bar you . . . and the rate is far better than my usual tutelage fees. Come in."

Beowulf and the City of the Dark Elves

Jeff Grubb

For five days and nights, Beowulf traveled in a single direction—upward. From the stone shores of Aelfdal, its beaches bleached and rounded like a shoal of skulls, he left his boat and companions behind and headed skyward. He threaded his way through the giant-strewn boulders above the bustling seaport, until he reached the plateau, then across that great grassland, its blades nothing less than golden spears heralding his passing, to the foothills proper, where the grasses turned to brush and then to sentinel pines and there nestled among those pines the trading crossroads at Gelth.

And from Gelth he moved upward still, and the sentinel pines around him clustered together to form a great battlement of forest, which rose above him and sealed out sun, moon, and stars.

And through that darkness Beowulf climbed. To an unnamed

outpost where hunters and lycamorphs traded pelts and prom-
ises, now he was past the outpost and upward still, the pines
scattered by great pillars of dark stone, their hexagonal sides
cut and finished at hands of an ancient empire, now toppled
down from higher peaks. The forest at last surrendered the sky,
and the moon lay brooding ahead of him, caught by snow-
capped peaks.

The road out of Aelfdal had now become a path and then a
trail, and then a hint of a trail, but Beowulf still moved upward.
Black-shadowed vultures watched his progress from the last bare
branches of the forest, and at last the trees surrendered entirely,
and still he moved upward.

With the forest's passing, the land became bare pasture,
studded with rocks and angular fragments, the lichen and scrub
grass, and in the shade of the rocks collected patches of snow
unmelted, though it be high summer. Goats looked up from their
grazing as he passed, but he saw no shepherds.

Five days and five nights, and even Beowulf's calves were tight
and clenched from the strain, and his lungs labored hard in the
ever-chilling air. Ahead and upward he could see the mountains
themselves loom overhead, and the rocks steamed in places from
underground fires. And after five days and five nights, he reached
the palisade of the town of Flambruk.

The dying sun still clutched the edge of the world when the
weary Beowulf thundered against the palisade with the pommel
of his blade. At last a worn-faced man poked his head up and
asked him his business. Now Beowulf spoke, his voice cracked
from disuse, and his words felt weak and frail in the thin air.

"I am Beowulf," he said simply. "My father was Ecgtheow and
my mother the daughter of Hrethel of the Geats. I have slain
giants and serpents and monsters and the mothers of monsters. I
come in the name of my liege Hygelac, for I am his champion."

The worn-faced man's countenance seemed to brighten. "And what be your business with us, Beowulf, champion of Hygelac?"

"My liege sends me to your Thane," he said, "on a matter of tribute."

† † †

"Of course, I always thought it a matter of time before Hygelac sent someone," said Gris, Master of Flambruk and the Thane of the Highlands. "One angers our lord at one's own risk, eh?"

Beowulf, for his part, managed a grunt and took a long pull from the drinking horn. They sat on the ground, at a low table in the center of the Thane's hut.

"I would not know," said Beowulf. "I have rarely angered him. And neither have you. He merely wishes to know if something is amiss."

Gris for his part was a heavy man, a muscular fighter in his youth but now given to the comforts and respect of middle age. His beard and moustache were full, and blond and heavy, and his hair lightened only slightly with age, gathered behind his ears in a loose braid. He rested on pillows on his side of the table, well made but also well used.

"Amiss," said Gris, and let out a sigh that sounded like a hillside subsiding. "Yes, you could say that. Do you know the nature of the tribute we owe our liege?"

Beowulf shrugged.

"Gold," said Gris. "Gold and amber and gems."

Beowulf looked about. Gris's home was more opulent than he had expected. Indeed, it matched that of any he had seen in Aelfdal. The ironwork within the house was excellent, and the hangings were thick and woven both expertly and recently. Great earthenware jars of grain and wine from the lowlands ringed the central room of the building. The Thane was indeed a prosperous man.

Of gold and amber, however, Beowulf saw precious little.

Gris followed Beowulf's gaze and smiled a yellow-toothed fence at the warrior. "Yes, you do not see that much gold and amber here. Because we in turn have been trading for these goods, and that trade has gone astray. As Thane, I hold myself responsible for this, not my people, and if you wish to depose me from my seat for my failure, you can do so."

Beowulf shook his head and grimaced at his cup. The wine was no sweeter than that on Aelfdal's shores, yet it seemed more potent. He said, "My lord remembers you well for your service in years past. He sent me here to encourage the restoration of that tribute, not to depose anyone. I would not do so without his leave. So tell me, who were you trading with?"

"Ah," said Gris. "That is a local secret, one that we do not share with most lowlanders, for fear of others coming up the vales to our land. And it was in keeping that secret I was mindful not to spread word of our difficulty downward. Again, my responsibility."

"You bear your burdens well," said Beowulf, "but we serve the same liege. Whom have you been trading with?"

Gris looked about, as if strangers were about to enter this hall, then stared at Beowulf.

"Elves," he said.

"Elves," said Beowulf.

"Elves," continued Gris in a low tone. "Elves from beneath the mountain. Shadow elves. Dark elves. Miner elves. Knockers. Cobolds. Spawn of Cain. Call them as you will, they keep their own cities, towns, and villages in the great range of mountains above us. There they keep their forges in the heart of the mountains, and their industry causes the hot springs to steam and forms pools of flame in the highest peaks."

"I have heard of the race," said Beowulf. "They say they are the finest craftsmen in the world, but chary to deal with."

"Indeed," said Gris, "but in exchange for our food and wine and cloth, they share their bounty with us, and we in turn send it down the slopes to Aelfdal and from there to our liege. Surely your lord makes gifts of gold torcs and necklaces dripping with amber tears? Do you never wonder where they came from?"

"Some are from spoils and booty, from wergilds and gifts of other leaders," said Beowulf.

"Indeed," said Gris, reaching for a simple pewter pitcher and splashing more wine into the warrior's horn. "But some of it is newly made, and it comes from the city of the dark elves."

Beowulf took another pull, and smacked his lips at the potency of the wine. "And from all this I assume that matters are not as what they once were."

"Alas, no," sighed Gris, and Beowulf wondered where the older man got all the air to manage such deep sighs. "Less than a year ago, there was a . . . falling out. Between them and us. So, no more gold. No more amber."

Beowulf stared at the dregs floating at the bottom of the horn. "No more tribute."

"Indeed," said Gris. "Though we do have much that we can offer. Our smiths are second to none in forging iron, and our goats produce excellent cheese and good wool." He managed a weak smile. "Perhaps if one would intercede with our liege it would make matters less difficult for us."

"Perhaps if one went to speak with the dark elves directly," said Beowulf.

Gris, Thane of Flambruk, literally winced, then leaned back on his pillows, beard against his chest. "Ah. And there our tale takes a darker turn."

"Darker?"

"The matter of the falling out," said Gris, with another unendingly deep sigh. "The elves from beneath the mountain, they made demands that we could not abide by."

"And those demands were?"

"Meat. Specifically the meat of children. Their liege got the taste for it, from his barbarous brothers further north. So they spurned our goats and cheese and woven cloth. And demanded the meat of children."

"Which you could not provide," said Beowulf.

"Could not and would not," growled Gris, shaking his head. "And within their mountain fastness, they have proved to be invulnerable. Worse yet, they have taken to raiding us for that which we will not provide. You notice our sheep and goats roam wild? That is because no family dares leave their children unattended. And of late they have broken into the town itself, and raided us for our youngest. We have lost many."

Beowulf felt a rage building within him. "And you have done nothing? You have not sought out these creatures?"

The Thane's face colored. "I have done nothing but, and wasted days and weeks chasing their raiding parties. I have put arrows into at least three with my own bow, by the dark of the moon, but have yet to rescue a single child, or dissuade the elves from their actions. Safe within their mountain, we cannot reach them. But now that you know, you can carry word to Hygelac of our plight."

"Or I can take care of that matter myself," said Beowulf grimly. "If it is only the ruler has gotten a taste for human flesh."

Gris nodded slowly. "I am sure that if their barbarous lord was slain, the rest of his kind would fall into line," he said. "Would that you return with even a small force of trained men, I am sure that we can—"

"I can take care of that myself," said Beowulf, standing now. "I was told to do what I could to restore the tribute. I think this falls within those bounds. Where do I find this City of the Dark Elves?"

Gris looked up at him, and slowly shook his head. But he pointed toward the mountains and said, "Up."

† † †

Beowulf arose the next morning to find that Gris's handmaidens had already packed food and water for him. Five men waited for Beowulf at the palisade gate.

"We will come with you," said the worn-faced man from the previous evening. All five were dressed in a clattering mix of armor pieces that had been passed down from their fathers—mismatched shoulder plates and borrowed greaves, all lashed over thick hides. They carried an ill-sorted arrangement of blades, axes, and hammers more suitable for the carpenter's shop than the battlefield.

"I can use a guide," said Beowulf pointing at the worn-faced man, "but I have no use for bringing my own village with me."

The worn-faced man nodded but did not stand aside. "I am Gundar. My son was taken by the elves." He motioned to the others. "Snorri and Alric have lost daughters. Sebbi and Bregnar have had sons taken from the fields. Bregnar's was but an infant. We will come with you."

Beowulf started to say, "Your children . . ."

". . . may yet be alive," said Gundar. "The slimmest hope is still hope."

Beowulf shook his head and started to say, "Your liege . . ."

". . . has granted us permission to aid you," finished Snorri, a thick-shouldered man. "We have asked to pursue the elves into their lair but he has forbidden us previously. Perhaps he thinks you will keep us alive."

Beowulf looked back at the longhouse. Gris stood in the doorway. The Thane gave a short, grim nod, then retreated back into the darkness.

Beowulf turned to the others. They had not disobeyed their liege previously, but now, with a real hope at hand, they were willing to risk their lives.

They might follow him regardless of his answer.

"Very well," said Beowulf. "We're going up."

† † †

The climb took two days. Even the pretense of meadows and scrub disappeared beneath a continual onslaught of grey rock. Beowulf saw more of the hexagonal pillars as well, but now realized that they were nothing more than dark shards that had fallen off the mountain cliffs themselves, leaving long vertical grooves in the sides of the granite peaks.

At first he was worried that the villagers would slow him down. Instead, it was he who labored up over every rockfall. The natives of Flambruk were surefooted and steady, and seemed unaffected by the heights.

Beowulf looked down into the valley beneath, and could not even see the sea in the murky distance. The corners of his vision lit with new stars as he stared. He shook his head and followed the others upward.

The group moved swiftly during the day, but insisted on finding a suitable cavern before nightfall.

The night belonged to the dark elves.

"They hate the light," said Alric. Beowulf had him pegged as being the good-humored one, the one who would make a joke in less-perilous situations. This was not one of those situations. "They come down in a single night to just above the village, when we used to trade. But always at night."

"What do these dark elves look like?" said Beowulf, looking out past the entrance.

There was a silence. Then Alric spoke up again. "They wear purple cloaks."

"They wear purple cloaks," said Gundar, "because we traded them purple cloaks. They hide beneath them. Gris probably knows what they look like. He would be the one to meet with them."

"Him alone?"

"Gris would take a couple guards, and his bow made of horn when they would meet, but among the meeting stones, only the Thane and the King of the Dark Elves would meet. Then his people would bring goods to the meeting spot, and would leave. And we would bring what we promised, and take their goods, and leave ourselves. And they would head up the mountain."

"And you know nothing of the King of these dark elves?" asked Beowulf.

"Only that he is as large as Gris," said Gundar.

"Larger," said Alric.

† † †

The snow did not hide in the shadows now, but blew up in drifts on either side of them, and while the sky was clear the wind churned up bits of ice and tossed them in the travelers' faces. Their breath puffed in the chill air, but did not rise, instead streaming after them like frustrated clouds.

On the second night, they could not find a proper cavern, and instead huddled beneath a slight overhang just off their path. They made no fire. As Beowulf honed his blade, the sword's edge danced in the moonlight.

"Does it have a name?" asked the thick-shouldered one, Snorri. "Your sword. Does it have a name?"

"No," said Beowulf. "A named blade often cannot carry the load that a name puts upon it. It will always fail you at the worst time."

Snorri nodded as if he understood, then said, "My own sword could stand a good whetting. I was wondering if . . . what?"

Beowulf stood up and moved to the edge of the overhang and motioned for Snorri to remain. Then he slipped out around the corner and was lost to sight.

Snorri edged forward, Gundar behind him. There was no sign of the Geatish warrior.

"What did you say to him?" said Gundar.

"I asked him about his sword," said Snorri. "I didn't mean to offend him."

"If you offended him," said Gundar, "you would know it sooner than this."

There was a hiss of metal and a sudden, truncated cry. More of a gasp than a cry, it was enough to wake the other three men and bring them to the edge of the overhang.

"Was that Beowulf?" asked Bregnar. "Did he cry out?"

"I don't know," said Gundar.

"It didn't sound like him," said Sebbi.

"I said I don't know," said Gundar.

"If it was him," said Alric, "does this mean we have to go back now?"

"We go on," said Gundar.

Bregnar shook his head. "You know Gris wouldn't have let us go off on our own, without him."

"We've come this far," said Gundar. "Whatever else happens, we go on."

There was silence for another moment. Then Beowulf returned, hauling something over his shoulder.

"It is good that there was only one," said Beowulf. "You can hear your skull-rattling worries all the way up the canyon."

He laid his burden down. It was the size of a man, but thin and pale, and wrapped in dark robes.

"What is it?" asked Gundar.

"Dark elf," said Beowulf. "I think. We won't risk a fire, but get a look at it in the morning. Here." He passed a slender sword to Gundar. "This should be better than the pig knife you're carrying."

Beowulf set himself down at the far side of the overhang. He let out a deep breath and closed his eyes. Within a few moments he was snoring.

The other five men looked at the shadowy corpse next to them.

"What do you think happened?" asked Bregnar.

"I don't know," said Snorri, looking at Gundar's new sword. "But I'm willing to believe that your new sword once had a name."

Alric said, "It has no eyes."

Beowulf grunted agreement.

In the harsh morning light, their guest's appearance had not improved from several hours previous. Its flesh was a pale violet, made paler still by the blood from its wounds, which pooled in a purplish puddle beneath it. Even the ragged gash across its chest and throat had purple, peeled-back edges. It had no eyes, instead large purplish bruises bulging slightly out from its skull above a thin, almost nonexistent nose with elongated nostrils, edged with flaps of skin. Its teeth were long and barbed, curling inward, its ears oversized and pointed. Its white hair was patchy, like mange. Despite its nonhuman appearance, it had on its face a look halfway between surprise and disappointment.

The elf was clad in a chain shirt, now ripped open from the warrior's attack. The links were black and slimy to the touch, as if they sweated their own oil. The robe it wore over everything was purple, made in the lowlands and traded.

"Scout" said Beowulf, "was only fifty yards away when I found him. Probably drew him to us with our noise." He looked at Snorri, and the thick-shouldered man looked out over the valley. Beowulf added, "We are close to their home. We should be careful."

Beowulf went to the far side of the overhang to get their gear. The other village men kept a healthy distance from the corpse.

"There is something else," said Gundar, who followed Beowulf. "You are grimmer than normal."

"Aye," said Beowulf. "This one was coming up the valley, not down it. It may have been following us. And it may not have been alone."

Gundar looked grim as well.

"Hello!" said Alric. "It has no palisade! What kind of city has no wall?"

"It doesn't need a wall," said Sebbi. "It's got the mountain itself to protect it."

Alric protested, "But it doesn't even have a gate! What good is that?"

Indeed, the entrance to the dark elf lair was nothing more than a steaming mouth in the side of the mountain. A small stream, its surface filmed with a weak rainbow of scum, flowed over rich banks of lichen and moss. A fog of water vapor billowed upward over the cavern's upper lip, green and thick from algae.

There were no guards visible.

"So we go in, kill the lot of them, and be done with it," said Bregnar.

"And who would make your tribute for you, then?" said Beowulf. "No. We slay their king, and any who choose to defend him. But no more than we need to."

Bregnar made a huffing noise but did not press the point.

Beowulf held a hand up for the others to pause, and padded slowly forward, his body crouched low, his blade drawn. He moved up to the entrance, and stood in the mouth of the cavern. The air from within wrapped him in its warmth. The cavern itself extended into the heart of the mountain, tipping upward as it drove deeper within its vastness. He could see greenish lights in the distance, and fires.

He waved for the villagers to follow, and peered into the depths below. A careful path of switchbacks had been built up to the entrance, looping back and again alongside the stream, which had been gathered into pools by stone dams.

The stonework and mortar of the dams was the equal of that which he had seen among the Geats and the Danes. In fact, it was on a par with the ancient aqueducts of the south, ruins of the now-lost empire.

The village men, in their motley of armor, clanked up behind him. "No walls, no gates, and now no guards," said Alric, swinging his axe against nonexistent foes. His voice seemed suddenly loud within the walls. "What kind of city is—?"

His life escaped with a single breath as a black-feathered arrow sprouted from his neck, his arm making a halfhearted attempt to reach it as he collapsed. From the direction from whence the arrow came two dark elves sprang out from the shadows. A third, behind them, stood with an ebony bow in its hands, reaching to its quiver for another arrow.

Almost all the villagers except Sebbi had their weapons drawn. Sebbi for his part could only kneel where Alric fell twitching, his blood darkening the sand floor of the cavern's entrance. The older man tried to hold Alric still, to pull the arrow from his friend's throat, but Alric thrashed, a bloody foam on his lips.

His compassion cost him, for the bow-elf caught Sebbi with its second shot. A second black flower bloomed, this one in Sebbi's exposed back. The older villager pitched forward, stone dead, over Alric's still-twitching form.

The remaining three villagers let out a cry and joined battle with the two sword-elves. Their heavy humaniform weapons were rusted and ancient compared to the oil-covered dark elf blades, but they were powered by anger and rage. On the far side of the entrance, the bow-elf wavered for a moment, looking for another clear shot. Then it opened its cloak and pulled from it an over-sized ram's horn.

Beowulf ran toward where Alric still twitched. He did not bother with the younger man, now glass-eyed and rasping, but instead picked up Alric's axe, and in a single, spinning motion flung it at the furthest elf, the one with the horn.

The bow elf had raised the ram's horn to its lips to wind it, but the axe caught it in the face. The pale creature made a soft, gasping cry and fell backward, the cloven horn clattering down the stones.

The other two elves, the ones with swords, rushed the surviving villagers; one of the elves already sprawled on the cavern floor, its darkening blood mingling with that of Sebbi and Alric.

The three villagers surrounded the last one. Its mouth lolled agape, showing rows of needlelike teeth. It made high, keening sounds. Each man in turn lunged forward, and the dark elf spun to parry the blow, though each attempt to press back the attack was met by one villager joining to help the attacked party, while the other human launched an attack from the other side.

The three were trying to attack the dark elf as if they were harrying a bear. They had their hands full from just the one survivor.

Beowulf grimaced.

He sprang forward just as the dark elf was attempting to launch its own attack, its sword thrust before it. The warrior brought his blade down hard on the dark elf's arm, just above the bracer. There was a satisfying snap and the dark elf pitched forward from the force of the blow, its knees giving beneath it, onto the sandy floor.

It curled up, facedown, cradling its ruined arm. It made a whistling noise that might have been a scream.

Gundar strode forward with his new blade, ready to strike the final blow, but Beowulf stopped him. Instead he rolled the wounded dark elf over on its side.

"You understand me?" he said.

The dark elf let out a high-pitched squeal of pain.

Beowulf poked it hard with his blade, not enough to puncture its jerkin, but enough to assure him that he could.

"You understand me?" he said again. This time the dark elf managed a nod.

"Where is your master?" said Beowulf, and the dark elf pointed at its own throat.

"They can talk," said Gundar. "How could they speak with Gris if they couldn't talk?"

"Maybe not all of them can," grunted Beowulf, and with his boot cleared a space in the sand right before the bleeding dark elf.

"Draw," he said. "Give me a map to your master."

The dark elf reached out with a palsied hand and dragged a yellow-taloned finger through the dirt—the entrance, and then inward, through a long series of convolutions, through a large chamber, up some stairs, across a bridge, and finally into a great hall.

"And the children?" said Bregnar. "What of the children?"

The dark elf made a gurgling noise and slapped the final, large space.

Beowulf asked a few more question, confirming a few of the more questionable squiggles by frantic, pained shakes of the head. Only when he was satisfied did Beowulf draw his blade across the elf's exposed throat and released it from life.

By that time Alric had quit squirming, and was as dead as Sebbi. Snorri and Bregnar took the remaining golden blades, but determined that the dark, oily armor was too small for their frames. They carried Alric and Sebbi's bodies to the side of the entrance down by one of the pools, along with the remains of the three dark elves. Gundar committed the map to memory and stomped it and the blood into the sand. Beowulf was down at the pool as well, but was swinging his sword through the water.

Beowulf climbed back up the hill, wet weeds in his hands.

"They're clever," said Gundar. "They hid from you, and waited until we were at the entrance to attack."

"Shove this into your armor," said Beowulf, putting the weeds into the worn-faced man's hands. He handed a fistful to Snorri and Bregnar as well.

Gundar gave him a questionable look.

Beowulf scowled back and said, "They did not notice me come forward, any more than I noticed them staying stock-still. We were both too quiet. Your armor clunks and shifts on your bodies, and told them where you were. Then Alric opened his mouth and confirmed that he was foe to them. Put the weeds and moss in the chinks of your armor to soften them. Speak no more than you have to, and then only in a whisper."

"Where are we going?" said Bregnar, softening his voice to a breath. "Where is their king? Where are the children?"

Beowulf pointed upward, into the heart of the mountains.

† † †

The mountain was hollow, or so it seemed to Beowulf, its heart a great vault tearing vertically through the bands of crystalline granite. Their path trailed upward along the wound in the heart of the earth, boring through rocks sometimes, other times pitching over narrow delves on web-thin bridges.

Beowulf moved slowly, and the men followed him, their clanking armor muffled by the plants.

There was light from above and below. Above it was soft, in shades of green, blue, and purple, alien constellations scattered against the dark grey sky. Beneath them it was red, and warmth struck their faces whenever the path took them along a ledge.

Beowulf looked down. Far at the bottom of the vault something glowed as red as a pulsing heart, a thick band of red overlaid with a crust of broken black. There was the sound of anvils below, but it sounded no more than an erratic metallic tapping this far above the molten surface.

These must be the forges, realized Beowulf, where the dark elves spun their golden blades and wove their dark, oil-covered armor, and set their nuggets of amber into filigrees of silver and bronze. There was industry down there, a regular clattering.

Yet who would they trade with, if all trade with the town had ceased? They could not eat gold or drink dark iron. Still they busied themselves, and far above them, Beowulf could see their thin figures moving spiderlike around the great blocks of magma, forging their weapons on moving platforms of rock.

There was motion in the passage up ahead, and Beowulf pressed himself against the outside curve of the wall and held a hand up. The village men—Gundar and Bregnar and broad-shouldered Snorri—all snapped to statues, their armor jingling from the suddenness of the motion, and moved against the wall as well.

A pair of shadows around the next corner grew larger.

Gundar raised his blade and Beowulf put a heavy hand on the man's shoulder. Gundar froze. A second set of shadows appeared behind the first, and four dark elves ambled around the corner.

Guards or merchants or blacksmiths, it did not matter, they were armed and armored . . . but their blades were in their sheathes, and they were moving slowly, leisurely, following a well-trod path that looped through the caverns. They were larger than the guards at the entrance.

None of the men even breathed as the four elves moved past them. The dark elves turned to each other and Beowulf heard their high-pitched mewling, the sound of kittens, alien in this hell-lit place. But they did not seem to notice the stock-still men, holding their breath, pressed against the wall not more than a foot away from them.

The guards moved past them and down the path. Bregnar let out a deep, exhausted sigh.

The last of the guards turned, its face raised, making quizzical mewling noises. The flaps around the lateral holes in its face flapped in a weak attempt at smell.

The men froze in place. Bregnar raised his hand to his mouth. Beowulf let go of Gundar's shoulder and raised his own blade.

The dark elf paused for a moment, mewling and sniffing. Then he turned back and loped to catch up to the others, now no more than shadows themselves in the flickering light from the hearths below.

The men moved upward through the heart of the mountain, knowing that the patrol would soon find the missing guardians from the cavern's entrance as well as their dead companions. The reddish glow dimmed behind them and with it the industry of the dark elven forges. Now they could see the source of the blue and green stars.

They were glass bowls; perfect spheres mounted on staffs of cold, sweating iron, the staffs themselves driven into the cavern walls. Within the bowls were fish and crayfish, denizens of some distant pool, the fish as blue as a dead man's lips, and the crayfish as green as moss on a gravestone. They were so pale that they radiated their own light, casting the caverns in shades of weak sapphire and emerald.

Now the stream, which had disappeared within the mountain soon after they had entered, reemerged, a brilliant cascade of diamonds among the other pale shades. The outside wall of the caverns formed its bed, and it collected in great pools behind stonework weirs, the fit of the stones as perfect as those near the entrance.

The sound of the rushing water made the men relax, but also covered the sound of the cavern's other denizens. And when they rounded a corner they were among the elves.

It was some sort of longhouse, carved deep within the mountains, where families of elves were sleeping, playing, eating. They were weaving silver cloth from the bellies of cave spiders and poised over engraved boards set with markers of precious stones. They were shaping tall pots of earthen clay. They had a hearth, not forging brass or bronze but for a large copper cauldron and its brood of smaller pots and pans buried among its coals. Older, frailer elves sat by the fire, and were either whittling long staves of dried wood or peeling some serpentine form of root. Children, or at least small versions of the larger dark elves, splashed at the raised pools, alternately luring and frightening the small glowing fish within.

One of the lankier, older ones, busy with a pegboard laced with silk, looked up from his work and transfixed the men with his sightless eyes. It let out a hissing mewl and spat in their general direction.

Beowulf stood away from the others, hefting his blade but not raising it in anger. The dark elf tilted its head toward him, let out another mewling noise, and returned to its work.

"Its like we're ghosts," said Gundar, and though he whispered, it felt like his words filled the vault.

Beowulf nodded. "We are deep in their lair. They see us, or smell us, or however they sense. But why would something dangerous be at their very gates?"

"We're spirits," said Bregnar. "We could slay those we choose and leave the bodies as a warning."

Beowulf stiffened at a remembered thought. Instead he said, "We are after their leader. It would do us little good to merely raid and leave their master unharmed. They will not bother us. Follow."

Beowulf took three steps forward, and Gundar and Snorri fell in behind him. The dark elves made no move to block their path, or to pay any attention whatsoever. It was as if heavily armed humans (or whatever the villagers would seem as to these creature's eldritch senses) were a commonplace thing among them.

Snorri said quietly, "You notice something?" His voice belied his nervousness.

Gundar hissed back, "What?"

Snorri said, "No women."

Gundar said, "Maybe the women look like the men."

Snorri made a disgusted noise. "What would the fun of that be?"

They were nearly across the chamber and Beowulf turned back to hush the men. It was then that he saw, Bregnar, already lagging behind, had stopped entirely, and was looking at one of the old root-skinners by the fire. The villager's eyes were wide and glassy, and one hand was clenched to his chest.

Beowulf hissed for Bregnar to follow, but the villager made no response. Beowulf looked at the target of Bregnar's attention—an old creature, with a leather cord and a crudely carved talisman dangling from around its neck.

Beowulf said, "Bregnar, no!" but it was too late. The villager reached out and snagged the cord with his free hand.

"This is Anol's," said Bregnar, his voice cracking and loud.

The dark elf hissed at the human and tried to pull away, but the leather cord noosed it. Bregnar spoke louder now. "This is my son's. I gave it to him. Why do you have it?"

The dark elf let out a short, sharp screech and all activity in the chamber stopped. Even the children by the pool were suddenly riveted, their eyeless heads swung toward the human looming over one of their own.

"What did you do with him!" screamed Bregnar. "Where is my son?"

"Bregnar!" shouted Beowulf, as Bregnar raised his blade.

And with that the chamber erupted as every dark elf, dozens of them present, and dozens more that appeared from the shadows, all converged at once. Golden blades flashed out of nowhere, catching the hearth light and the glow of the cavern fish.

Bregnar was overwhelmed in an instant, completely surrounded by the slender, pale forms of the dark elves.

Thick-shouldered Snorri let out a shout and leaped forward to help his friend. Beowulf lunged toward him, but his fingers closed on empty air as the brute of a man surged into the mass of twisting bodies, pulling them off and throwing them aside, trying to find Bregnar at their center.

Gundar charged forward as well, but Beowulf was quicker this time, snagging the worn-faced villager by the back of the neck and dragging him close to him.

Gundar tried to shake loose, but the warrior was too strong.

"We have to help them!" shouted Gundar.

"They died when they raised their weapons," said Beowulf, pulling the villager back toward the upper entrance to the chamber. Next to them a waterfall filled one of the numerous pools.

The battle before them was a boiling mass now of pale-fleshed elves and dark robes, all of them pounding, slashing, and beating something at the heart of their mass. They took up a rhythm as a group, their arms all rising and falling in unison.

Of the two dead men, there was no immediate sign.

Something surged to the top of the pile—a dark shadow roughly the shape of a man's torso. It was tossed above the roiling mass once, twice, and then was swallowed again.

The two survivors stood at the uphill side of the chamber, near a narrow entrance. Beowulf turned to that entrance as it filled with the form of another dark elf guard.

Gundar threw himself to one side, against the wall of the pool, but Beowulf leapt forward, skewering the guard with a single blow, up beneath the chest plates of his armor, ripping aside the oiled chain, through the soft cushion and into the softer, wetter flesh.

The guard sank to its knees, but let out a piteous cry as it did with its final breath.

The mob, further downhill, paused for a moment, and let out its own mewling questions in response.

Beowulf cursed and shoved Gundar over the wall of the dammed pool. "Get in and get under!" he snapped.

Gundar protested, but Beowulf shoved him in, then dove in after him, scattering the pale-moon fish as he plunged to the shallow bottom.

Gundar thrashed in the cold water, sputtering from the shock. Beowulf reached up and pulled him under, and gathered him in, and fled underwater to the far wall, frog kicking in the chill flow. At first Gundar thrashed, and Beowulf held him tightly, and only when the villager had ceased his struggles did the warrior push him up toward the surface for air. Then, his own lungs near bursting, he raised his own head.

The commotion had died down almost as quickly as it had begun. The chamber had returned to normal—dark elves grooming each other, playing, eating. The same venerable creature was poring over his game board, undisturbed in the riot. The same old wrinkled elves were shucking roots, including the one with Anol's talisman.

It was as if nothing had happened. The only change was broth overtopping the edge of the cauldron and hissing down the side, leaving new paths along its weathered flanks. Something had been added recently to cause it to overflow.

Of the men, or even the dark elf Beowulf slew, there was no evidence.

Gundar sputtered next to him, his teeth clattered, "Why do they not attack?"

"You are right," said Beowulf. "We are ghosts. They do not see as we see, or sense as we sense. In this hellish cold, we are chill against a chill background, with moss in our armor. If they paid attention, they could see us. But they will not pay attention."

The warrior slid toward the edge of the pool, near its inlet by the narrow door, and climbed over the rim of the weir. Gundar followed him, sputtering and clattering. He bent down and picked up his shield, discarded when he had gone over the side.

"You let them die," he managed through chattering teeth, at last. Beowulf said nothing, and he said again, "You let them die."

"I did," said Beowulf. "And I will have to face your friends later in the cold land of the dead. And I will thank them."

"Thank them? For what? Their folly?" Gundar hissed, a lidded pot near explosion.

"The patrol will have found the dead entrance guards," whispered Beowulf. "And two humans. Two more humans are found up here, attacking the longhouse of the dark elves. They will think we are done. We are cold and we are silent. If we do nothing else foolish, we should reach their King's Quarters."

† † †

Up rising passageways away from the communal chamber and to a stairs.

Up the stairs to another passage, which bent around and opened out of the great cavern.

Now there was only the faintest heat from the inferno below, and the softest tapping of the hammers. Then up another staircase and across a great span and at last to the great brazen doors of the King of the Dark Elves.

Four guards stood by the doors, their armor the color of night, and their capes made of dark metal links, which shone and swam in the surrounding light. They bore spears tipped with gold, and heavy bladed swords hung from their belts.

"I will draw them out," said Beowulf. "You can stab one of them from behind. If more appear, run. They may have allies nearby."

Gundar just stared at the warrior. "The children," he said. "They're dead."

Beowulf paused for a moment, then said, "Most likely."

"You knew."

Another pause. "Such creatures rarely take hostages like real men, and if they do, they talk trade soon after."

"You didn't say that when we were in the village."

"Would you have believed me then, when we were in the village?"

Gundar paused for another moment, then said, "I have a better plan."

† † †

At the far end on the bridge, Gundar slammed his stolen sword against his shield and shouted, "You are dung!"

The heads of the guards turned as one toward the sudden disturbance.

"You are the dregs of a bleeding woman's chamber pot! The soft heart of a diseased midden! Child eaters! You are whoresons and lie with the poxed! You are cowards!"

He smashed his shield with his sword again, and the guards charged him.

"Cowards!" bellowed Gundar, and then turned his heels and fled, back across the great span and down the staircase, toward the communal chamber.

The guards pursued him. The last of them was a bit slow reaching the staircase and another shadow separated from the wall and was upon him.

The guard had its blade up at once but Beowulf beat it aside, and leaned in close against the armored dark elf. The warrior dropped his own sword and gripped the dark elf's blade arm at the wrist.

The dark elf let out a hiss and lunged forward to bite Beowulf's arm. With his free hand, the human warrior drove his dagger home, into the creature's neck. The elf lurched against the force of the blow, then slumped against the cavern wall.

Beowulf muttered a prayer and pulled his dagger loose. The prayer was not for the elven corpse but for the man who he would have to see in the cold land of the dead. Far below him, the corpse's three brothers chased Gundar around the bend overlooking the great cavern and down the second set of stairs.

† † †

That the doors swung effortlessly inward surprised Beowulf not in the least. As he pushed them open he half-felt weights hidden within the hollow centers shift into new positions, holding the gates open for him, then easing back into place.

Beowulf stepped out into sunlight.

Above him was the tip of the mountain, carved out at its apex with great windows, like his own lord's keep. These windows were made of colored glass, shattered and reassembled with blackish putty between the shards. It made the room feel like it was overlaid with flowers.

The room itself was pale stone, polished and shaped like it was liquid. A great reception chamber, perhaps, where the king could lord his wealth before subjects too blind to see? The entrance was framed with braziers, and the coals popped merrily within them.

At the center of the room was a dais with a stone couch, upon which rested a bundle of silk pillows. The couch was surrounded by small chests, silver boxes, and earthenware jars.

Another low pool was to Beowulf's left. At first Beowulf thought it another dammed stream, but this was empty of water, and instead was a pen. Five huge creatures, the size of overfed boars, rooted around in the scraps and bones that littered the bottom of the pen.

No, not boars, but rather monstrous caterpillars, overstuffed slugs that moved along on stubby feet shod in horn.

One of the slug-things turned toward Beowulf, and the warrior saw its face. It had purplish bruises instead of eyes, flapping sheets of skin over slitlike nostrils, and long needlelike teeth.

Now he knew why he had not seen any female dark elves elsewhere in the city. The creature gave a hiss and a mewling sound, expecting food.

"You're too early," said a melodious voice, and Beowulf saw now that the dais was occupied, and the large bundle of silk was the King of the Dark Elves. The creature rose to its feet and it was like a mountain suddenly made flesh, making the maggot women in the pen look svelte.

He rose and kept rising, a giant half again Beowulf's height. He was nearly naked, the pale flesh hanging in the thick bundles on his frame, covered by a rainbow robe of silk scraps, sewn and re-sewn to form a robe.

His face was fat as well, his neck invisible beneath the jowls, his black, bruised non-eyes almost dripping down to a rubbery maw filled with askew teeth. His hair was a white mane, and reached down his back . . . and on his bulbous brow rested a thin diadem, set with a white pearl at its center, the pearl in turn inlaid with a disk of blue turquoise.

The Elf-King looked partially melted, and did not stride forward as much as ooze across the room.

"I said you are too early," repeated the King. "It will be another month before we have everything ready. Of course, if you want to pay me in advance . . ." A worm of a tongue appeared at the corner of his mouth, tasting the air. "No, no, I don't smell the blood of the newborn. Who are you, stranger?"

"I am your vengeance," said Beowulf, "for the children and their lost parents."

The Elf-King laughed, and his form glistened and roiled as he did. "Of course." He turned slightly back toward his dais, presenting a fat flank to Beowulf. "I knew it was only a matter of time," he said simply.

Beowulf did not bellow a warning cry, but crossed toward the behemoth, his blade drawn.

The Elf-King spun in place, a mountain moving with the grace of an eagle. When moments before there was an expanse of silk-covered fat, there was now a hardened metal blade drawing against Beowulf's own, sliding along the length of the warrior's sword and biting into the crosspiece. The Elf-King twisted his wrist, and the warrior had the choice between having his blade wrested from his grip or being pulled aside by the Elf-King's strength.

Beowulf followed the force of the blow and dropped to his knees as he slid across the smooth marble floor. He rolled and rose again.

The Elf-King had a sword in each hand. They were mighty blades, but could have been mere stubby daggers in his grip. Their hilts were made of spun gold, and their blades had the dark shine of the elven foundries to them.

The Elf-King laughed, and held one of his blades forward. "Naegling, which means Iron Kinsman," he said. He held the sword in his off hand forward. "Its sister, Haedling. That means Starbite. They are superior blades, each one taking two months of folding and refolding of their steel to forge. They are weapons suitable for a king."

Beowulf looked at the giant monster's face—two dark patches of where the eyes should be, beneath a diadem of drawn silver.

He charged again.

The Elf-King made a wide, broad horizontal stroke with one blade, at the level of a human's head. Beowulf dodged beneath the cut, expectant of a follow-up from the off-hand blade.

But that blow did not come.

Instead the mass of fat and skin surged forward as the Elf-King slammed into Beowulf, belly-first. The human warrior thought it would be soft, but instead the creature's flesh was hard and firm as a filled wineskin.

Beowulf spilled backwards again. This time his sword came loose from his hands and danced, jangling across the floor.

"I hope you try harder," jeered the Elf-King. "I know you're only the first, and when you fail to return, they will send another, and another, and so forth. So I do need the practice. I don't get enough as it is. My followers are no match for me, though they try. A Cyclops in the Kingdom of the Blind, as it were."

And he laughed again, and Beowulf launched himself at his discarded sword.

The Elf-King's laugh ceased like a pot with the lid dropped, and in a blur he was upon the warrior. Beowulf did not reach out to grab his sword, and this was fortunate, for one of the gold-hilted blades cut the air between him and his target, and would have removed his arm as well. Instead the warrior dropped down, sliding on the polished floor, carrying himself and his blade away.

He rolled and when he rose, he had his sword once more in his hand.

"Better," said the Elf-King. "So they will send another and another. And eventually they will send one who almost bests me or they will run out of children and I will sue for peace, promising them some small bit of my horde." The ruler smiled and his teeth were sharpened pegs. "At least until the next crop is ripe."

Beowulf let out a howl and charged again, spittle flying from his lips. The Elf-King seemed surprised this time, and made only a clumsy, halfhearted attempt to turn his blade.

Beowulf's sword bit deeply into the giant's stomach, then stopped, mired within the rolls of fat. Then, like a buoyant log in a flood, the sword bounced back out from the flesh.

No blood seeped out from where the blade struck.

"Your heart is mighty, manling," said the Elf, "but your weapons are primitive. Naegling could pierce my flesh, perhaps, but not your puny blade. Let me show you."

Now the giant's off hand was moving, and Beowulf brought up his sword to catch and turn the blow.

Instead, Haedling struck Beowulf's sword a third of the way up its length, and shattered the human sword. A rain of razor shards whipped around both man and elf, and Beowulf felt something bite deep along his cheek.

"See what I mean?" said the Elf. "Poor craftsmanship. You think your lord would give you a decent weapon—after all, I traded him enough over the years. I will have your head delivered to the Flambruk. Your body I will give to my wives. And I think I will double my demands. Yes," he licked his lips again, "children don't last as long as they used to."

Beowulf looked up at the giant, his shattered blade in one hand. His eyes were locked on the elf's corpulent face. He reached to his belt and pulled out his dagger.

"Not giving in to the inevitable?" said the Dark Elf. "Good. As I said, I need the practice."

Beowulf flung his ragged sword at the King's face. The giant swatted it aside with his off-hand blade, laughing, but he did not see that Beowulf flung his dagger as well, in that same instant.

The dagger smashed into the King's forehead. It would not draw blood, but it was not intended to.

Instead it skewered the pearl mounted on the King's diadem, the pearl set with the disk of blue turquoise. The blade fell away, but the white orb was skewered, and now leaked blood and tears down the Elf-King's face.

The Elf-King roared and slashed with both blades to where Beowulf had been, but he slid backwards now, and the gold-hilted blades slashed through empty air.

The Elf-King bellowed again, and swung his blades randomly, cursing. Beowulf remained still.

"You think you can hide, do you?" snapped the Dark Elf, his face a rising purple. "I can feel you here." A rough sword-swing through space. "You can run, but you won't escape me."

Beowulf held his breath. His lungs were already strained and bruised.

The Dark Elf muttered a curse and stepped backwards, toward his dais.

Beowulf held his breath.

The Elf-King carefully laid down Naegling on the topmost step of the dais carefully, his ears pricked for the slightest noise.

Beowulf held his breath.

The Elf-King reached for a small box among his assorted treasures, made of silver and carved with the image of three ancient human women squatting around a cauldron.

Beowulf held his breath. His chest ached as if a kraken had him in its grip.

The Elf-King opened the box lid. The clasp made a soft snap.

Beowulf exploded with activity, crossing the room as the stale air left his lungs in a screaming rush.

The Elf-King wheeled at the first noise, thrusting his blade forward and downward. The human warrior twisted as his charged, the dark blade passing inches above him. The giant pulled his sword back to protect himself, by instinct, but again the giant had mistaken Beowulf's target.

Instead the warrior grabbed Naegling from the dais with one hand, and kicked the silver box away with the other. The box skated to the edge of the dais and toppled over, spilling its contents on the steps.

They were shaped like pearls, and each one inset with a disk. Some blue, some green, and some brown. They bounced softly down the steps.

The Elf-King bellowed and brought his Starbite down hard on Beowulf. The human warrior raised his own gold-hilted blade, and dark metal met dark metal. The elf's blow was heavy but hesitant, and Beowulf turned it aside.

The giant tried to recover, bringing his blade back, but Beowulf was already within his reach, and brought his own blow down, hard, on the giant's knee. Naegling bit deeply into the elf's flesh, and the metal slid through muscle and sinew. Purplish blood spurt from the wound as Beowulf struck something vital.

The human warrior staggered backward a half-step now and the dark elf, unable to support himself, dropped to his knees. Then Beowulf charged him again.

The dark elf could not hear the sound of Beowulf's feet, or smell the musky scent of elven blood on him, or sense his rage. But all he could do was bring up Haegling to block the assault.

Beowulf met the blade at the third-point up its length, and smashed the dark elf's blade into shards. The Elf-King dropped the shattered remains of his sword, stung by the force of the blow.

The Elf-King opened his mouth, perhaps to plead, or to curse, or to pray.

Beowulf did not care. He swung his elven-made blade in a

powerful arc, the blade meeting the Elf-King's hypothetical neck where it joined the shoulders.

Even then, he could not sever the king's head with a single blow. The Elf-King made a grunting sound and fell backward, and it took two more strokes to finish the job.

† † †

Beowulf staggered back through the weighted doors, across the bridge, past the guard he slew, down the stairs to the first turn overlooking the great cavern beneath, and there found the body of another guard, the links of its chain shirt sliced open above a ragged tear in its chest. As he started down the second set of stairs, he heard the sounds of steel against steel from the chamber.

Beowulf, desperately pulling the air into his lungs, began to run. Gundar was a bloodied mess, but most of the blood that coated his arms and shield was a deep purple. He stood on the body of another guardsman, and two more dark elves were also sprawled on the ground at his feet. The surviving guardsman crouched before him and slightly downhill, about to launch an attack. Behind the guardsman was a mob of elves, waiting for their chance.

Gundar smacked his sword against his shield, and screamed an obscenity. The last guardsman lunged forward, and Gundar stepped quickly back, his shield up, catching the force of the blow. The dark elf hesitated, and the villager used his shield to beat aside the attack, driving his own blade home in a straight thrust. The elven-made blade bit deeply into the dark elf's belly. It hung for a moment, then dropped its own sword, and slid to the floor to join its comrades.

The mob now inched forward, muttering and keening. Gundar raised his shield again.

"Hold!" shouted Beowulf, and Gundar jumped from the sound. Beowulf strode forward and stood alongside Gundar.

"Well met, warrior," said Gundar, not taking his eyes from the mob. "Been there long?"

Beowulf ignored him, instead holding up his grisly trophy. "Behold your king!" he shouted.

The mob stopped as one creature, its leaders puzzled. One of their numbers carefully moved forward, picking its way among the bodies of its fallen toward the pair.

Gundar took a step back and kept his shield up.

The dark elf stopped a foot from Beowulf's offering and tilted its head. Its nostril-flaps flared and quieted.

It reached forward and tentatively touched the cooling flesh of the Elf-King's head. The touch became a caress, and something rippled beneath the bruised skin covering the eyes of the living dark elf.

The dark elf let out a low, mewling noise, which rose into a keening wail. Gundar shivered at the sound of it.

Beowulf stepped forward, and the dark elf stepped back, still keening. Other hands reached forward, touching their king's face, and the cry spread, first through the chamber and then spilling out into the great cavern, doubling and redoubling until the heart of the mountain itself was mourning.

Beowulf held the severed head up like a lantern, and the crowds parted before him. Now dark elves were dropping to their knees, and some were tearing at their clothes from the pain.

Gundar hung close behind Beowulf. He whispered, "At what point do you think they will get past the shock and start getting angry?"

"I don't know," said Beowulf, "but I trust your sword should it come to that."

It did not come to that, and the two men spiraled downward.

More dark elves issued from the depths, but that was only to touch, wail, and weep with sightless eyes.

The two men reached the entrance. There was no sign of their fallen comrades.

They started down the mountain, to Flambruk.

† † †

They reached Flambruk in the early hours, Gundar's hallo rousting the gate guard and gaining them quick entrance. Gundar and the guard spread out to gather the others.

Beowulf strode into Gris's hut, unannounced.

The older, fatter man rose from his pillows when Beowulf entered, his face a combination of expectation and dread. "What news do you bring?"

Beowulf set down the head of the Dark Elf-King on the low table, the blood from its neck clotted into a rude pillow.

Gris brightened visibly. "Wonderful," he chuckled. "With a show of force, and their ruler dead, they should be more than willing to resume trade. You have served your lord well, Beowulf, champion of Hygleac."

"And you serve your lord not at all," said Beowulf, pulling his new, elven-wrought blade.

Gris took a step backward. "What do you mean?"

"The Dark Elf-King greeted me as YOUR servant. Apparently the trade continued, even though none of it made its way as tribute to Hygleac." Behind him the other villagers, led by Gundar, filtered into the room.

"There was no trade," said Gris firmly. "The dark elves made demands no one could agree to."

"Not in daylight, no," said Beowulf. "But quietly, by the dark of the moon, dark elves came down from their mountainside with their gifts and returned with smaller, more valuable parcels."

The Thane thundered, "You overstep your bounds, champion!

You were asked to reestablish the tribute. With their horrible king slain, there should be no trouble. Your task is complete. Report that to our liege."

"True," said Beowulf. "And should I also tell him that you would trade the children for your own riches?"

The Thane laughed, and it was a flinty, brittle laugh. "You have been ensorcelled by the dark elves, champion! What did he say? I have no riches here."

"No?" said Beowulf, and strode forward.

Despite himself, the Thane flinched, but Beowulf did not strike against him. Instead, he strode past the Thane, to the nearest of the large earthenware jars that lined the room.

He struck out with Naegling, and the reddish clay of the sides ruptured. From within spilled grain, but also a cascade of golden chains, bits of amber, and jewels that the grain had been covering.

It was a small avalanche, and slid into the room.

Beowulf stirred the pile with the tip of his sword. "There is enough here for the wergild of Snebbi and Snorri and Bregnar and Alric, and for their children lost and those lost to the rest of the village. The rest should be sent down to Hygleac, as tribute owed."

The villagers in the room made dark noises. The women were shooed to the back, and weapons now appeared in hands previously empty.

Gris looked at Beowulf, and at the mob. He bit the edge of his moustache. "I think I would choose to accompany you to Hygleac myself."

"You are needed here," said Beowulf.

"I demand your protection!" said Gris, hotly. He looked around for his own weapons, but they had disappeared in the growing crowd.

"I would not think of overstepping my bounds," said Beowulf, "but I will make your concerns clear in my report. You!" he turned to Gundar. "You are now the Thane's chief assistant. Should something happen to the Thane, you are to rule in his name until a suitable replacement is chosen by our liege."

"And make sure the tribute continues?" said Gundar, his eyes locked on Gris.

"Of course," said Beowulf. He reached into his vest and pulled out a circlet of silver, its clawed socket bloody and missing its prize. "When the dark elves wish to talk, use this to trade. Whoever rules there will want it, desperately."

Gris drew himself up to his full height. "You cannot leave me."

"As you said, my task is complete," said Beowulf, resting the tip of his sword on the low table. "And I go to report to my lord."

With the tip of Naegling he pushed the head of the Dark Elf to one side, leaving room on the table for another head to be placed alongside it.

The crowd parted as he left the Thane's hut, and closed behind him like a trap. By the time Beowulf reached the front gate, the screams had begun, human at first but quickly becoming wet, sobbing, keening wails.

Beowulf did not look back, and started the long journey down to the sea.

BEOWULF AND THE
MASTER OF HIS CRITICS
Interlude 2

°✝°

"Where did these stories come from?" the Master inquired. "Various researchers have spent many years tracking them down."

"They are obviously the work of different hands?"

"Well, they had different translators . . . and then synopsisized from the poetry to the prose form."

"Why? Did you think I couldn't read the originals?" The Oxford man seemed quite offended at this slight.

"No, of course not . . . but not everyone involved in this project is such a scholar. Should you accept our offer, all of the originals will be available for your casual study."

"Are these composed from fragments?"

"Some."

"Dated?"

"I don't know."

The Master drew back on his pipe, and commented pedantically, "Of course, you don't know. Did you know that the original fragment is ambiguously dated?"

"Well, yes."

"That there are simultaneous references to what seems to be both a pagan setting and a post–Judeo-Christian setting?"

The Cambridge man decided it was safest to concur.

"Yes."

"Which means . . . ?"

"What you said."

The master shook his head.

"Which means a post-original conception editor probably copied the text during the post–Christian era . . . which probably explains why a Danish hero-warrior is at the center of an English epic. Your associates obviously didn't send you to impress me with your knowledge."

"No," the Cambridge man conceded.

BEOWULF AND THE TITAN

by Lynn Abbey

✣

"Health to our king!" Beowulf declared as he stood with his mead cup held high.

The thanes in the hall loudly echoed his wish.

"Health to all Geat-folk!" King Heardred replied, lifting his cup. "And land for our sons!"

Their eyes met, Beowulf's and his king's. The bonds between them were strong as ox leather boiled in oil. They were kin. Beowulf had called the old king uncle, though they were much the same age. When Hygelac was slain and Heardred but a boy, Beowulf, a proven warrior, could have rightfully claimed the crown.

Beowulf had wanted nothing of crowns or thrones, but the thanes and the old queen persisted and he agreed to stand in Hygelac's place, raising Heardred until the boy could become the Geat-folk king, as now he was.

Heardred was the image of Hygelac: the same yellow-gold hair, the same summer-blue eyes, the same temperament, too. The wisest of men in most things, Hygelac had had one flaw: He believed that Geat-land was too small for the greatness of the Geat-folk. Hygelac had hungered for new land, started wars with his neighbor-kings, and lost his life in battle against one of them.

No man loved Geat-land more than Beowulf. He would have fought to the death had another king threatened one rock or tree, but the All-Father had matched land and folk together. The lands of the Finns, the Scyldings, or the Half-Danes had been made for other folk. They never tempted him because they were not—and could never be—Geat-land.

Leave them be, he'd said to Heardred, not once, but a thousand times during the years he'd had charge of the boy.

And, in his first full season of kingship, Heardred had forgotten every word.

The thanes and Geat-folk in the mead-hall echoed their new king's enthusiasm. Beowulf retreated to the wall shadows. The *wyrd* of kings passed from Hygelac to Heardred. The Geat-folk champion had striven to raise a king who would not repeat his father's mistakes and, it seemed, he had striven in vain.

That was Beowulf's wyrd and he strove to make peace with it.

That battle still raged in Beowulf's mind when Hygd, the old queen, mother of Heardred, appeared at his side.

"It is as we feared," she said simply, understanding, as Beowulf did, that wyrd could not be thwarted. "Yet, I think there is no small part of my son who does what he does because it is not what his champion-cousin would have him do."

Beowulf sipped mead and pondered the old queen's words. "A son must step outside his father's shadow," he agreed. "I have stood father to Heardred longer than Hygelac did."

"Just so," Hygd replied.

She had been little more than a child herself when she delivered Hygelac's son and was still a beautiful woman, though it had been understood from the beginning that she would never become another man's wife. Geat-folk would not accept a woman's rule, but they respected her wisdom. Beowulf waited for Hygd's next words.

The not-so-old queen smiled with her eyes alone and said nothing.

"I need to leave Geat-land," Beowulf reasoned. The thought had not occurred to him before that moment, but once born, it, and its complications, grew quickly. Silently, he ticked off the halls he could not visit. "I cannot go where Heardred covets. He will see betrayal, provocation."

The smile faded from Hygd's eyes. "You'll think of something."

Beowulf watched Hygd walk away. If she had not been Heardred's mother . . . If she had not been the old queen . . .

Though an adventurer in his youth, once Beowulf had returned to Geat-land, he'd had no desire to leave it and little curiosity about the lands beyond. He knew of the Western Isles, where the descendants of distant cousins dwelt in a land that was both green and damp. To the near north lay the halls where Beowulf had lived his adventures, the same halls Heardred now coveted. Forests covered the east. The Geat-folk valued tall trees and straight timbers for their boats, but they were not a forest-loving people. Far to the south, there was an empire where men wore soft cloth draped around their shoulders and the emperors hired men to fight for them.

Gold was precious to the Geat-folk, but money was a useless, foreign notion. Beowulf could scarcely imagine hiring himself to anyone, unless it would serve the Geat-folk he left behind.

Beowulf made his decision at midwinter, when the sun rose and fell without clearing two handspans above the horizon and the snow lay deep as his thighs. There'd be no travel for months, until the mud hardened after the spring thaw. Much could happen before then, so he shared his decision with no one, except the bard, Aelscyg. Each winter night thereafter, the champion of the Geat-folk toasted his king, as if nothing had changed.

Aelscyg could be trusted with any secret. The bard was near the oldest man among the thanes and Geat-folk who came together around Heardred. He'd been born when Swerting held court in the Geat's mead-hall and sung for Hrethel, Hygelac's father before he sang for Hygelac. Now he sang for Heardred. Men did not live as long as Aelscyg had lived without learning to keep another man's secret.

The old bard had the gift of languages and he had traveled. In his youth, he'd visited the southern empire, harvesting their tales for his kings' amusement and picking up their language as well.

Beowulf prepared himself for the south through word lessons with Aelscyg, which had not progressed far beyond the words for sword and battle and the proper way to address an emperor when word came that a stranger had come into Geat-land—and a true stranger at that, not merely a visitor from another northern land.

Honor and hospitality demanded an escort. Heardred commanded his champion to lead it.

Beowulf selected five men and together they set out into hoary daylight that froze their breath in their nostrils. Darkness had fallen when the Geat-folk came to the stranger's campfire. He jumped up to meet them and they were not sure that he was a man at all, so strange was this stranger's appearance, so odd his chattering language. Standing straight, his head did not rise above Beowulf's chest. His shaggy hair, where it was not covered by a fur-lined, pointed cap, was dark as the sky overhead. His skin was the sallowest the Geat-folk had ever seen and his eyes . . . !

The stranger's forbiddingly dark eyes showed no lids, but were hidden behind slits in his flat face.

"Monster!" Brythnor shouted from Beowulf's right.

He drew his sword, but Beowulf stayed the attack by clasping the other man's arm in a mighty grasp.

"We are charged to escort this stranger to Heardred's hall, and escort him we will."

Grumbling, Brythnor sheathed his sword. Beowulf turned to the stranger and hailed him, though it was clear that the stranger understood no more of the Geat-folk tongue than they understood of his. With gestures, then, the men communicated, Beowulf pointing back the way the Geat-folk had come and the stranger pointing into the shadows where a small, sturdy horse waited patiently among trappings that were as unfamiliar as the stranger himself.

The Geat-folk were unwilling to rest beside such a strange man, so the seven set off at once, despite the darkness, and returned, weary and bone-cold, to the hall near high-sun of the next day. Heardred, having been warned by his lookouts, awaited them with a blazing fire and warm mead. Like Beowulf, the young king was astounded by the stranger's appearance, but mindful of a host's obligations. Heardred welcomed the stranger who had the sense to reply with a bow and make a show with empty hands as well as with words no one understood.

Heardred called for heated mead, which Beowulf and his companions welcomed and which the stranger drank in suspicious sips. Aelscyg followed the mead into the hall, rubbing his eyes, as it was not the bard's habit to rise before midafternoon in winter. At Heardred's command, Aelscyg attempted to make sense of the stranger's language. He questioned the man in all the northern tongues, then moved on to the tongues of folk the Geat-folk neither knew nor fought. In all cases, the stranger responded with words that echoed no language the bard had heard before—and bards measured their wealth in accumulated languages.

As the fruitless interrogation continued, the Geat-folk followed their king out of the hall until only the stranger, the bard, and Beowulf remained. Beowulf would have left, if he hadn't been the target of the stranger's agitation. A Geat who gestured like that would find himself answering a challenge, but there was little honor in challenging such a small man whose only weapon was a bow as strangely strung as he was himself.

Then Aelscyg ventured a few words of the southern language Beowulf had barely begun to master. The stranger grinned and chattered anew. Beowulf didn't recognize a sound the stranger made, but the bard was nodding now, so the champion fetched his king back to the hall.

"He calls himself Elmaz, of the Didon," Aelscyg explained when they were all together again. "He's from the east . . . beyond the forests."

The Geat-folk exchanged doubtful glances. As they understood the world, there was nothing beyond the eastern forests except sunrise. Hemnyr stood with every intention of challenging the yellow-skinned stranger as a liar. Aelscyg met Hemnyr's eyes before the accusation could be made and went on with the stranger's story.

"They lived well until the king of the Tarvar commanded his *vekka* to summon a dread spirit and turn it upon the Didon."

More glances were exchanged around the hall. "Didon" and "Tarvar" were mere sounds but vekka was a word the Geat-folk knew. Vekka dwelt in the far north, where superstitious folk chose to worship rocks and trees instead of the All-Father. Superstitious folk gave birth to vekka—men and women who sold their souls for bits of dark power.

When he mentioned vekka, Aelscyg captured Beowulf's

attention. Though he stayed in the shadows, the Geat-folk champion listened closely as the bard continued—"The very ground trembled and a great cloud covered the sun's rise. The women and children of the Didon covered their eyes in fright, but the worst was yet to come. The cloud parted and the spirit emerged, striding out of the Tarvar land. Elmaz says the spirit towered over them. Its feet crushed their homes. It seized their finest warriors in its fists and tore them limb from limb. Not even their animals were spared.

"By nightfall, the Didon had been driven off their land. With a heavy heart, their king summoned Mirgul, his bard, and asked, 'What have we done? What can we do?' Mirgul climbed to the highest place. Through his tears—for he had lost everything that day save his own life—Mirgul sang the Didon's tragedy to the stars.

"And the stars sang back.

"They showed him the vekka delving deep into the earth where stands a prison, ancient beyond reckoning. The vekka spoke a single word. The great doors were sundered and the dread spirit emerged. Mirgul sobbed as the stars revealed what he, himself, had seen: the Didon's utter destruction.

"Mirgul repeated his king's question, 'What can we do?' and the stars stretched their light-bearing fingers to the west.

"They point to us," Aelscyg concluded. "Elmaz says the stars showed Mirgul a tall and fair champion who fought without fear and vanquished dread spirits with his hands alone."

There wasn't a Geat in the hall who didn't know how Beowulf had slain Grendel. Aelscyg needed only the barest encouragement to sing the tale and Beowulf, himself, had been known to recount his adventures over a cup of mead. The story was known wherever mead was drunk on a cold night and no Geat was surprised to hear that the stars had sung of their champion to a bard of the distant Didon.

Beowulf, though, insisted that the tale be told correctly. "It's true I slew Grendel with my hands, and his mother, too, but for all that they were fell creatures, they were flesh and blood. They bled and died of their wounds. They weren't spirits."

Aelscyg scowled. "Spirit or flesh, it matters not. The stars themselves have guided this man to the Geat-folk hall, in search of the Geat-folk champion."

A Geat at the back of the hall slammed his mug on the table, making a crash that drew everyone's attention. "Hear him, Heardred! Send forth our champion." He slammed the mug again. "Glory to the Geat-folk!"

Twenty thanes echoed the call.

Beowulf made a fist where it couldn't be seen. He squeezed his fingers against his palm until the veins on his forearm bulged. He studied Elmaz of the Didon: a stubby man with an oddly colored, flat face and sooty, lank hair. Elmaz was a lesser man, lesser, even, than a half-Dane. He'd been born to lesser folk who couldn't raise a champion of their own and hadn't held their ground against a vekka's conjuring.

What glory would flow to the Geat-folk, if their champion bestirred himself for the likes of Elmaz or the Didon?

Yet again, what glory would flow to the Geat-folk or their champion, if that champion hid himself in the southern empire in the hope that his absence would awaken wisdom in a beardless king?

If the choice before Beowulf was fighting a spirit or hiding, then there was no choice at all. His wyrd was champion, not hired warrior.

"With my king's permission and with the All-Father as witness," Beowulf said, "I will go with this Elmaz and champion his Didon."

Hygd met his eyes with a fleeting smile that was lost to another round of cheering.

Though his decision was newly made, Beowulf already envisioned himself leaving the hall quietly with the little Didon as his only companion. He failed to reckon with his own fame. Heardred's regency years had been quiet ones. The younger Geat-folk, bored with peace and hungry for adventure, clamored to share their champion's glory. No few of the veterans, sensing a last opportunity or, perhaps, chafing under the caprices of a young king, joined the chorus.

Beowulf didn't want a cohort; Heardred didn't want to empty his hall of its best warriors.

If either had spoken his heart's thoughts . . .

If both had spoken and realized that, in essence, they wanted the same thing . . .

Once they'd been as close as father and son, but when their eyes met across the mead-hall, Beowulf beheld a stranger. He said nothing of his preferences; and neither did Heardred. Ignoring the gulf between their king and his champion—or completely ignorant of it—eleven Geat-folk swiftly swore unbreakable oaths. They would follow their champion to the land beyond the forests.

Any hope Beowulf had of a quick or quiet departure vanished. Heardred would provision his champion, but the newly sworn companions needed time to settle their affairs and gather provisions. Days, then weeks, slipped by. Beset with impatience, Beowulf retreated to the practice ground where he put every sword in Heardred's armory to the test.

Aelscyg found him there in the steel-gray light of a late-winter morning.

"I have dreamt," the bard said after clearing his throat loudly enough to alert the champion to his presence.

Beowulf finished his stroke, slicing deep into a straw man's midsection, before resting his sword's tip in the earth. "You have learned something. Is the stranger not to be trusted? Has he told untruths?"

The bard shook his head. "No, nothing like that . . . but there is something that he didn't say, perhaps doesn't know."

Beowulf raised an irrate eyebrow.

"Elmaz said the western stars sang back to their bard, so I went out last night and asked the eastern stars to sing to me."

"You said you dreamt."

Aelscyg shrugged. "Do I ask you how you wield a sword?"

Beowulf allowed as all men were entitled to their mysteries, and the bard continued.

"I saw the land you will visit. The Didon are all much like Elmaz, and so are their enemies, the Tarvar, but neither the Tarvar nor the Elmaz are the first people of their land. Those were the Tochari . . . and the Tochari were taller. Many of them were blue-eyed and as fair as any Geat. The Tochari had mighty enemies, but they had mightier gods and the mightiest of them took the gods of their enemies and cast them into prison far below the earth. That's where they were when the vekka freed one of them—the stars sang a word . . . a name, I think: Vrunus. He's the worst of the Fallen Ones, but there are many more in that prison, and worse . . ."

"So sang the stars?" Beowulf said with a touch of skepticism. He'd heard what Aelscyg and other bards had done to his own tale.

"Beowulf, I looked down, and there was no bottom; but there were *things* . . . creatures, monsters that no man of flesh and blood could hope to stand against."

"You're telling us not to go."

"No. I'm telling you to be careful, and I'm sending my son Oswyn with you."

Oswyn was a clever lad with curly hair, too slender to wield a sword properly, and no more Aelscyg's son than Beowulf was himself. The bard had returned with the boy after one of his wanderings. Since Aelscyg had no true children, the Geat-folk accepted that, in the fullness of time, the sweet-voiced Oswyn would be their bard. But take Oswyn on a hard journey with danger, maybe death at the end . . . ?

"Keep him here. Teach him what you know."

"I've taught him and what I haven't taught him, he's learned for himself. He jabbers away with Elmaz in the Didon tongue and when you need him to, he can do what I did last night."

"Dream about singing stars?"

"I'd go with you myself, just to witness the battle, but I'm too old, so, I'm sending Oswyn. Don't argue with me. I serve the Geat-folk, same as you. I've already spoken with King Heardred. He agrees; Hygd, too."

Beowulf didn't stop to argue. He limbered his sword and took a swipe at another straw man. It and the pole behind it split cleanly and fell in pieces to the ground.

Aelscyg retreated and kept his distance until that morning when Beowulf and his companions were at last ready to follow Elmaz south and west. The bard strode up, leading his son and one of Heardred's best horses. They exchanged whispered words before Oswyn mounted and took his place amid the eleven sworn thanes. Beowulf felt eyes against his back, especially Heardred's eyes. He ignored everyone, except young Oswyn himself.

"You'll get no help," he snarled to the lad.

"I'll help you, my lord," Oswyn replied calmly.

No Geat would have borne the look Beowulf shot at Oswyn, but, then, curly-haired Oswyn wasn't a blood-born Geat.

Beowulf gathered his reins and gave the signal for the journey to begin. He rode in front of Elmaz and until they reached the land beyond the forests, he would stay there.

They rode south, through lands speckled with greening fields and peasants who ran for shelter the moment they spied northern warriors. Then they rode east, into the uncut forests where trees had grown since the beginning of time and sunlight scarcely touched the ground. They were the first since snow-melt to travel the cart-way that Elmaz had followed through the hulking trees. The mat of fallen leaves still covering the narrow track muted their horses' hoof falls.

Beyond the closest trees, the shadows were as dark as any cave. No Geat would admit it, not to himself and certainly not aloud, but they mistrusted those shadows. Speaking in whispers when they spoke at all, the Geat-folk kept too close to Elmaz's cart-way. At night, they built fires larger than springtime warranted and bade Oswyn sing the familiar songs of Geat-land's seas and rocky shores.

It was uphill and down through the forest until they came to a noticeably steeper decline that brought them to water as broad as Geat-land's broadest sea arm, for all that it was freshwater, not salt. While Beowulf weighed the dangers of fording such wide, unknown waters, Oswyn huddled with Elmaz.

"There's a boatman a day's ride south along the shore," the bard's son said, interrupting Beowulf's thoughts. "Elmaz says he'll take us across for a token."

Heardred had sent his champion off with gifts for the Didon chief and a purse filled with coins and bits of silver and gold the Geat-folk had gathered from other lands; tokens for the boatman would not be a problem. Beowulf reined his horse southward, following a road that was somewhat wider and better kept than the forest cart-way.

Like all the northern peoples, the Geat-folk knew how to build boats and built them well. They were not encouraged by the ramshackle boat they came upon the next day. Brythnor and Hrothgar swore loudly that they would not set foot on its decks and the other Geat-folk, including Beowulf, thought much the same. But the Didon were on the far side of the water and

Beowulf approached the boatman who knew enough words from the various northern dialects to make himself understood.

He shook his head when Beowulf offered him silver bits for the use of his boat. He shook it again when Beowulf added a small gold ring to the collection in his palm.

"How much more?" Beowulf snarled.

"Not for all the gold you carry," the boatman replied in the same tone.

Years spent standing at the rudder had toughened the boatman. He stood nearly as tall as Beowulf and was, if anything, broader across the shoulders. When Beowulf demanded passage, the boatman held his ground and pointed toward the river.

"See them whitecaps? Them's the river maids, and they'll have you an' me both off the boat and in their bellies in an eyeblink."

Beowulf studied the water where there was, indeed, a cluster of white-capped waves. The winds were quiet, but a shoal could kick up white water in any weather. "Steer around it."

The boatman spat a laugh. "Them's the *maids*," he repeated. "They'll swim after the boat no matter where I set her."

Beowulf understood, then, that it wasn't rocks that roiled the water, but water beasts. The Geat-folk called them nickers and he'd slain the largest of them all when he'd followed Grendel's mother into her lair. He stretched a knot out of his shoulders and patted his sword hilt.

"Get me out there, and I'll take care of them."

The boatman laughed until Beowulf drew his sword. Brawn was no match for that. He cursed Beowulf with the names of gods the champion neither recognized nor feared, then, with a yard of steel still leveled at his throat, climbed into his boat. Beowulf followed alone, sword in hand.

As the boatman predicted, the white-capped water came toward the boat like an arrow. The boatman ceased his cursing and began his prayers. The white waves held their distance until the boat was a good distance from the shore, then a handful of heads broke the surface.

Maids, the boatman had called them, and there was something female about their faces, but nothing beautiful. Their skin was gray, their large eyes were a sickly, unblinking yellow-green, and their teeth, which showed when they opened their mouths in a ghastly chorus, were both numerous and sharp-pointed. Weedy hair, longer than Beowulf's sword, swirled in the water around them.

"You've slain us now," the boatman muttered as the maids encircled the boat.

Beowulf said nothing. These water beasts were smaller than the nickers who dwelt off Geat-land's shore and, though there were more of them, he had no doubt that he'd prevail over them. From experience, he knew his sword would be useless; it took named steel to rend that cold, gray flesh. He sheathed the blade—now that they were surrounded, the boatman was no threat at all—and unbuckled his sword belt. The belt and all his armor went into a pile at the boatman s feet.

"Hold these for me," he said to the boatman, "until I get back."

A gray arm heaved onto the railing. The hand bore five fingers, but there was froglike webbing between the knuckles and long, black claws at the end of each finger. The claws clenched into the rail and the river-maid's face appeared. She hissed like a serpent and reached for the boatman who immediately abandoned his post beside the rudder.

Beowulf got the maid's attention with a whistle, then gathered himself and dove over her head into the frigid water.

The maids swirled around him, all grasping claws and gnashing teeth, as he sank. Nickers weren't fish and neither were the river-maids. They didn't have gills and needed air when they fed. Beowulf had reasoned that they'd have a lair nearby, a lair where he could breathe and fight, if he could last that long.

Beowulf bled from a score of gouges and his lungs were burning when the substance surrounding him changed from water to air. He fell hard and gasping, but was on his feet in a heartbeat. The maids came at him in a hungry swarm. They got in each other's way, fighting amongst themselves as much as they fought against Beowulf. In the jostling conflict he couldn't get a good enough grip on any one neck to wring it fatally.

Then, seeing that they pulled one another's hair as they struggled, Beowulf got the notion to lock his fists around the weedy tress that flew close. A few swift wrist twists and he had a grip that couldn't be shaken.

The champion of the Geat-folk cracked the maid like a whip. Her shrill cries stopped abruptly when her neck broke. The other maids hesitated and fell silent at the sight of tarry blood seeping from their sister's mouth. Before the maids could renew their attack, Beowulf settled onto his heels and began to swing the dead one around by her hair. The whirling gray-skinned corpse made a more-than-adequate club that Beowulf brought down again and again until all the ghastly maids were stretched out senseless on the rocky ground.

Beowulf knelt beside each maid, wrapped his hands around her leathery throat, and twisted hard until the bones within snapped. As each maid died, the air-filled chamber on the river floor shrank. It disappeared altogether with the last maid's death. With a desperate kick, Beowulf swam for air.

The feckless boatman was making for the river's far shore when Beowulf broke through the surface. With an angry roar, Beowulf swam after the boat, seizing the rudder and wrenching it from the boatman's grasp as he clambered aboard. From his knees, the boatman swore that he'd lost faith and, believing the maids had taken Beowulf, had been too afraid of the Geat-folk on the near shore to return there. He was lying, but he groveled well and Beowulf couldn't read the river's currents well enough to manage the boat himself, so he let the boatman live.

By midafternoon, the Geat-folk, Elmaz, and their horses were across the river.

"How much farther?" Beowulf asked Oswyn who repeated the question to Elmaz.

The little man jabbered and gestured toward the east.

Oswyn was frowning when he turned again to Beowulf. "He says he'd been riding for three months when he came to the river."

To the man, the Geat-folk swore oaths of disbelief. When he'd set eyes on the wide river, Beowulf had been certain that they were near the edge of the world, near the place where the sun rose.

"Three months?" he repeated. That was twice again what they'd ridden. The champion looked back toward the river where the boatman was already headed home and far from the shore.

"It took Elmaz almost a year after he crossed the river to find us. We'll do better now. Elmaz says we'll follow an arrow's path from here on and be home—his home—by summer."

"A year! Your father never mentioned that. It's a wonder if any of Elmaz's people are left." Beowulf sighed and mounted his horse. "We follow," he told the other Geat-folk and gave a nod to Elmaz who got his horse moving east.

For a week the east bank forest was the same as the west bank forest had been, allowing for the difference each day made as the trees awakened. Then the cart-way became a single-file path that ended at a village where the people spoke a language neither Oswyn nor Elmaz understood and worshiped a blood-reeking wooden stag three-men tall. Warily, the Geat-folk traded for food and arrows.

There was no true path beyond the stag-worshiping village, only the trails made by hunters and their prey. At Beowulf's insistence, they broke from Elmaz's straight line, zigzagging north and south and sometimes west until the champion believed they were out of the villagers' reach.

After a month in the eastern forest, the trees at last began to thin. A hot summer—as a Geat measured heat—had just begun when they entered a sea of grass. From horizon to horizon, the steppe was without a tree or rock to stand as a landmark. Beowulf's first thought was that it was as flat as a smith's anvil, but as that first day of grassland riding wore on, he realized that the land heaved in great, shallow waves that could easily hide a stream . . . or a raiding party.

In the forest, the ancient trees had imposed their silence on puny men. It was different on the steppe, but no less quiet. Once, in the distance, they'd spotted a bird circling high in the cloudless sky; other than that, they'd seen no animals and nothing living that wasn't rooted in the earth.

Come late afternoon, Elmaz gave his horse its head. The dun ambled south by the sun and brought them between two land-waves where a soggy patch of ground offered water to those blessed with patience. Elmaz herded the Geat-folk to higher ground for their night camp, then, returning to the seep, he set small, grass-loop snares and gathered rock-hard turds from its verge.

"He's mad!" Brythnor hissed in Beowulf's ear. "We've followed a madman into a mad land. The All-Father has cursed them. We're doomed."

And Beowulf was inclined to agree as the strange little man made a heap of the turds and dried grass in the middle of their camp.

"The forest was bad enough," Hrothgar griped, "but at least we had something to eat! What manner of god commands an altar like that?"

Elmaz paused in his labor. His unkennable dark eyes studied first Hrothgar, then Beowulf, reminding Beowulf that if Oswyn had mastered the Didon language during their journey, Elmaz might have returned the compliment.

"Not now," he cautioned Hrothgar in a tight-lipped whisper.

They bedded down hungry and discovered that the steppe was not entirely empty. Swarms of insects descended with night's darkness. Some homed in on eyes, noses, and ears where their incessant buzzing was enough to keep a man awake or drive him mad. Others had blood-thirst and left stinging welts in their wake.

In desperation, Beowulf covered his head with his saddle blanket. He sought sleep's refuge without finding it.

What manner of god, indeed, received the Didon's worship? A poor god, if that heap of dung and straw was his altar. A cruel one, too, if the steppe was the land he provided. If Beowulf hadn't given his oath to his king and his god—but he had and such oaths could not be broken, not for insects and dung.

At sunrise, Elmaz checked his snares and retrieved one stringy rabbit and a variety of small creatures, all of which Beowulf would have called "rats" and thrown into the midden. But Elmaz skinned them with alarming speed and skill. He threaded them onto stalks of pithy grass before striking sparks onto what they'd all mistaken for an altar. Bones and all, the ratty meat cooked quickly. Elmaz offered charred stalks to each of the Geat-folk while the larger rabbit sizzled above the pungent flames.

In the north, hospitality was an honor-bound virtue and there was no greater affront than to refuse an offering of food or drink. But rats? Beowulf's mind said *No!* in the strongest terms; his empty stomach begged to differ and the weighted stalks stayed where they were in his fist, neither flung into the far grass nor brought to his mouth.

Elmaz bit into a morsel he'd saved for himself. He chewed carefully; the Geat-folk could hear tiny bones crunching. Elmaz spat those out before swallowing.

Every Geat had done something similar with fresh-caught herring, even to searing it over an open fire.

But rats?

As Beowulf pondered, Oswyn took a bite. The boy chewed and spat and looked a little green as he swallowed. His smile was tentative when he said a few words to an obviously concerned Elmaz who had devoured his first rat and was nearing the tail of his second.

If the boy—a bard's son and no true Geat, at that—could stomach Elmaz's hospitality, then Beowulf judged that he could hardly toss it away. And if their champion would gnaw a rat off a weed stalk, then Hrothgar, Brythnor, and the other Geat-folk could hardly refuse to follow.

It was, by far, the least appetizing meal Beowulf had ever eaten, but two months later, he spat as well as Elmaz and scarcely noticed the gamey taste.

Oswyn had taught Elmaz a good many northern words, more, Beowulf suspected, than he admitted to. He was careful with his words when the flat-faced man was within earshot. Elmaz had his own sense of pride and would not speak imperfectly to the men destined to free his people from the Tarvar. He spoke only to Oswyn and through him revealed that the Didon did not eat vermin by choice and vastly preferred a feast of horsemeat with curdled milk.

One evening, no different than any other starlit evening, from the crest of a land wave, no different than the hundreds they had crossed before, Elmaz raised his arms and traced imaginary lines among the stars. The next morning, the party changed direction, trekking more nearly south than east as they had been since leaving Geat-land. A fortnight later, the first dark rocks appeared amid the grass. Another three afternoons and they were in hill country, leading their horses along treacherous rocky paths.

Eighty-eight days—Beowulf had kept count—after leaving the forest village, they came upon an abandoned hearth.

Elmaz leapt down from his horse. He scratched among the char and ashes, then, throwing his head back, he let loose with a howl that would have raised the hackles on any wolf.

"What now?" Beowulf demanded of his bard's son as Elmaz's wailing continued. "Are we too late?"

Oswyn relayed the questions and returned.

"Elmaz says we wait here. The Didon will come."

The Didon arrived before sunset, about a score of them, adults and children together, on foot, emerging from the rocks. None of the Geat-folk had heard them approach. They shared Elmaz's appearance: sallow skin, lidless eyes half-hidden in flat faces, and dead-straight black hair, but where Elmaz was wiry, they were gaunt. Their clothes were both patched and tattered. No few of them limped. Beowulf needed a moment's concentration to realize that, despite their tunics and trousers, all the adults in front of them were women.

One woman separated from the rest and, with a cry between joy and pain, ran to embrace Elmaz. A child of perhaps seven or eight and so scrawny Beowulf couldn't guess if it were a boy or girl followed close behind the woman. The youngster wrapped arms around Elmaz's hips and swayed from one foot to the other as husband and wife assured each other that they had survived.

Then the woman—but not the child—stepped back. She took Elmaz by the wrists and spoke rapidly. Beowulf couldn't see Elmaz's face, but tears streamed down the woman's. He nudged Oswyn whom he'd called to his side when the Didon appeared.

"Do you understand?"

The lad shrugged. "It's names, one after another. I thought I heard the words for brother and son. I think she's naming the people who've died since—"

Elmaz wrenched his hands free. He covered his face, then leaned down on his wife's shoulder.

"This is everyone who's left?" Beowulf asked. "Only women and children? What happened to the men?"

Oswyn left Beowulf to stand beside Elmaz. The lad waited for the man to compose himself, but before that happened, an older man with silver in his black hair made his way slowly down the path the others had used, leading a cohort of men. The silvered Didon was as gaunt as his people and his tunic was nearly as ragged as theirs. He had the gait of a man in considerable pain, but there was gold wrapped around the horse-tail staff he used to steady himself and he had the bearing of authority.

The Didon men matched their leader's pace. None that he could see wore steel larger than a hunter's knife, but they all seemed to sprout a quiver of arrows over one shoulder and slung Elmaz's strange, short bow over the other.

Beowulf thought of his armor bundled up in his horse's pack. Its metal was proof against arrows. If the bow were the Tarvar's chosen weapon, as it was for the Didon, the Geat-folk would have an easy path to glory. Then, when the silvered Didon stood before him, Beowulf repeated the clasped-hand gesture Elmaz had offered Heardred at their first meeting.

Elmaz had disentangled himself from his family. Together, he and Oswyn made the introductions: Zulgat, king of the Didon and Beowulf, champion of the Geat-folk, foretold by the singing stars.

A man stepped out of the cohort behind Zulgat. There were feathers bound in his hair, black scars etched into his cheeks, and a strand of what appeared to be knuckles and bits of leather hung around his neck. He closed his right eye and, cocking his head, subjected Beowulf to a thorough, silent study.

Beowulf bore the inspection with increasing discomfort until the man surprised him utterly by throwing a handful of pale powder at his face. The powder stung and blinded him. For a heartbeat, the champion was defenseless, but not his men. The air rang with the sound of drawn steel as the Geat-folk, who went nowhere without their weapons, prepared for slaughter. The feathered Didon shouted words Beowulf couldn't understand.

As Beowulf's vision cleared, he saw the Didon men with their arrows nocked toward him. Oswyn and Elmaz together hurled themselves between the Geat-folk and the Didon.

"A mistake!" Oswyn cried as Elmaz, Beowulf hoped, said the same thing in the Didon language. "He didn't believe you were a man."

"All-Father!" Beowulf swore. "What did he think I was?"

Oswyn asked and received several replies. "A spirit. An evil spirit like the Tarvar guardian, the one my father named Vrunus. He says"—the lad chewed his lip anxiously—"he says we did not look like men. We look like Vrunus, only smaller."

"Not men!" Beowulf's anger blossomed. He was a Geat, the finest of men, and their champion, to boot—the finest of the finest! Then wisdom got a handhold on his anger's neck. If he'd been born among men like Elmaz and Zulgat, he might not have known what to make of a Geat, either.

"And, are we men?"

"Oh, yes. You did not burst into flame when his powder touched you."

Beowulf threw his head back and laughed loud and long enough to avert disaster. Weapons were lowered and put away. He embraced Zulgat and the powder-throwing Didon who, when introductions were complete, proved to be the bard Mirgul.

Through Elmaz and Oswyn, Zulgat invited the Geat-folk to a feast deeper in their rocky stronghold. The horses were unloaded and led away by Didon herders. The Geat-folk shouldered their packs and followed the Didon. Beowulf made himself last in line. He held Oswyn beside him, whispering, when they were almost alone . . .

"That Mirgul, he's vekka, isn't he? Your father said bard, but, on my life, that man's no bard."

"Elmaz said he was like my father. He sings. The Tarvar, they have the man who's vekka."

Beowulf thought a moment. "It all depends on what you meet first. Meet a Geat first, and the Didon are wild men. Meet the Didon and we're . . . what? Monsters? Spirits? Things to be set on fire?"

"Friends," Oswyn corrected. "Champions. They believe we were sent by the stars."

The oldest of the Didon, the youngest, and the weakest waited in a natural stronghold. Altogether there were about sixty of them. Another slightly smaller band hid in the rocky hills a day's ride north and a third had split itself off in the spring and headed south. That was all that remained of Elmaz's people who had numbered over a thousand before the Tarvar raised Vrunus, their guardian.

The Didon had lost their herds when they lost their lands. For over a year, they had subsisted by hunting what little game the steppe had to offer and stealing their own horses back from the Tarvar herd. The remains of such a stolen beast formed the backbone of the "feast" laid before Beowulf and his companions. Beowulf would rather have eaten one of Elmaz's rats. At least the rats were fresh.

The next morning, Zulgat gathered everyone around him. He said many things Oswyn couldn't understand and one very important thing that he did. Zulgat assumed their star-sung champion would need to study the Tarvar guardian before he could fight it, and Zulgat meant to provide that opportunity. Scouts were ready to guide the star-sung champion deep into the Didon's lost land where they could get a good look at Vrunus.

Beowulf readily agreed. There wasn't anything he liked about the steppe and precious little he liked about the Didon he'd sworn to champion. If he liked what he saw, he'd challenge Vrunus on the spot and get the killing over with. The sooner the confrontation, the sooner the Geat-folk could leave this forsaken place.

Mirgul dusted them all with a sooty powder he said would hide them from the living Tarvar, though not—the Didon had learned through sad experience—from Vrunus. The powder itched and raised a rash on Geat-folk cheeks. For two days they suffered as they rode beneath a relentless sun, then the rash subsided and the hiding began. They kept to the troughs between the land waves, huddled for hours in the crushing heat, and crossing from one trough to the next trough only after sending a scout on foot to the crests.

Neither the Tarvar nor the Didon built halls. In the best of times, the Didon had lived in tents. The Tarvar still did, staying in one place for a week or a month, following their herds from one grazing ground to the next. The Didon scouts knew where the main Tarvar tents *should* be, but not precisely where they were. When their first guess proved wrong, they studied the grass and sniffed the air like dogs before striking out in a new direction. Their second guess proved wrong as well and a heated argument arose among the scouts. Beowulf pulled the Geat-folk back, lest they be drawn into an argument they didn't understand and could only lose.

The eastern sky had bloomed to lavender when two of the scouts mounted their horses and galloped away. That left three scouts who told Oswyn that it was time to ride north. Beowulf passed the order to the other men, but his heart was worried.

"Did they say why two of their own ran away?" he asked Oswyn, wishing he had taken the time to learn something of the Didon language himself and didn't have to rely on a boy whose beard had just begun to shadow his chin.

"Not directly, but I caught a few words as they argued. This place where we're headed now, it lies in the Tarvar lands, where the Didon were never welcome. Mirgul's powder will not protect us there."

"Mirgul's powder does not protect us now. Even this far from home, we have the All-Father's protection. It is all the Geat-folk ever have, all we ever need."

Oswyn nodded, because it was expected, but he was not reassured.

"There is more?"

Another nod. "The last time they crossed Tarvar land, Vrunus came upon them. Ten men died. *Eaten.* Their heads bitten off while they still lived."

Beowulf sat back in his saddle. That said something about the size of the enemy he expected to vanquish, something he had not quite known before. "And you are afraid?" he said to the bard's son.

Oswyn neither spoke nor moved, which was answer enough for Beowulf.

"It was much the same with the Fallen One named Grendel," Beowulf went on in a deliberately casual tone. He suspected he was lying, suspected that Vrunus would prove larger than Grendel. Not that that mattered. "He could not stand up straight in Heorot, and that hall was far greater than Heardred's. When Grendel came, he tore good men limb from limb and, yes, he ate of them, too. Men were his prey. When I swore to King Hrothgar that I would defeat his curse, I thought to fight with my sword, but my sword was not my weapon that night. I fought Grendel strength against strength, with my hands. I tore his arm from his body, as he had rent so many of King Hrothgar's good men. He ran away, because the Fallen have no bravery."

"Were you ever afraid?" Oswyn dared ask.

Beowulf thought a moment. "No. It is my wyrd to be champion of the Geat-folk."

"This Vrunus is a terrible thing."

"Grendel was a terrible thing, his mother, worse."

The bard's son stared at his hands.

"Ach!" Beowulf reached out to clout the boy lightly on his shoulder. "I make no sense of this land. One hill is the same as the next, but if we turned west right now, I think, in time, we'd come to something that would show us the way home. You could sing a tale of our adventures."

"But not how you slew Vrunus."

"No, not if we ran. Would you have us run?"

Oswyn shook his head and they continued north.

When the time came, only four of them—Beowulf, Oswyn, and two of the scouts—made the pre-dawn crawl to a row of tall stones that people who'd died long before the first Tarvar or Didon was born had erected on a land-wave crest. The stones' shadows would conceal them from Vrunus, Oswyn said . . . or so the scouts hoped.

The Tarvar camp lay far enough away that people could be seen individually, but not distinguished one from the other. At a glance, there were at least twenty black tents and maybe twice that number as their silhouettes blurred in the sunrise light. The four Tarvar herds clumped outside the tent. Beowulf had never seen so many horses at once.

But neither people, tents, nor horses held his attention; that went to Vrunus.

The Tarvar guardian was painful to behold. He was shrouded in a dazzling glow, like sunlight scattered on the sea. Within that shroud, his shape shifted constantly. One moment Vrunus's head rose as high as the rare steppe clouds overhead. Then he grew smaller, but not *small*. As Beowulf watched, Vrunus was never shorter than the height of seven of the Tarvar at his feet.

At the tallest, Beowulf could discern the guardian's features and though he would never mistake Vrunus for a Geat, it was fair to say that he did not look at all like the Didon. His hair was rust colored and surrounded his face like a wild wreath. His face wasn't flat but sloped back from a prodigious nose. Save for their size, the guardian's eyes were unremarkable, which was to say they were lidded, not half-hidden in dark slits. In truth, Vrunus most resembled Oswyn whom Aelscyg had brought up from the Imperial lands far to the south of Heardred's hall.

Like a berserker, Vrunus clothed himself in untrimmed hides that he'd tied at one shoulder and across his loins. The garment fit him whether he was great or smaller. He'd shod himself in flimsy shoes, little more than leather slabs laced around his feet and up his massive calves. He carried no weapons that Beowulf could see, though by the size of his fists, Vrunus didn't need any.

The guardian trod a path that roughly circled the Tarvar camp and its herds. Remarkably, his footfalls did not make a sound, even when he came closest to the stones where Beowulf and the others hid. Nor did the grass break beneath his massive feet and, though Vrunus blocked Beowulf's view of the sun, he did not cast a shadow.

Grendel had cast a shadow. He'd walked naked, like the beast he was, but he and his mother had cast shadows.

Beowulf clenched his fists. The veins in his forearms bulged, the veins in his neck, also. His pulse hammered throughout his body. Strength against strength, the champion of the Geat-folk feared nothing under the sun. But a thing never shorter than seven men together that cast no shadow?

Beowulf forced himself to relax; his heartbeat steadied. He was ready to leave the stones' shadow. Not to challenge Vrunus; it was too soon for that. He needed to think and plan as he had never done before.

Both Didon scouts seized Beowulf when he attempted to ease backward from the stones' shadows. With frantic whispers they made him understand that leaving their shelter by daylight was dangerous beyond contemplation and that they needed to stay where they were, still and quiet, until nightfall.

So Beowulf did his thinking in sight of his enemy. By midafternoon, when the sun had come around to kindle fire upon his back and he would have sold his soul for a mouthful of water, he had his strategy: Bring Vrunus down. Anything that could be laid flat on the ground could be vanquished. And his tactics: Get behind the guardian and slice through the sinews at his knee and ankle.

After a blood-red sunset, the observers slipped away from the stones. The Geat-folk pummeled Beowulf with questions when the party reformed. What did Vrunus look like? How would they fight him? Beowulf let Oswyn describe the Tarvar guardian; bards were best for that. He answered the other questions himself: Geat-folk and Didon together—as many as could mount and ride— were to swarm toward Vrunus. There was risk, and there would be loss if the Didon tales were true, but someone would survive to hamstring the mighty guardian.

To a man, the men before Beowulf nodded, each believing that he'd be the one to bring Vrunus down. Beowulf said nothing to discourage them. Next to the All-Father, a warrior's belief in himself was the faith that kept him safe. Even if that belief were rooted in something perilously close to lies. To be sure, Beowulf had faith in the All-Father who ruled the world and protected the Geat-folk; and he had supreme faith in himself and his wyrd. What he lacked was faith in the swords Heardred had given them months ago. They were forged of the finest steel made in the north, but steel had not brought Grendel down and Beowulf doubted that it would have any effect on a fell creature without a shadow.

The champion nursed his dread throughout the journey back to the Didon stronghold but kept it hidden when he told Zulgat what he had seen and what he would do.

"When?" the tattered king asked.

"Soon," Beowulf answered. "Soon."

By *soon*, Beowulf meant several days during which he intended to ransack his mind and memory for better ideas. *Soon* had a different meaning to the Didon—or, perhaps, Oswyn, who knew nothing of Beowulf's crisis, and had let his own faith get ahead of his translation. Either way, by Zulgat's decree, *soon* became *the riders will leave tomorrow.*

The women prepared another feast. Choking down his meal, Beowulf gave silent thanks that the Didon were starving and, feast or no, the portions were small.

One man did not eat with them: the Didon bard, Mirgul. Beowulf expected Mirgul would make an appearance eventually and he did. The man had added more feathers to his hair and wrapped himself in a horse-tail cloak. A veil hung over his face, yet he had no difficulty finding his way to the fire. He carried what looked to be the shoulder bone of a long-dead horse and shoved it deep into the embers. The fire quickened with blue flames that drew a gasp from the Geat-folk and evoked a communal keening from the assembled Didon. They made sound from the depths of their throats that was as unnatural as the blue flames.

Just when Beowulf thought the wailing would overwhelm his

wits, the flames shattered into a cascade of blinding sparks. The Didon fell silent as Mirgul rooted through the embers with his bare hands. He raised the charred shoulder bone and brandished it in the moonlight. In the unbroken silence, Mirgul sat cross-legged and, without lifting his veil, pored over the bone, twisting it and turning it until he had studied it entirely. When the bard was finished, he discussed the bone with Zulgat, then laid it in Beowulf's lap. He made a speech of which Beowulf understood not a single word.

"What did he say? What do I do?" Beowulf asked Oswyn who'd been clever enough to move closer as Mirgul approached.

"The Didon believe the future is known to the flame and written on the bone. Mirgul told Zulgat that Vrunus would be defeated. Now, he's told you that you will fly like an eagle and burrow through the earth before you defeat Vrunus."

"He's mad. They're all mad. No, worse than mad, they're vekka, every one of them."

Oswyn recoiled. "Must I tell him *that?*"

"No. No. How did Zulgat reply?"

"That his heart had taken flight with joy."

"Say that. Say whatever you think wisest, but do not listen to what this vekka has said." Beowulf stressed his words for the benefit of the Geat-folk who'd overheard the conversation. "Men do not fly. Men do not burrow. We will fight Vrunus with steel and strength. We will bring Vrunus down and then we'll slay him."

After handing the bone to Oswyn, Beowulf walked away from the feast with a churning stomach and a troubled conscience. He didn't return until the camp was quiet, then he found the blankets where Oswyn slept. Laying a hand over the lad's mouth, he awakened him and led him out of the camp.

"Your father said you could do what he had done—dream a song from the stars."

There was moonlight enough for Beowulf to see Oswyn's eyes widen before he nodded.

"How is it done?"

"A potion of mead infused with special herbs."

Beowulf's shoulders sank. He hadn't sipped mead since leaving Geat-land.

"I have enough," the lad quickly assured Beowulf. He withdrew a lacquered vial from within his shirt. "My father said I would need it."

"Will it show you the future, also?"

Oswyn shook his head. "Only the All-Father knows what will be. The stars reveal what is and what was."

"Ask them to reveal Vrunus's fault, the crack that will bring him down."

"But—?"

"Ask," Beowulf repeated. The word was not a request.

Oswyn broke the vial's waxen seal but hesitated before putting it to his lips.

"I will watch over you. You will be safe."

The lad's expression clearly said safety was not his chief concern but he said nothing aloud before sipping down his father's potion. Within heartbeats, Oswyn was slurring his words like a mead-hall veteran. He swayed on his hips as he sat. Beowulf caught him and eased him to the ground where he was instantly asleep.

Twice while Beowulf watched, the bard's son stiffened and whimpered with terror. He clawed the ground like a dog caught in a nightmare and gave Beowulf a solid kick in an unguarded shin. Then, with the waning moon still well above the western horizon and the eastern one dark as pitch, Oswyn's eyes opened.

"What did you learn?"

"Learn?" the lad mumbled. "What? Where am I?"

Beowulf buried his face in his hands. He should have known better than to waste his hopes on magic. The bards' potions were as useless as Mirgul's powders. They'd fight Vrunus with steel and the All-Father would collect their souls if that were not enough.

"Come on."

He offered a hand to the groggy lad who reached and then withdrew.

"Wait . . . wait. I can remember now; it's becoming clear." Though the night was far from cold, Oswyn wrapped himself in his arms. "There is *no* fault, Beowulf. Vrunus is more powerful than my father saw from Heardred's hall. You cannot imagine his power. He would destroy the Tarvar as well as the Didon, if he could."

"If he could? Vrunus has power beyond my imagination, yet he cannot destroy the Tarvar?"

"The vekka controls it. There is a golden strand around Vrunus's neck. The vekka has the other end wrapped around his wrist. If the strand were cut!" The lad squeezed himself tight.

"If the strand were cut, then the vekka would lose control of the Tarvar guardian? How thick is this strand? Could a sword slice it through?"

"No! No, you mustn't! Cut the strand and Vrunus's full power would be unleashed. Nothing would stop him. Nothing could. Not even the All-Father. Whatever we do, we must not cut the strand until we've slain Vrunus . . . and maybe not even then."

So, they were back where they started, with swords, faint hopes; and a new warning not to cut a thread of gold. "Did you learn anything else?" Beowulf asked without optimism.

"I saw something at the Tarvar camp that we didn't see when we were there: a pit."

"We were too far away—"

"No, when my father dreamt with the singing stars, he saw the Tarvar vekka summon Vrunus from a pit. I saw the pit. It is in the Tarvar camp . . . near it, anyway. Just to the east."

"We would have seen a pit large enough to expel Vrunus."

"It's hidden. I don't know how. But it's there. The pit my father saw. The pit with Vrunus's prison at the bottom. Beowulf, you could throw Vrunus back into the pit . . ."

"Lift him over my head and throw him?" Beowulf chuckled bitterly. "Even I don't have the strength for that." He offered his hand a second time. "You tried, lad. You tried. We'll all try."

"We'll bring Vrunus down, just like you've said."

"Maybe—but not you. When we get there—if the Tarvar are where they were before—you make your way to the stones. You watch and remember; and if worse comes to worst, you go back to Heardred's mead-hall and tell our tale."

Thirteen Geat-folk and twenty Didon left the stronghold after dawn. They rode directly into Tarvar land, hoping to find their enemies where they had last been seen and in this, at least, their hopes were fulfilled. Oswyn protested his exile to the stones but Mirgul was likewise charged with witnessing the battle for Zulgat who had remained at the stronghold. Beowulf would have preferred to leave Aelscyg's son with anyone but the man he considered a vekka, not a bard, but, so long as he wasn't the only chosen witness, Oswyn was willing to stand apart.

Beowulf saw no reason not to attack as soon as Mirgul and Oswyn had slipped into the stones' shadows. As imposing as Vrunus was, the guardian circled the Tarvar camp alone. Beowulf had spotted no sentries the first time he'd overlooked the camp and he expected none now. He'd been assured that Vrunus didn't sleep and any advantage his men might gain by surprising the Tarvar as they slept would be more than offset by confusion wrought by darkness, since the moon had shrunk to a useless sliver.

"We attack when we arrive," Beowulf told all the men. "When we see that Oswyn and Mirgul have made their way to the stones."

The Didon muttered among themselves. To a man, they knew Vrunus's power. Fear showed on their flat faces. Waiting would not change that. Except for Beowulf and Oswyn, the Geat-folk still had no good notion of what Vrunus was. Brave and bold as they were, they'd be dumbfounded when they laid eyes on the Tarvar guardian; and waiting wouldn't change that, either.

"If we begin now, we will be riding home by sundown."

The men liked that thought, even if they didn't entirely believe it.

Beowulf embraced the bard's son, but not too heartily, lest the others suspect the doubts in the champion's mind. He would not touch Mirgul and, judging by Mirgul's stance, the so-called bard felt the same way about the Geat-folk's champion. They dipped their chins and went their separate ways.

Left to their natures, both the Geat-folk and the Didon would begin a battle in a tight-knit swarm that would make them much too vulnerable to Vrunus's great fists. As they neared the Tarvar camp, Beowulf commanded each of them to stay yards away from the others, even as they neared the guardian. He commanded the swordless Didon to aim their arrows at Vrunus's eyes as they charged; and to break away when they came within the guardian's reach. The Didon could harrow the Tarvar camp, taking vengeance on their old enemies. That, Beowulf hoped, would keep the Tarvar from forming a counterattack as he and the other Geat-folk brought Vrunus down.

It went without saying that Beowulf expected to be the first to dash around the guardian's leg and make the first hamstringing cut. But, as it happened, Beowulf's horse was not the fastest in the headlong charge toward the Tarvar camp. Both Hrothgar and Brythnor were in front of the champion and, fools that they were, they forgot everything Beowulf had told them about keeping distance between themselves.

The Didon were excellent archers, when confronting man-sized enemies, but their arrows flew long rather than high. They never came close to Vrunus's eyes and gave no protection to the brave fools racing toward the guardian's feet. With his first back-hand clout, Vrunus hurled Hrothgar and his horse far away from the camp. On the return swing, Vrunus seized Brythnor about the torso and lifted him into the air.

Beowulf heard the Geat's screams as the guardian brought him headfirst to his open mouth. Teeth the size of wagon wheels clamped shut and Brythnor screamed no more. Then Vrunus tossed away what was left and caught himself a wayward Didon.

Beowulf had not quite believed that part of the Didon tales, but seeing it for himself raised a blood anger in his mind. He had never succumbed to the *berserkerang* before, then again, he'd never seen a man's head bitten off. The world around the Geat-folk champion turned red, except for the guardian's massive right leg, which Beowulf saw with extraordinary clarity.

Unsheathing his sword, Beowulf raised his battle cry. He swerved his horse around the headless Didon corpse when it crashed to the ground, then brought it to the outside of a hip-high anklebone. Mustering all his strength, Beowulf sliced his sword through a tendon as thick as his neck.

The blade passed through something. By the All-Father's truth, Beowulf had felt resistance against his swing, but when he was done, there was no blood, no wound, nothing to say that he'd accomplished anything.

Made mindless with rage, Beowulf leapt down from his horse and swung wildly, repeatedly, and futilely.

The Geat-folk champion never saw the vast hand swooping toward him. It slammed against his spine, knocking him senseless. As thigh-fingers closed around him, Beowulf's mind cleared just enough for him to keep his sword and sword arm free by holding them over his head. With his feet no longer touching the ground, Beowulf slashed at whatever part of Vrunus his blade could reach.

Suddenly, Beowulf was upside down. Vrunus shook him as a

cat might shake a mouse and, to his shame and consternation, Beowulf lost his grip on his sword. He felt the sting of a thousand wasps as he was brought within Vrunus's sparkling shroud and shaken again.

For a heartbeat, panic nipped at Beowulf's mind. He beat it back. While he lived, he had his wyrd. If he died now, it would be fighting, not screaming. Beowulf saw what there was to see: Vrunus's gaping mouth, his teeth, the ground so far below him now. And, by the All-Father's mercy, there was a pit! A soot-black, bottomless pit large enough to swallow Vrunus, for all the good that did.

If there was a pit, perhaps there was a golden strand circling the guardian's neck?

The strand, too, was there where Oswyn had seen it, well beyond Beowulf's reach.

The strand danced in the wind Vrunus made as he moved. It descended, a brilliant streak through sunlight. It billowed above the Tarvar camp before coming to an end within the silhouette of a man seated beside the pit.

Shove the vekka into the pit and the golden strand would bring Vrunus down after him!

The perspective changed.

Beowulf was on his way to the guardian's mouth, on his way to death.

He would not scream.

No conscious thought guided Beowulf's hand at that last moment. He grasped Vrunus's upper lip because it was his wyrd to fight strength against strength. The fingers that had snapped the river maids' necks and torn an arm from Grendel's shoulder, dug in. A blast of breath as hot as the forge and foul beyond measure enveloped Beowulf as he squeezed and twisted with all his might.

He did not wound Vrunus, did not even draw blood. But Beowulf surprised the guardian and, in his surprise, Vrunus preferred to get rid of an annoyance rather than devour it.

Beowulf flailed thin air. Even as he tumbled, he recalled Oswyn's words: "You must fly like an eagle." A man had no wings, but he could spread his arms wide. He had no tail feathers, but he could open his legs as he'd opened his arms. The tumbling stopped. His cloak furled upward, like a sail, and though Beowulf did not exactly drift to the ground, he fell more slowly than he might have.

Ribs broke when Beowulf struck the ground. He lay there a moment, unable to breathe or think, but he'd been through worse—much worse—before and got to his feet before any of the Tarvar surrounding him had thought to slit his throat. The All-Father, it seemed, had guided the falling champion to the place he wished most to be: within the chaotic Tarvar camp, in sight of a seated man with feathers in his hair and bones hung around his neck.

The Tarvar swarmed. Beowulf beat them back with his fists until he sidestepped to a hearth where he armed himself with a firebrand. He couldn't help but notice, as he maneuvered toward the vekka, that the pit he'd seen so clearly moments ago was no longer visible and neither was the golden strand.

They're there, he told himself as if he were a first-beard like Oswyn. *Have faith in what the All-Father revealed.*

The vekka didn't twitch until Beowulf's commotion was almost upon him, and by then it was too late. With a final surge, Beowulf closed the gap between them. He closed his eyes as he lifted the Tarvar high above his head. Beowulf found the pit in his memory and turned. At that moment, the vekka—who surely knew about the pit—began to thrash and writhe, but nothing smaller than the champion had ever escaped his grasp.

Beowulf heaved and, for an instant, the vekka flew free, then, through some foul miracle, the Tarvar's hand closed around Beowulf's wrist and he, too, found himself falling, falling beneath the ground, into the pit. He had scarcely begun to accept this bleak twist of fate when he and the vekka holding onto him were jerked to a stop.

The golden strand!

They rose slightly. In his mind's eye, Beowulf saw Vrunus standing firm. What a fool he'd been to think that the weight of one mortal man—or the weight of two—could drag the likes of Vrunus into the pit from which he'd come. The vekka must have had a similar thought; or something else inspired him to let go of Beowulf's wrist and, before he could form another thought, the champion was falling again, alone through darkness.

Beowulf braced himself for the fall's end, for death. Neither came.

How long could a man fall? Long enough to make peace with himself. How deep could the pit be? Deep enough that Beowulf not only slept, he was still falling when he awoke.

And that happened not once, but nine times.

As it happened, Beowulf was awake when he met the ground, an encounter he had not expected to survive, much less stand up from with no more pain than he might have felt after slipping on the Geat-land ice. There was no light at the pit's bottom, not from the sun or the smallest candle, yet the landscape was not dark. And it was a landscape, as if at some unappreciated moment Beowulf had gone from falling down a pit to falling from heaven to a new and gloomy world.

A thousand questions crowded Beowulf's mind, not least of which was whether he was as alive as he thought he was. But Beowulf had never been a questioning man, not once he'd turned around.

The fall had dumped Beowulf on the doorsteps of a hall high

enough for Vrunus to enter without ducking his head. It had doors of solid brass . . . doors that had been blasted off their hinges and leaned like broken wings against the ash-colored walls. Words in an angular script were written above the door. They resembled runes, but Beowulf could not read them.

A thud at his back pulled Beowulf's attention away from the doors: The vekka had come to the end of his downward journey. He'd risen to his knees but had not seemed to realize that he was not alone when the ground shook with a third arrival.

Vrunus landed on his feet, still as tall as seven men together, but now as substantial as rock. He stood closer to the vekka than to Beowulf, and that was good luck for the champion, because Vrunus pounced at once on the Tarvar. Roaring words Beowulf didn't understand, Vrunus squeezed and squeezed his fist until the little man's head flew off.

That convinced Beowulf that he, himself, was alive and needed to take cover. He hauled himself up the chest-high steps and raced for one of the brass doors, though he had no illusion that he could shelter behind it for long.

"*Kronos!*"

As soon as he heard the word that burst through the open doorway, Beowulf knew in his heart that Kronos, not Vrunus, was the guardian's true name.

Kronos replied with bellowed words that might have been names or curses, or perhaps both. There was no mistaking the hatred in them.

A boulder the size of an ox shot through the doorway. Kronos dodged, then picked it up and tossed it effortlessly back the way it had come. Another three boulders flew out, and six more after that. Kronos couldn't dodge them all, but appeared unharmed when they struck his thighs and torso. He grabbed one that had fallen close by his feet and hurled it at his as-yet unseen attackers.

Kronos's aim was good. He drew a cry from one of his as-yet-unseen attackers. Beowulf dared a glance from the shadow where he hid toward the open doorway. The champion of the Geat-folk was not an easily frightened man, but retreated swiftly. Aelscyg had warned him: There were worse things in the prison from which the Tarvar had freed Kronos.

Huge as he was, Kronos was a man. The three monsters that emerged onto the landing no more than twenty paces from Beowulf's hiding place were nothing at all like men. They had no feet, no legs, no heads, nor faces. Instead, they had arms, countless arms radiating out from an unseen center. Using a few of their arms as legs, the monsters stood about half as tall as Kronos.

While Beowulf watched in sickened disbelief, the nearest monster raised two of its arms and a boulder appeared—simply appeared—between its hands. Then it raised another pair of arms and the monsters beyond it did likewise. A volley of five boulders flew toward Kronos who caught one and ignored the others. He threw the one he'd caught; the middle monster rolled backward, lifting some arms, stiffening others. It wasn't hurt and it quickly rejoined the fight.

The monsters appeared to have an endless supply of their magical boulders. They lobbed many more than Kronos could lob back at them. His aim was better, perhaps because he had eyes. He never missed, not that it made any difference. Neither he nor the monsters seemed able to deliver a decisive blow. The battle might come to a draw when both sides were buried in boulders. They were already two-deep in the yard where Kronos stood, one-deep on the monsters' landing.

Beowulf was planning his eventual escape when a lightning bolt reduced a number of the boulders to gray powder.

"Kronos!"

Once again, the single word echoed through the gloom. The many-handed monsters folded their arms as if they had a hundred or more faces to protect. Kronos shouted another name, another curse. He picked up a boulder and hurled it in a new direction. Another lightning bolt sizzled and the boulder turned to dust.

A man—a white-bearded man in a long white robe—strode into Beowulf's sight. In every way, the newcomer was greater than Kronos and the monsters knew it, too. They bent their elbows and raised their many hands in supplication. Kronos raised a fist, instead, and began to grow as he'd grown outside the Tarvar camp. The white-beard lifted his hand . . .

Beowulf had the sense to cover his eyes before the lightning bolt burst forth. Even so, he was blinded for a heartbeat. He heard and felt, but did not see, Kronos fall.

Whatever could be laid flat on the ground could be vanquished.

As Beowulf's vision cleared, he saw the three monsters shamble forward. They seized Kronos by the arms, legs, and hair. They dragged him over the boulders and into the prison.

The white-beard lifted his hand. Beowulf pressed his hands hard against his eyes. This time there was no blast, just a breath of wind and dust. When Beowulf opened his eyes again, the boulders were gone. The white-beard lifted his hand a third time. The great brass doors were restored to their rightful places and Beowulf's hiding place was gone.

Ever the champion, Beowulf stood straight. He called upon the All-Father to protect him as the white-beard took notice of him and raised his hand . . .

"For nine full days our champion had lain on the ground," Oswyn sang.

There was tension in the young bard's voice, but none in Heardred's mead-hall. The Geat-folk knew how the story ended. Their champion had awakened, hale and whole. He'd told them of Kronos's fate, of the many-handed monsters, and of the white-bearded man who might, or might not, have been the All-Father. The surviving Geats—only seven, including Beowulf and Oswyn—had feasted with the Didon, then journeyed back to Geat-land.

Beowulf, standing in hall's shadows with a cup of mead, did not correct the lad when he strayed. As with the slaying of Grendel, the story of his encounter with Kronos no longer belonged to him.

BEOWULF AND THE
MASTER OF HIS CRITICS
Interlude 3

°✝°

"Notice the allusion to the Titans simultaneous with a metaphoric Christian God of some sort."

"Yes . . . though I am sure that those who sent me will be better able to engage you in conversation on these matters."

"Harrumph."

"Excuse me."

"Would you prefer I comment on the cannibal elves and the disgusting worms?"

"Does this mean you are interested in the project?"

"You still haven't told me what the project is."

"A well-funded research study into the concurrent mythos of the Beowulf legend in Germanic culture."

"Poppycock."

BEOWULF AND THE ATTACK OF THE TROLLS

by Wolfgang Baur

°‡°

The moon was so thin, it could have been scratched onto the sky with a needle.

Beowulf stood at the steering oar, watching the shore as his hand-picked crew of ten Geatish warriors pulled at the oars. The sky was dark but flecked with stars, and they rowed toward a small notch of fields and pastures cut out of the surrounding forest. The pine-black hillsides of the fjord rose up to enfold the longship on either side. Behind them, the winds on the sea pushed them north and east, into the shore. Straight ahead were the lights of Skaggarheim, the village where they hoped to drink the guest-cup and shelter for a day or three while the storms blew themselves out. The homelands of the Angles, Saxons, and the Geats were many days travel to the south, a warm place where the Geatish king had given him a gift-dagger with a silver-wrapped hilt and an amber pommel, wishing him luck.

The journey seemed more rash with every wave that broke around the dragon-head prow.

Salt spray encrusted Beowulf's beard, and he pushed the smooth oak steering oar to the right, correcting their course. The lights grew slowly larger, and he could make out the dragon-shaped prows of four longships—the village held at least forty or fifty Norska warriors. The darkness of the forest on all sides was so deep that Beowulf saw just a flicker of movement along the shore, toward the village. He steered a little closer to the shore and saw them, at least a dozen wild-haired creatures taller than any man. They noticed the ship and began running toward the village. They leaped as high as stags over the fallen logs and among the boulders of the rocky shoreline, outracing the longship toward Skaggarheim.

Beowulf knew they meant to steal the livestock or take slaves.

"Row harder, you motherless dogs! Trolls! Trolls on the shore!"

The longship leaped forward like a horse put to the spurs. Each stroke of the oars ripped into the sea, and the white wake gleamed in the black fjord.

The trolls moved faster, even through the forest, outrunning the longship.

Beowulf saw them reach the wooden palisade, a dark wall of pointed logs that protected the village and its animals.

The trolls jumped up, grabbed the points at the top, and pulled themselves over in smooth, powerful motions.

Moments later, the first screams echoed down the fjord.

† † †

The trolls moved quickly, snorting the air, bellowing war cries, tree branches slashing at their thick skins. Their moss-backed leader struck down the sleepy sentry before he uttered a sound.

The humans around them, half-asleep, panicked, and the trolls took their pick of the fattest goats, the meatiest ponies, and the best of the villagers.

† † †

Once the Geats' longship came close enough that their course was set toward the pebbled beach, Beowulf lashed the steering oar in place, unwrapped the bundle of axes, and moved along the keel, placing an axe close at hand for each rower. His own weapon of dwarvish steel shimmered a fey green in the starlight—they had come north to find more such steel, to buy or trade with the dwarves of the north.

Beowulf carried the axe to the prow, gripped his shield straps tightly, and made the quick leap from the longboat to the shallows just as the longship ground against the shore. He ran, knees high through the shallows, then faster to the shore where no palisade stood.

The closest troll was dragging a pony out of the village by its reins, but when it saw him it bellowed a challenge. It dropped the reins and turned to face him. It held a long spear in one hand, a mass of daggerlike claws—all the weapon it needed—in the other, its mouth filled with long curving tusks larger than those of a full-grown boar.

Beowulf's pace never faltered.

This bravest of the Geatish warriors let his rush carry his axehead up and through the troll's ribs. The ash and iron shield turned the troll's spearpoint, and Beowulf twisted around, trying desperately to pull the axehead out of his foe. The axe was stuck, and the troll raised its free hand—as Beowulf let go of the axe to avoid being clawed and drew his dagger as he slipped to the left. He stayed close to keep the troll from thrusting its spear.

Beowulf realized he had misjudged the troll's height, for it would have stood twice as tall as a man but was heavily hunched over, hiding the length of its arms. The warrior pushed his shield into the troll's face as a distraction and stepped in close, swung his dagger, connected. He let the dagger go. The troll's hand, heavy as falling timber, grabbed him by his armored leather shirt and threw him into a wooden plank wall. Beowulf stumbled but kept his feet, and now he was weaponless against the troll—his shield could hold it back but nothing more. He grabbed a torch from beside the longhouse door and waved it to make the flame dance. If the troll rushed him, it was over.

The world drew back; the tip of the troll's iron spear and its flexing claws were all Beowulf saw. He thrust the torch into its face, lighting up its black eyes, forcing it back and singeing its hair. Its wounds were bleeding heavily, and its movements slowed: the axe in its ribs would cut down this tree before long. In the meantime, it was watching him just as carefully, and its spear thrusts were deliberate, quick as Thor's lightning. Three thrusts, each a little slower, and only the first cut Beowulf, right along the thigh, a scratch. As the troll recovered from the third thrust, Beowulf stood behind his shield and chased the spearpoint forward, grabbed the handle of his green dwarven-steel axe in the troll's ribcage, and pulled hard.

The axe came loose with a gout of black blood, and the troll howled. Its claws caught Beowulf just above the ear and tore the helmet from his head. He tumbled with the blow but again stood up at the end, and he kept his grip on the blood-soaked rowan haft of the axe. The blood poured from the axe wound in a river, and the troll rushed forward.

Beowulf stepped aside.

It rushed a second time, and again Beowulf stepped to the right, this time using his shield to deflect the spear and swinging the recovered axe in a short arc to the troll's head. He struck, and the troll staggered. Its spear was still pointed at Beowulf, even as its eyes blinked and lost focus. Beowulf waited, and the troll fell.

Behind him, Beowulf could hear his men approaching at long last. He knew they had secured the longship, oars shipped, hull brought up above the tide. They cried in wonder at the size of the troll. Beowulf was already pulling his dagger free from the beast and moving into the village. He shouted, "Get torches and work together to chase them out!" A scream was cut short just inside the gate; an old thane wearing glittering gold armbands was struck down at the entrance to a blockhouse built of logs. Several trolls were on the roof, trying to get into the blockhouse through the smokehole—others were fighting to get in through the main entryway.

The next few minutes were a strange sort of raid, looking not for plunder or defenders but searching for the hulking hairy figures of the trolls in firelight. The Geats moved in groups; the trolls moved faster but fought alone. Beowulf and the Geats walked down the length of the long winter blockhouse, weapons tightly gripped, and twice were surprised by the speed of the trolls' rush and the strength of their spear thrusts; they shattered Ragnar's shield to flinders, they snapped Yngvar's spear with one hand, and they knocked the village's thane senseless and bloody. But the Geats fought well, drawing the trolls away from the villagers and pushing them slowly out of the palisade. More and more villagers came to help, and soon the last troll had jumped over the wall and back into the forest.

"Your spears are reeds!" shouted Beowulf. "Run to your hills and caves." They fled, but Beowulf did not follow them into the forest, the trollhome, where they would see him clearly and he would stumble through the dark.

Norska bodies littered the ground, their flaxen hair bright on the black dirt. One was a child, four were men who died with spear and axe in hand, bound for Valhalla, and two were women. One of the men was an old thane; a young woman at his side cradled his head, picking bits of dirt out of his beard. In a purple cloak trimmed with silver, she looked like a *valkyrja*, ready to carry the old thane to Odin's halls. Beowulf walked over to her and knelt in the dirt beside her. "Your father?"

She turned on him and Beowulf stepped back at the fury in her eyes. "He was Ottar, the thane of Skaggarheim!" She turned to a man who stood beside her, leaning on his spear. Her eyes narrowed and she frowned. "Uncle Ulli, why aren't you pursuing your brother's killers?"

The man glanced at Beowulf and said, "Salveig, the woods are dark, and they are swifter than we. I will follow their tracks in the morning."

Beowulf said, "In the morning they'll be over the hills and miles away. But let them go far from here."

A red-haired thrall ran up, bowed his head, and spoke. "Ulli, the boy Hálfdan and two of the ponies are missing. The ponies should be easy to track."

"You are both cowards!" Salveig glared at them. "Hunt them now, or give me a spear and I will do it myself."

At that moment, they heard a boy's voice from the forest, screaming at first, sheer panic and pain and naked fear. A troll roared, somewhere not a bowshot away. Salveig grabbed Beowulf's spear and pulled him toward the settlement gate. "That's Hálfdan. We must go get him."

Beowulf pulled back his spear and planted his feet. "It is a trap. They are using the boy to draw us out onto their ground."

"He's suffering!" Salveig's cheeks were flushed and tears glittered in her eyes.

Beowulf said, "You and yours are all fine fisherfolk, woodsmen, and goatherds. But you are not reavers or blooded slayers, bear-sarkers, skinchangers."

"Are you sure?" said Salveig. "We live hard and fight harder. My father, Ottar, knew the runes and led a raid against the Letts. I can throw an axe. *We* are not helpless."

"Have you any skinchangers among you? A scout as quiet as the leaves? If we knew where they hoped to catch us, we could catch them in our net instead of falling into theirs."

"I know these woods better than anyone," said Salveig. She took Beowulf's dagger from his belt, checked the edge with her thumb, and pulled a dark bearskin cloak around her shoulders. "They'll never see me, and when I return, I'll lead you right to them." She walked out without a backward glance, hunching over as she reached the trees and disappearing completely. Beowulf knew then that he would stay and help Salveig and the Norska men, for her sake.

The boy Hálfdan's cries echoed from the forest for long minutes, and then went silent just as the light turned from grey and white to pink. Salveig was still in the woods. The people of Skaggarheim wept, the men held their wives, and Hálfdan's little sister screamed until she was exhausted, inconsolable. Beowulf made himself useful, putting out the smoldering fire on the shingled roof first, then binding wounds with the ease of much practice. Wounds could wait; fire never did.

When there was nothing else to do, he walked the length of the wall, which went from the shore on one side of the village to a small watchtower on an enormous rock at the other, again on the shore. Standing on a narrow wooden board at the palisade gate, Beowulf waited for Salveig to return from the woods. He heard the birds sing to greet the coming dawn, and the weight of regret fell on his shoulders. He should never have let her go alone into the woods.

A second, true dawn came, and the chieftain's brother Ulli called for a gathering in the longhouse, to decide what to do next. The people chattered among themselves, grieving and planning and hoping that Ulli might know what to do. Hálfdan's sister sat silently and watched the adults and always stayed near one of the armed men.

Salveig returned an hour later in full morning light, her face full of fury, but with no news. She threw Beowulf's dagger down at his feet. Her eyes were as bright as the promise of snowbells and crocus, blue and dry and icy as the alpine meadows.

† † †

Dawn broke over the mountains and spilled into the Skaggarfjord. The golden light did nothing to improve the look of the troll dead by Beowulf's hand. If possible, it looked even uglier by sunlight than by torchlight. Its hairs stood up like bristles, its nose was enormous and flattened, its hands curled like claws. Its tusks were yellow and filthy, and its leather cloth smelled of stone and moss.

Beowulf put all the Geats on the wall, in case the trolls should return by daylight, though the Norska thought it unlikely—trolls were creatures of darkness, either the darkness under forest branches or the full dark of the new moon. They rarely moved into daylight (some people thought they would turn to stone if the sun caught them; the skald Eilert of the village called that an *eventyr*, an old man's fable, though he said that far north, in the land of the midnight sun, the trolls ruled the stony forests for six dark months of the year).

Beowulf strode into the longhouse. The noise of a hundred and fifty people filled the Skaggarheim hall to the rafters. The thane Ulli and his carls and freemen debated and drank. Were the trolls passing through the territory or staying? Should the villagers stay and bury the dead? Every man spoke his mind loudly, and the women as well. The younger women and boys brought ale and mead, roast goat, and a goose stuffed with chestnuts and honey. Salveig spoke softly to her uncle, who shook his head at her every word.

Ulli stood and spoke first, the chief's silver *rhyton* full of mead in his hand: "The trolls are stupid things, always hungry, fiends for our flocks. We should not waste our lives in fear every night, and we cannot ask Beowulf and the Geats to fight for us all summer. No, I have a better plan than cowering behind a wall: We should pack our goods and ship out the longboats for a while, go to the Torsen steading in Hammarsfjord and winter there. We will feast with them, fish with them, and the trolls will simply leave after the first snows. There's nothing for them here without us."

"What if they don't leave?" shouted one of the Skaggarheim carls.

"We could join our two clans together. My brother Ottar and their *huscarl* Terkild were almost blood brothers, they fostered together with Frøydis and Pentti. And their women need company!" Some of the men hooted and banged the table with their knives and fists. Others kept silent and stroked their beards.

In the end, it was Salveig who answered him. "Uncle Ulli, the men of Hammarsfjord are good friends, and if we were broken here, I would agree with you. But we can defend what we have, and we must stay and fight. The trolls will not leave if we run away. They will just find another village to slaughter."

"But not Skaggarheim!" said Ulli.

"You think they will not follow us?" said Salveig. "And honestly, we have eighty goats, ten ponies, and almost one hundred fifty clansmen here. Six longships will hold no more than a third of us, and the ponies don't travel well. Who will stay behind while your men pull the oars?"

Beowulf stepped forward into the firelight. "I am happy to stay behind. My warriors can guard your homes and flocks." The audience murmured with excitement. Beowulf waited a moment for silence, then spoke again. "Yes, you should go fishing, or visiting the neighbors, and the Geatish warriors will feed the goats, and cut the hay for the ponies, and fight the trolls. And in time, we will go raiding for wives and thralls, and call ourselves the thane and jarls of Skaggarheim. While you go and join the men of Hammarsfjord as guests, whose company grows stale."

The murmur was less joyous. Several of the Skaggarheim men fingered their knives or seemed to be dreaming up a toast to the Geats, but several of the women laughed. Salveig spoke again. "You might make a fine thane for us while Uncle Ulli goes to consider strategy in the southern fjords. Perhaps some women will stay behind so you do not need to feed all the goats yourselves."

"This is foolishness," said Ulli, ignoring Salveig and facing Beowulf squarely. "You mock us and call us cowards, though we have made you our guest."

"I mock nothing," said Beowulf. "You should prepare your nets for fishing and pack your trunks with clothes and gifts for the Hammarsfjord steading."

"We could stay," said a man to Ulli's right. "Beowulf thinks we can fight them. At Hammarsfjord they will call us lemmings, to flee so quickly."

Ulli snarled. "Names are wind and words. Staying will bring us nothing but death and ruin. What if the trolls set fire to the houses? What if they smash our ships and fishing boats?" Small flecks of foam marred Ulli's beard.

Beowulf smiled like a wolf, all teeth. "They haven't yet. They live under the mountains and barely understand fire. We are many, and strong, and once we find their caves or huts, we can raid them as they have done to us. When we defeat them, the *skalds* will sing of our victory. Those who die will be remembered by our children and their children as trollkillers. What are you afraid of, old man?"

The young men of the fjord cheered. Some of the married women frowned, but from that point on it was decided. Despite the lives lost, the people of Skaggarheim would stay and mourn their dead at home. They trusted Beowulf and his Geats to defeat the trolls or to drive them away.

After the moon set and the mead ran out, Beowulf left. He saw Ulli speaking to some of the greybeards and heard a few dark murmurs. They would do nothing until he failed, then seize their chance, or better still, they might slip away in one of the longships, leaving the braver hearts behind.

Beowulf hoped they had the courage to flee.

† † †

That afternoon, the trolls slid through the shadows at the edge of the forest, watching the palisade where men stood watch. They were too big and heavy to move entirely silently. They snapped tree limbs and sent rocks rolling along the forest edge where the pines threw the longest shadows, but never quite showed themselves.

The trolls peered closely under the grey, clouded light. The village wall was old but siegeworthy, built of heavy, wet oak and ash logs. All day, they watched villagers brace the wall and clear the brush away from the fields around it. The sunlight burned the trolls' eyes, but they marked the lowest point in the wall and the water to either side.

† † †

The noise in the woods did not go unnoticed. Beowulf ordered some pitch torches prepared, to burn in the fields during the night. By nightfall, the village was ready to fight, spears and axes sharp and hardened.

Beowulf asked Salveig and Ulli to gather the men and women. They stood before him along the shore in the twilight. He waved toward the palisade and said, "If the trolls come again, they will come in the darkness. I will give this ring to the man who first raises the alarm." He held up his best ring, a thick band of carved gold granted him by Heardred, king of the Geats. The villagers drew in their breath.

"But if someone wakes me for nothing, for a squirrel or a fox or an owl moving through the forest, I will throw that man in the fjord!" The villagers laughed and raised their drinking horns.

† † †

An hour later, Beowulf told the oarsman Øyvind and his warriors Ragnar, Gjurd, Gudbrandr, and Yngvar to sleep near the doors of the longhouse, and told his three best lookouts—Dagfinn, Hrothwulf, and Albin—to stay awake on the wall watch and wake him after half the night passed. He was sure that if the trolls came back, they'd return deep in the night, in the hours before dawn when men's souls shivered and their courage faltered. He needed rest, and he found sleeping furs in the longhouse guest chamber.

No sooner did Beowulf put his head down on his sleeping furs that evening and cover himself than he heard an alarm, the wooden clapper along the north wall near the fjord. He threw his cloak and boots on and grabbed his spear, shield, and axe. The light outside the longhouse was greying with the light before dawn—Dagfinn should have woken him hours ago. He ran to the wall, and Albin pointed to the woods.

"Where are they, Albin?"

"Dagfinn went out along the shore after a deer. He didn't come back."

"No shout?"

Albin shook his head and pointed. "He went there."

Beowulf saw the waves dark along the shore, barely glimmering under the new moon. "It was a stupid thing, to go out."

"If you had seen this stag, you might not think so. Antlers like a king of stags."

"Tell the Skaggarvolk and all of us. No one goes outside the wall until dawn."

The trolls never came to the wall that night, and Dagfinn never returned.

† † †

The next few days belonged to the people and the nights to the trolls.

The goats went out each morning with three or four herders, the women going to the stream never went alone, and at night, the walls were watched. It wasn't clear whether the trolls were staying or moving on, content to have taken a few people and ponies away. Nonetheless, Beowulf was sure they were lurking nearby, waiting for the Norska wariness to fade.

The fourth night, Beowulf lay down on the sleeping furs just after sunset and slept early. The missing boy's family and Salveig were the only ones who still wouldn't speak to him. The danger seemed past, and Ragnar had said that perhaps it was time to leave.

Possibly the trolls had left, but there was no way to prove it. Beowulf snorted to himself. The trolls were trying to lull them into foolishness. Beowulf practiced a night alarm with the villagers, sending each man to his place along the palisade, at the longhouse entrances, and up in the watchtower. They moved quickly, though he pressed them for more speed. As long as they stood together, the village was safe: the fjord at its back, brush cleared away from the palisade wall, new firepots placed at the single gate and the watchtower. The men of Skaggarheim grumbled, but they were already learning to work together when they heard the alarm.

Beowulf considered. If he wanted to find the trolls, he'd have to divide their forces, some to scout the dark pines in strength, others to hold the palisade and protect the village. He'd much rather the trolls came to meet them at the wall, where the Norska folk were ready, and more than ready.

† † †

In the knife-cold waters of the Skaggarfjord, ten trolls swam along the shore, past the wall to where the boats rested on the stony shore. Their swimming was as jerky and silent as frogs slipping beneath a lily pad. They drew themselves out of the water silently, dripping saltwater onto the stones, then pushed their spearpoints into the longships.

The meat in this village would all be theirs.

None would escape by sea.

Slowly, hunched over in the darkness after moonset, the trolls walked up the undefended shore into the village. They hid their bulk in the black night, and their claws padded silently on the packed earth beside the small guest longhouse—the larger hall could wait. In the space of a dozen heartbeats, ten trolls were all within the hall, and the red work began.

† † †

Beowulf woke instantly from his sleep and for a moment thought Salveig had crept into his room—then the smell of salt and mud hit him, and he rolled out from under the sleeping furs just before the spearhead landed. The guesthouse was lit only by the embers of a banked fire, and the light was quickly swallowed among the blankets, dark furs, and pillars. He had a small room to himself, but his men and a few of the Skaggarheim thralls slept nearby.

Beowulf could see the figure in front of him, hunched under the rafters and silhouetted by the light from the hearth's few remaining embers.

Beowulf wore neither his mail shirt nor his helmet, but his axe was in one hand and his sword, single-edged and pointed, in the other. He heard the distant crashing of trolls and fights elsewhere in the guesthouse but ignored them. The troll in front of him blocked the way out, and it was shaking his sleeping furs off its spearpoint with the flick of its wrist. "Geats, to me!" shouted Beowulf. "Die on your feet!"

Beowulf rushed the troll, and it moved that spearpoint fast as an arrow. Beowulf almost impaled himself on it but managed to knock it aside with his sword, stepping off balance and leaving himself open to the spear-butt, which the troll swung with equal speed, knocking the great Geatish warrior back to where he started. Without his chain shirt or his shield, Beowulf could not deflect the spear or afford even glancing blows. He considered throwing the axe, but it was risky. If he missed, he would have just a single weapon against the much larger troll.

He hesitated, and in that moment, Salveig pushed aside the hanging next to the troll without announcing herself and half-stepped into the room. She was unarmed, and the troll grabbed her by the neck and lifted her off the ground effortlessly, and then it backed out of the room. Salveig's eyes bulged and her cheeks turned bright red as she kicked and clawed at the troll. It ignored her, watching Beowulf carefully as it stepped back the way Salveig had entered, through the leather door hanging and into the larger chamber beyond. Beowulf pursued, leaping and throwing aside the hanging an instant after the troll—and almost getting speared for the second time that night, this time the edge of the spearhead raking along his ribs like fire. If he'd been wearing his chain shirt, it would barely have slowed him down. As it was, he was bleeding, and every step brought a fresh gout of blood.

The troll spun away and fled, Salveig screaming now, hefted over its shoulder. She stabbed it twice with a knife before the troll casually grabbed the knife by the blade and threw it away. Beowulf hesitated. He couldn't throw his axe at the troll without hitting Salveig, and the creature could run faster than he did.

Faster than a torch flicker, it was outside the guesthouse and into the chaos of the village; a fire burned somewhere, and men and trolls were fighting in the light and smoke. Ashes settled into his beard, the smell of burning thatch mingled with the smell of blood and offal in the dust.

Beowulf grabbed a shield from a fallen man, and jumped up onto the low eaves of the guesthouse for a better view. The wooden shingles were slippery beneath his feet, and almost as soon as he stood up straight he slid back down toward the ground, but not before he caught a glimpse of six or seven more trolls jumping back over the palisade, men and women slung over their shoulders. Some of those Norska were limp and lifeless, others struggled and screamed, but all were help-less in the trolls' enormous claws. The trolls reached the edge of the forest just as Beowulf leapt from the roof down to the street again.

He could not track the trolls through the forest in the dark, but he would use his rage against any troll still within the walls—and he had seen his men surround one of the trolls against the shore, bleeding. One tried to swim away just as Beowulf threw his axe; the axe landed between its shoulder blades, and the troll thrashed in the water, churning up pink foam. "Give me another axe!"

roared Beowulf. His lead oarsman, Øyvind, handed him a small throwing axe, well-balanced, the blade heavy and the haft smooth from long use. Beowulf held it at the ready for a moment, his arm motionless till he saw the troll's head rise above the water, and then he threw, the second axe catching the troll in the skull, stunning it and sending it from standing upright in the waist-high water to splashing into the tiny waves, saltwater closing over its head and mouth. The body twitched six or eight times, then hung still in the water, drifting with the incoming tide. Beowulf swam out to recover the axes, then organized his men to watch the wall and the fjord against any return.

Beowulf felt the sharp pang of strategies he might have used, if he had been wise enough to think of them in the heat of battle. He might have taken the village dogs to stay hot on the trail rather than let it grow cold. He might have covered himself with blood and allowed himself to be captured with Salveig, dagger hidden in his chain shirt. It probably wouldn't have worked; half the troll's victims were unconscious or dead as they were taken away.

Somehow, he should have followed Salveig.

In those few minutes, the villagers' shock and grief turned to anger at the trolls and at the Geats. Beowulf knew that the losses from this second raid were worse than the first: another six Norska men dead, five women and another boy missing. The people were enraged, and if their longship had not been leaking and swamped with seawater, the Geats might have shipped out in the middle of the night.

"Salveig is gone!" said Ulli, pointing at Beowulf. "She fought because you told her to."

"No," said Beowulf, hand on the haft of his throwing axe. "She fought because she was brave and bold, as a Norska woman should be, a bear in defense of the children." Beowulf's despair pricked his heart; his eyes burned and his orders hung in his throat. Then he looked carefully at Ulli's furs, the spear in his hand, the clean leggings and carefully plaited beard. He looked quite presentable for a thane whose village had just been overrun.

"I see no blood on your spear, Ulli," said Beowulf. Thane Ulli stood there for a moment with his mouth open.

"I need volunteers to go with me into the forest, to bring back the women and children. Who will go?" said Beowulf. He looked at his own men: Half were wounded, and Albin was the only one who stepped forward. "Ulli? Men of Skaggarheim? Women?" He stared at the smoke-smudged faces.

Ulli said nothing, but one boy stepped forward and said, "Hálfdan was my little brother."

Beowulf looked hard at his second man, with his smudge of a moustache and thin arms and legs. He couldn't be more than fourteen, maybe less. He carried a knife and an axe for cutting firewood. "And what is your name, boy?"

"I am Kulli Andressen."

"How many times have you shipped out to raid along the Oder or the Seine?"

"None, but—"

"How many monasteries have you plundered?"

"None, but—"

"Does your mother know you want to follow trolls into the woods?"

"My mother is Salveig's sister, Ulla."

Beowulf hesitated.

He wanted to tell the boy to wait. He would soon be stronger, his reach longer, his skill sharper . . . but the boy was not in a waiting mood, and without someone from the village along, things would be even worse when he returned. He needed the village men to stay and protect what was left.

"Very well," said Beowulf. "Tell your mother you come with the Geats, and that I swear by my blood and Odin's beard you will return to her." It was a foolish oath, but he swore it anyway, hoping to force it to come true. "Get your spear and axe, boy, some water skins, and five ponies."

"Five, sir?"

"Me, you, Albin, one for Salveig or anyone else we come back with, and a spare."

"But they took five, Marta, Grunhild—"

"I'm sorry, boy. Two were already mortally struck when they were carried out, and the others may not last the night if the trolls are hungry." The boy's face paled. "Quick, now, ponies!"

The boy ran to the barn as if the trolls were already on his heels.

† † †

The forest was dark, and darker still the further the trolls marched into it. Their wailing captives were soon silenced by the rigorous pace. The four-tusked troll tracker. The sound of horses in pursuit was as loud as a glacier calving into the fjord, each hoof-beat a distinct thud on the forest floor.

The trolls began covering their tracks.

† † †

Beowulf rode in front, his shield slung over the small horse's pommel, torches lighting the way through the woods but also announcing their arrival. Tracking the trolls was easy at first: broken branches, bits of clothing and hair, and the churning foot-prints of eight or nine trolls were clear enough. Soon, though, the troll tracks stopped in a small clearing leading up into the stones and hills, beside a brook.

They might have gone along the water, hiding their tracks, or over the stone, where only a few lichens grew and their footprints would hardly leave a trace. And indeed, the trolls' tracks seemed to vanish into the hills or along the stream.

Albin was the one who found the lichens scraped from the stone and a few threads of purple, the color of Salveig's cloak. The trolls must have either dropped her from her struggles or thrown her down to silence her.

Beowulf howled with frustration: The stream would have been easier to follow, limited to upstream and down. Tracking the trolls over the lichens took slow, careful hours up and down slope, and they lost the trail at least a dozen times.

Their torches made them perfect targets for an ambush, but the trolls never came—Beowulf was sure they were feasting on the flesh of the fallen. Albin said nothing, but the strain on his face was plain. Kulli was relentless, and his young eyes were sharp, again and again finding the path that Beowulf wanted.

"They are going to the Rødå spring," said Kulli. "That's the only place anyone goes up this valley."

"You're sure?" said Beowulf. "Because if we lose them and have to find the trail again come morning, I'll thrash you and send you home to your mother."

Kulli met his stare. "I'm sure. And I'll mark this spot in case you need to find it again. Without my help." He took his axe and cut three quick strokes into the beechbark; the wood within shone like a white rune in the dim light. They mounted up on the ponies and left the mark behind, riding as quickly as they dared in the dark, torches streaming behind them like bright red banners.

† † †

The ride to the spring was short but steep, no more than two miles over rock, switchbacks, and through dense copses of birch and pine along a small stream. The ponies' hooves clattered on the stones every time they had to cross the streambed, a noise that seemed to echo their arrival.

"How close are we?" said Beowulf.

"Not far—see where the rocks come together?" said Kulli.

Even through the trees, Beowulf could see it, a semi-circular bowl of stone, like the Roman stages in the south, with an overhang of stone and trees. Two bowshots away, maybe three. They should have pulled up sooner.

"Put out the torches, and leave the ponies here," said Albin. "If they catch us in this narrow gorge, there's nowhere to run."

"You mean, if we catch them," said Beowulf. Albin grunted. "Kulli, stay with the ponies."

"You can't make me stay," said the boy.

"True. But if the ponies are alone, they are more likely to make noise or wander off."

"I brought hobbles, and the grass is good here. They'll stay until we return." The boy stuck his chin out, expecting an argument.

Beowulf saw no need for one; it would waste time. "Hobble them quickly, and make no noise." He leapt off, removed saddle and blanket, then looked to his own armor and blades. As soon as the hobbles were secure, Albin quenched the torches in the stream with a hiss. Beowulf secured the boy's shield, axe, and spear, loose but ready.

"To the spring, quietly."

The woods were stirring in the night breeze, branches soughing, leaves covering the sounds of their movement. They traveled single file for speed, Beowulf in the lead, Albin in the rear. All went well until Beowulf saw a scattering of white beneath a large pine: not the white of pine sap, but a small human skull, a boy or girl's skull, and the elongated bones of ponies. Beowulf hesitated, then picked up the skull. The bone was not dried out, but still flexible. The kill was recent, and the size was a match for the boy Hálfdan. Only then did he notice the rest of the carrion: deer antlers, ribs from a bear, goat hooves, human hands and skulls. Each thigh, rib, and other bone was stripped of every bit of flesh. Not even wolves stripped their prey this clean. They'd been boiled clean or the flesh had been nibbled away. He dropped the skull back onto the silent pine needles.

"Is there a way around the back of that hill, Kulli?" said Beowulf.

"It's a climb up. Loose stones," said the boy. He was whispering, and kept looking at the skull at Beowulf's feet.

"We will give these bones a fine funeral soon, a proper one. But right now I need to know: Do you think the trolls can climb up that hill from the spring?"

Kulli thought about it for moment, but was interrupted by a ram's horn voice that carried through the trees. The deep rumble of troll speech was interrupted by a higher-pitched shout.

"I'm going closer to take a look," said Albin.

He slung his shield over his back, crouched low, and stepped toward the voices. Without another word, all three abandoned the idea of the cliff climb and approached slowly through the holly, juniper, and brush along the wall of the valley. Normally each footstep would require careful steps into the dark shadows, shifting weight slowly. But as long as the trolls and their captives were shouting, they would hear nothing. Beowulf and Albin moved quickly and low; covering this ground if the troll camp was silent would have taken much too long.

At last, they saw the stony glen itself.

The grey light before dawn was creeping up the sky, though the darkness beneath the pines and birches was still deep. The trolls had built their camp in a bowl-shaped widening in a narrow defile, a gorge with a stream and only two ways in, along the streambed to the spring or down the steep slope of the cliffs above the spring. The pool of the spring itself was a black spot with water welling up from the depths of the earth. The overflow formed the stream, a bubbling section already wider than a standing jump would cross.

Around the pool six trolls stood towering over two corpses, a live but terrified woman cringing and howling, and Salveig, standing and shouting down the trolls. Salveig's dress had clearly been dragged through the leaves—her blonde hair entangled with bits of leaves and branches, her blouse torn and mud-stained, and her face red with anger.

She looked magnificent, an earthbound valkyrja, unbroken.

Salveig and the trolls were shouting at one another, and it seemed that the trolls understood her.

"You are fools, the Geats will come for you, and their leader, Beowulf, the great warrior, will kill the rest of you with his own hands. He killed Grendel and his mother—do you really think a pack of Norska fen trolls frightens him? They are probably coming soon, with the dawn, you worthless raiding crows. Keep your claws off me." The trolls shuffled nervously, unused to a hellion instead of a meal.

Beowulf grinned. She did care for him after all. And the distraction would make the attack much easier.

As Salveig spoke, Beowulf quickly looked at the other woman in the camp. She was young, a thrall with shoulder-length black hair and a scratched face, and she held a hand to her face where it bled. She alternately screamed and wept, and she was paying no attention to the living. Each time she withdrew, her dark hair obscured her face, and she rocked back and forth beside the two corpses. Each time, one of the trolls poked her with a claw, playing with their kill, making her turn again from weeping to screaming. Salveig tried to stay between the dark-haired woman and the trolls, but it was impossible.

Beowulf's heart bloomed with joy to see a woman so bold and so fearless even when surrounded by her murdered neighbors.

The bodies were grisly.

One gutted body hung from its ankles lashed to a tree branch, slowly dripping blood from fingertips as if it were a sheep or goat being trussed for a midwinter fest. A four-tusked troll stood over the second, slowly removing its intestines and innards, which it placed in a large, shallow wooden bowl. The visible captives were clearly being prepared for a troll's meal. The missing boy was nowhere to be seen. Salveig and three other trolls stared at each other. Her shouts and threats seemed to amuse two of them; the third troll shuffled nervously, glancing in the direction of the village and the fjord.

Beowulf signaled to Kulli and Albin to hold their position and ready themselves. Albin propped a spear near a beech tree and took throwing axes in each hand; the boy held an axe and spear, both slightly too big for him to use effectively for long. They were as ready as they could be to fight twice their numbers, but Beowulf feared that their hurry would get them all killed. They needed to keep the trolls off balance; Salveig helped, but if all six rushed Albin and Kulli, it would end very quickly.

"Ready?" he whispered.

"Ready," said Albin. "We'll hold them here. Where are you going?"

"Closer. Close enough to smell them. And maybe flatten them."

Beowulf stepped forward slowly and took a smooth round stone the size of a belt pouch and circled to the cliff side of the camp, away from the covering noises of the spring and the stream. He moved quickly past yews and aspen, confident that Salveig's shouting covered the noise of his movement more effectively than water sounds could. He looked up at the cliff again, scanning the rocks.

Beowulf stared at the six trolls, one baring his tusks and flexing his claws at Salveig, a second grabbing the shrieking woman by the ankles and yanking her into the air as a woman might pick up an unswaddled newborn. She certainly shrieked like a newborn, but much louder, her voice echoing from the bowl of the valley camp. Beowulf looked away; death in battle was one thing, this butchery was something else entirely.

The woman's voice stopped.

The four-tusked troll taking out innards and intestines had finished with the dark-haired corpse and turned to the new corpse, blood turning to steam in the cold air. The troll who was staring at Salveig grinned, his mouth as wide as a frog's, filled with teeth to grind bone to dust. Salveig stood silent at last. She was the only one of the prisoners still standing, and she wouldn't be for long. Already, one of the trolls was poking her with a curled claw, trying to make her scream.

Beowulf stopped looking at the troll butchery and concentrated on the rocks above the camp. The waxing dawn light helped, and he thought he saw a section of stones that seemed to include a boulder as big as a pony. There was no time left to climb the cliff and check the size or use his back to start it rolling. He hefted the round stone from the stream and said a bitter word. He drew his arm back and judged the distance to the stone above—more than a spear cast, less than a bow shot (and throwing up from below was always tricky)—drew breath, threw the rock, and missed. The rock clattered in the stones above the camp, but nothing moved.

The troll poking at Salveig stopped and cocked his head. The four-tusked troll looked up from its task, pulling intestines from the raven-haired thrall, her tears ended. The mutter and grumble of trollspeech made the others watchful; their enormous heads turned to scan the forest.

Their eyes would find him soon enough, so he did not wait. He hefted his best throwing axe and threw at the stone at the cliff top, and struck it on one side. It pivoted slightly and then, achingly slowly, rolled down the slope, deflected by a sapling but still coming toward the troll camp, and toward Salveig. The trolls were confused by the sound behind them, and turned just in time to see stone and rock falling among them. Beowulf saw one struck directly in the back by the enormous stone, then rock dust obscured the view.

The fight that followed was desperate; four trolls rushed his position and only the trees kept him alive, because their trunks and branches kept the trolls from overpowering him with numbers. Beowulf's second axe wounded one as it rushed him, and his spear flickered in and out among the tree trunks and branches as quick as fire, drawing dark troll blood with each stab. He wounded all of them, but the pain didn't seem to slow them. Shouting for Albin and Kulli to advance, he moved quickly between the trees, crouching low under their claws, his shield slowly torn to shreds. He threw away the straps and took a better grip on his spear. Seeing him shieldless at last, the trolls gathered and again tried to flank him.

Beowulf knew the rush was coming that would finish him.

He put his back against a mossy tree trunk just as Albin struck a troll through the ribs, and he heard Kulli's shout as he threw an axe. The rib-struck troll crumpled almost instantly, the axe-struck troll turned and clouted Albin above the temple more by luck than anything. The trolls were thrown into confusion and fell back; Beowulf drew and threw his king's gift-dagger at the four-tusked troll, striking it squarely in the eye. It clawed the blade out and ran, shouting in pain, hurling the dagger deep into the woods.

The sun broke through the trees.

Beowulf could no longer hear the trolls crashing through the trees, and eerie silence filled the glen where havoc ruled just moments before.

Kulli shouted, "Albin! Albin, get up!" The man was on the ground, his skin on his skull torn away and the skull itself cracked and bled. Beowulf looked once more to be sure the trolls were not returning, then knelt beside Albin and removed his helm.

The wound looked bad, as wounds to the head often were. "Speak to me," said Beowulf. And Albin replied but without understanding, the wound in his temple oozing blood, his voice weak and whispery. He called to his mother and his wife. The speaking was good; he might live.

"His wound is too deep, boy. Help me get him on a pony." The boy moved slowly to help, and Kulli's wide eyes kept returning to Albin's torn skin and the white flecks of bone beneath. The two struggled to put Albin on the animal. "Take him back to the shore and keep him talking. Don't let him drift into the embrace of the choosers of the slain."

"What about the women? What about Salveig?"

"I will chase them a little further," said Beowulf. "Go." Kulli turned and left. Beowulf watched the boy go, leading his friend and the extra pony.

Beowulf searched the camp once and found the intestines of three women. He found no tracks of Salveig's leading into the forest; one of the trolls must have held or carried her. Their tracks led straight onto the rock slope. No matter how hard he searched all that day, he could not find the dagger from his king or the troll tracks leading off the rocks.

† † †

Beowulf did not return to the village but wandered the pines searching for Salveig—or her bones—for several days. The trolls had abandoned their camp by the Rødå spring, and Beowulf wanted more than anything to find their new campsite, but still it eluded him. At first he thought they would seek water again, and followed streams and searched the shorelines of mountain tarns. He found troll tracks everywhere and nowhere, sometimes leading to a stream and vanishing, sometimes disappearing on the peaks and stones. But their camp was well hidden, and he never saw smoke from a fire. His beard grew matted, his plaited battle locks caught leaves and moss, his armor flecked with spots of rust. He searched alone, impatient for dawn each day, when light might reveal some sign he had overlooked before.

After the fourth day, he stopped lighting fires at night and ate only when berries or small game fell into his hands. He thought he heard Kulli's voice, or maybe Yngvar's, calling through the trees. He ignored it.

Each night, dreams haunted him with the sound of Salveig suffering beneath a troll's claws. He stopped building shelters and slept curled around his axe.

When he woke up in a meadow where a herd of red deer and two fawns grazed silently all around him, their graceful nibbling and calm eyes reminded him of Salveig. He watched them move around him, unafraid of him. Beowulf remembered his hunger, his ship, his men. He should bring them venison as an apology for his mad and foolish wanderings. When he rose to throw his spear, the deer moved as one, kicking their hooves high as they scattered from the meadow.

† † †

When Beowulf stopped his wanderings and returned to the village, he saw the Norska were once again at their tasks outside the walls, fetching water from the stream, herding the remaining goats and ponies. Albin embraced him. "We feared for you in the woods alone. Did you find them?"

"No, nothing. I go searching again tomorrow."

Albin frowned. "Do as you must. But I did not come north to wander the woods with you. I came to visit the dwarves of Hammerfjord and buy their axes and chain shirts. If you do not lead the men, I'll lead them for you. We'll sail as soon as my wounds have mended and I can pull an oar. In Dagfinn's place."

Beowulf spoke to Hrothwulf, to Guđbrandr, and to the others of his men. Half seemed to enjoy the village women; Hrothwulf was also recovering from troll wounds, each day a little stronger but still not fit to pull an oar. They were all gentle with him except Albin. The other men all spoke of travel, of their king, of home. Beowulf was sure they all thought he was still slightly mad. He felt an unfamiliar urge to abandon his longship and its crew, a feeling he would have described as foolish a month ago.

He walked to the longhouse, smelling the wood burning to smoke salmon and the damp wool at a weaver's spindle and loom.

The village headman, Ulli, stood at the entrance, splendid in a deep-green wool cloak trimmed with ermine. "You and your Geats have been good guests here," said Ulli. "I wish to thank you for the strength of your spear-arms and the protection of your shields. Allow me to give you a parting-ring, one that belonged to my brother. We call it hunter's luck."

"I cannot take a parting-ring until we ship out to the ocean road again. And I cannot do that until I find Salveig or her killers."

"You and your Geats don't know the trolls as we do. Salveig is *bergtagen*—taken under the mountain, where she is a slave or servant or supper for the trolls. She is of them now. The Salveig we knew and loved will never return to the light of the sun, but you must gather a warrior's peace. You slew four trolls, more than any man in this village or any Norska I know. You drove them away, and for that we are grateful."

"I cannot rest."

"Stay then. But she is lost to us. Take another woman." Ulli turned and walked away. Beowulf washed at the stream, entered the longhouse, ate, and slept until the pink and hopeful light of dawn spilled in through the smokehole. The boy Kulli was waiting for him, and he handed Beowulf four long blonde hairs, and said, "I found them at the Rødå spring."

Beowulf said, "Thank you, Kulli. Tell the men I need a few more days."

Beowulf sharpened his blades, picked up a second axe and a fresh skin of ale, and returned to the forest.

† † †

He camped near the spring that night and his dreams ran wild, each worse than the last.

He dreamed of Salveig enslaved, her hair torn away, poked by claws, bled and wounded, tortured endlessly by the trolls beneath the mountains. He woke in a sweat and spent the day searching the abandoned troll camp for signs that they had returned, but the signs were mixed and ruined by wolf spoor and new grasses that held no sign. As the afternoon wore on, he built a hunter's blind atop the cliff over the clearing, pine branches and a few stones arranged to hide him from view below. It wasn't much, and he could have built better, but part of him wanted the trolls to find him. The end might be quick, but it would be glorious, and the trolls would fall around him, felled by his axe and spear. Even a mighty tree falls to the small axe.

At sunset, he heard a rumbling like trollspeech, but loud as thunder. The entire cliff wall below him shrugged and shifted, and one of the stones of his blind tumbled into the dust.

Beowulf poked his head over the side and looked almost straight down. He saw the stone itself split in two halves, then stop shifting. Between the smooth edges a black tunnel led into the hillside below him. Walking out of the tunnel was a troll wearing scraps of fur and cloth and carrying a belt over one shoulder. It was wide through the legs and untusked, and Beowulf was sure if he crept a little closer he could try a spear cast or axe throw. If the trolls came out from under the troll mountain one at a time, he could stay here very patiently indeed.

The troll was moving, and the sun's light was fading from the sky. Beowulf's tread over the pine needles was silent, but when he brushed aside a bit of birch bark, it crackled slightly, no louder than the stream. Still, the troll heard him, and its head turned. He saw its mouth moving, tuskless, as if chewing something over, ears slightly tilted. He readied his spear for the long cast, a little too long for this light.

A branch shifted in the canopy and a bit of light filtered down through the trees to where the troll stood, illuminating its clear eyes like spring and lighting up a shock of tousled, muddy yellow hair. Under the warty skin and warped growth of new bone, it was Salveig.

The spear froze in Beowulf's hand.

He stared.

Salveig the troll looked for a moment longer in his direction, but seemed satisfied and returned to gathering firewood, bark, and stones into her bowl. Beowulf watched her as she moved about her tasks and recognized her bold stride, her grace oddly transformed by trollish limbs. The belt around her shoulder held a dagger, and the pommel was amber. Beowulf wept, and let her go, and his troll-madness left him.

After the troll mountain tunnel groaned and closed behind her, a new sorrow took its place, his heart frozen into river stone. The madness had been more comforting.

Ulli was right.

She was "of them" now.

The moon rose, fat and full. Beowulf worked in the night's chill, first chopping away a few trees over the mountain tunnel, then pushing at stones the rest of the night, until finally he used a tree branch to lever the grandfather of all stones down the slope, kicking and clattering and taking all its cousins with it in a dusty slide that buried the tunnel completely.

He rested, the sweat turning to clammy damp in the night air. The monsters were sealed within the mountain and it would be many seasons before they would ravage these villagers again. He slept on the mountain stones, and in the morning he walked back to the human world of simple things.

There was work to do.

Beowulf greeted the goats at the edge of the village, gathered his spears, and helped pull in a villager's fishing net at the shore. He walked back to see if he could keep Albin away from a crossing he understood, the cold crossing into gnawing death. He gave Kulli a young man's golden ring for his help, with his thanks.

Beowulf kept a warrior's silence about what he had seen at the troll tunnel, and he counted the wounded men left to him.

Salveig haunted his dreams with pleadings and accusations, fiercely at first, and then less and less. He kept telling himself she was dead.

The Salveig he knew was no more. Salveig the warrior maid had passed on to the halls of her ancestors. All that was left was a monster, no different than Grendel's mother, a horrible troll who would eventually meet a violent and ignoble end.

It was the way of such things with trolls.

† † †

Beowulf and the Geats repaired their storm-tossed ship over a few days, carving oars, splicing the lines and patching the sail while Albin slowly recovered. His speech was slow for a few days, and his eyes did not seem as bright as they were, but he had killed a troll and survived. The other men called him "Albin the trollslayer" and "Albin longspear."

Beowulf said nothing.

Albin should return to Geatland a hero, for he was one and he would not go reaving again.

Beowulf spoke to Ulli just once, to haggle for supplies, and on the first clear day with a westerly wind, the Geats pushed the longship off the round stones of Skaggerheim and set sail further north.

He'd have to explain to the king how he lost his dagger.

It seemed a tale worth telling.

BEOWULF AND THE MASTER OF HIS CRITICS

Interlude 4

°✝°

"Now this one was interesting."

The man from Cambridge feigned interest, though what he really wanted was a drink.

"Some think Grendel and his mother were trolls."

Even a sherry would do.

"The children of Cain covers an awful lot of territory."

The Master had not even offered the visitor a cup of tea . . . not that that would have slaked his thirst.

"And the trolls are part of the Northern mythos. Some say that daylight turns them to stone. Is that what you believe?"

"I'm afraid I try to avoid trolls at all costs."

"As well you should, though certain writers can have fun with them."

The man from Cambridge was heartened. Did he detect a spot of interest on the Oxford man's part?

"And this one with the wraith harkens back to the repetitions of the original text with all of that traveling to and fro."

Maybe he would come with him to see the other artifacts.

BEOWULF AND THE WRAITH

by Ed Greenwood

°‡°

Beowulf peered vainly through the howling snow, a thousand-thousand tiny white wet flakes racing at his eyes, and silently cursed the King of all Orra. For about the third time in as many breaths.

If Ealdred had been able to curb his lusts until the dry end of spring, and wed Mara, Princess of Arbion, then, the King of the Geats and the worst of his thegns wouldn't be out trudging through wet, knee-deep snow, wondering if it would reach as high as their chests before they froze.

He looked back the other way. Orthnoth was waving, relaying the signal; the arrow was almost formed. Straight they'd march, into the blinding whiteness, men shouting if the marchers ahead veered to shield-wise or to sword. Straight on like an arrow instead of circling blindly in the snow until deadly chill froze bones and the last sleep beckoned. Straight on to where grim Argundrar had been clearly visible—a dark line of trees wise folk stayed well away from—before the fierce storm had howled down suddenly upon the Geats.

Wise men didn't march for days in deep winter, especially into lands not their own, lands of dark and fell repute, where hearth-fires were few and monsters many.

But then, no one had ever accused the Geats of being wise men.

Smiling grimly at that thought, Beowulf turned, raised his arm—only skalds were fools enough to demand heroes draw blade or axe to wave about in wet like this—caught the watching stares of his foremost thegns, and let his arm fall.

Then he turned and started walking again, on into the wet numbing whiteness, awaiting the shouts that would mean he'd strayed off spear-straight.

Rotting draugr take Ealdred

. . . And eat him, toes first

. . . And let the *draugr* be not some armored walking dead shuffling out of a warrior's tomb, but Ealdred's grandmother

. . . Followed by all of his wild-haired long-dead aunts, too.

As if all those spirits heard his thinking, the storm winds rose into a mocking moan.

Growling, Beowulf the King of the Geats bent his head against them, and strode on.

† † †

Indeed, Mara of Arbion must be something to make Ealdred hurry her so to a bridal bed. In haste that summoned a dozen kings striding through the storms and snows of deep winter. Not since the days of Grimli Giantsbones . . . but no, the time for such remembering was when the shield-ring was up, the fire crackling strong within it, and every Geat had eaten. If they weren't ringed by wolves and the watchful eyes of creatures far worse than wolves, by then, and too busy fighting to remember anything.

Beowulf trudged on, through blinding, deepening snow, until trees loomed up suddenly out of the storm like armed and waiting sentinels . . . dark, huge sentinels; so many waiting giants, thirsty for Geat blood.

He drew his sword.

Argundrar wasn't a place he'd have willingly led his best battle-thegns into, even on a bright morning in high summer. So here he was, stepping into its trees in this cold, with nightfall coming soon, at the head of too many proud, untried younglings with good names and flashy swords, and too few battlewise and wary grayblades. Most of the few veterans with him were too old for the march, let alone this weather; only their pride and their family names were keeping them warm.

So Beowulf and his far-from-best thegns would be spending a night in the very den of the ever-hungry wolves. Skalds often said the wolves and "dark magic" of Argundar were what had kept Orra and Geatlun from ever making war on each other. And here he was, chilling his boots in the Wolfwood itself. Draugr take Ealdred.

† † †

Tramping down the snows warmed them. The youngest thegns even hopped and shuffled through a brief mockery of dance steps, laughing, before they propped their shields on their spears, and downed their sacks of food and gift-gild. The older thegns stood watch in a ring, facing out, and did not laugh.

Sighing the soft cold sighs of racing wraiths—sad, hastening *hugr*—the storm winds rose higher, snow stinging Geat faces.

Beowulf led the first cutting-band.

The work was swift: there were many dead branches, and the rest were frozen and cracked off at a single tug.

When he set down his load, Uthgar, Groa's son, was muttering, "Why light fires? Won't the wolves smell the smoke, and come hunting?"

"They smelled us long ago, sunu," old Hrori answered. "Even before they heard all the branch-breaking. They know we're here. And as for knowing, be sure your hands know where your every knife is. Guard your throat and behind your knees."

"I've killed wolves before," Uthgar said shortly.

"That is good," the old thegn replied. "Let us all hope you do so again."

"What do you mean—"

"Wolves snap and snarl," Beowulf observed from right behind Groa's get, keeping his voice deep and flat. "Geats do not."

Young Uthgar stiffened as if he'd been slapped, and then spun around and got out, "Yes, my king!" in a single gasp.

Beowulf grinned, clapped him on the shoulder, and said, "I need your fierceness. Guard it well."

"'Ware, all!" The call came from but three men away, along the ring: old Eadulf, who had the eyes of a hawk. "Firelight, yonder!"

Thegns of the Geats were neither sheep nor careless children, to all turn their heads at once to look away from the dark forest they were standing guard against, but those who could darted swift looks sidelong to see Eadulf's pointing axe—and the tiny red glint of distant reflected glimmering on its end.

Beyond, there was a light in the depths of the Wolfwood.

† † †

The thegns did not wait for their king's command. As the skalds sang, Geats did not cower in the dark awaiting trouble, but went and met it, well armed.

"And if this, ahead, is a trap?" Uthgar murmured, as they trudged through snow that groaned under them with cold, branches all around creaking in the icy winds.

"Then we shall see it," Hrori said flatly. "Use eyes, now, not tongue."

"But—"

"You should be a skald, Uthgar Many-Questions. Or a priest. They talk like falling water, where thegns are not so foolish. Be a thegn."

Uthgar opened his mouth angrily, so Beowulf murmured softly, "Be a thegn."

Uthgar's mouth closed, and he flushed and bent his head.

And then they were standing where they could see, and no one was acting the skald.

† † †

In silence the Geats stood still and watchful, gazing through the storm-swaying trees, Beowulf their king staring as hard as the rest.

It was no fire that Eadulf had seen, but lanterns of goodly glass, such as only great temples had. Two lanterns, each as tall as a man, metal cages with a point beneath and another above, that stood out from a stone wall like great sentinels impaled on spears of stout iron, flanking an arched wooden door. Flames danced and spun inside the glass with no logs to feed them—glass their warming fury should have cracked like axe-struck ice in this cold.

About then the Geats became aware that the howling of the storm was around them and behind them, but the open space in dark Argundrar they beheld was still and calm, with not one flake of snow falling . . . or fallen.

In the lantern-light they could see dark, wet, dead leaves and the usual litter of rotten branches underfoot in that glade, but no hint of snow. The thegns said not a word to each other, but more than one made the sign that warded off fell magic or ghosts, and leaned forward a little.

In a moment they were all leaning in the deepening cold, like so many wary corpse-ravens a-peering, silently and suspiciously.

The lanterns, and the door between them, adorned an end wall of a building that stretched off into the dark trees for farther than a Geat could hurl a spear.

The Geats had come to a great dark hall, of strong stone gray with age, nestled among trees that had grown up alongside it and arched their branches over its roof-shakes, so as to hide it from anyone standing not near.

"I mislike the look of this," Hrori muttered. "This may look like a king's hall, but to me it smells like a dead-barrow."

Uthgar frowned. "I smell nothing."

"He was speaking as a skald does, sunu," Orthnoth growled.

"But—"

"Sometimes thegns are fools."

"So I am told," Uthgar said heavily. "Often."

Beowulf chuckled—and found himself shuddering in the cold. He was among the largest, strongest men in Geatland, but the chill was deep in him now, clawing.

Aye, thegns were shivering all around him, the storm flailing their helms and shoulders, ice-rime cracking as they moved.

"We can die within—perhaps—or die out here, of cold certainty," Beowulf told them, and strode forward, hefting his sword in his hand.

Men drew breath behind him in sharp apprehension, half-expecting him to blaze up into flame or face a draugr rising out of the ground like mist, the moment his boots touched the snow-bare ground of the glade.

Beowulf did not stop to await foes or doom, but strode deliberately across that silent, open space, giving the lanterns sharp, swift glances—had they flared more brightly at his approach?—and then laying his hands upon the door.

Which swung inward, as silently as any ghost, opening into—a fair, high-beamed feasting-hall, and true firelight at last.

† † †

A few paces into the crackling warmth, Beowulf paused to turn his blade point down to show he came with peaceful intent . . . and to stare about. The hall looked to be all one great room, and no person or food could he see in it. Smooth-worn flagstones beneath his boots, and blazing hearthfires, two along either wall, great cradles of stone around rushing flames that sought chimneys he'd not remembered seeing when he was outside. Between them, two lines of stout tables with benches drawn up to them, running away from him a long, long way, to—blood of the Einherjar!—the most splendid sword Beowulf had ever seen.

A thing of magic and wonder, as blue as the night stars, pulsing as if it was calling him. Floating upright at the back of the hall above a hearthfire greater than the rest, hanging in the air point down and as upright as if set on a peg—where there was neither wall nor peg.

The blade moaned softly at the sight of him, as if in greeting, but Beowulf was lost in gaping amazement.

He took a step forward, his own sword feeling suddenly heavy and clumsy in his hand, and swallowed. His mouth was suddenly dry, the cold fallen from him like a doffed cloak.

I must have that sword.

Beowulf never knew if he'd growled those words aloud or just thought them as fiercely as a battle-shout, but as if in answer, the sword blazed up into blue fire. He turned, then, to see if his thegns had followed him—they had—and beheld two bright blue dots on every face and snowy cloak he gazed at. His own eyes were blazing blue fire with his longing!

His thegns were all crowding into the hall now, spreading out to the walls to make room for those behind. There were soft curses of amazement and desire. Every hand hungered for such a blade.

Well, then, let it be a treasure of Geatland, which every thegn could wield for a time. Aye, every—

Beowulf turned again to look through the blue fire, at that beauty of—

Darkness fell, deep and utter, silent and sudden. Beowulf glanced swiftly all around, but saw nothing. All was as black as if he'd been blind-hooded. No blue flames, no hearthfires, not even the faint night-glow of the racing white snowfall from behind him.

"Fell magic," someone—Hrori—growled angrily, from not far away. Beowulf heard the boots of many thegns scraping on flagstones as they turned wildly this way and that, seeking light, or a foe.

"Get out!" someone shouted. "Back out quickly! Through the doors!"

There was rolling, echoing boom like a clap of thunder, as the great doors that had opened so softly under Beowulf's hand now came crashing shut. The king heard stout fists striking them, men growling as they hurled their strength against them, and then the despairing, disbelieving shout: "The way is lost! Curse of the Vanir, the way is lost!"

Several answering shouts arose, the confused and angry cries of men in battle, cut and in pain, lashing out in fury at a foe. And then shrieks of dying agony, the pounding of running boots as the thegns raced toward the unseen fray, and more shouts. Swords clanged and rang, wounded men groaned—and Beowulf swallowed the curse he felt like spitting, and instead flung his arms wide and roared, "Stop, all of you! Swords down! Stop slaying each other!"

No one stopped, of course, the darkness driving their fear and frenzy.

Indeed, full-blooded battle seemed to erupt all around him, men shouting and then screaming horribly as they died.

Beowulf cursed, snatched his axe from his belt, and hastily crouched down to avoid being sliced by someone lashing out blindly. Sword and axe raised, he strained to hear just where his thegns were around him. So many were untried younglings, eager to taste their first blood in battle. They'd die gaping in disbelief that the first blood they were tasting was their own. They were dying, right now.

Yet they were Geats, swift to strike, but neither fools nor madmen. They couldn't all be just turning on each other.

Who was attacking in the darkness, so silently and bloodily?

Beowulf shook his head, furious, frustrated—and still blind. He could see nothing, nothing at all. Even in deep Niflheim and in howling Hel skalds said there were horrors to be seen, which meant men saw, so there must be light enough, of a sort, to see things. But this . . .

Swords flickered like cold flames, visible now for a moment here and a moment there, too swift to truly light the darkness, reflecting back the cold glows of—what?

Wraiths! Glowing for a moment with the escaping lives and souls of Geats, then darkening into dark shadows that raced and swooped, twisting in and among the dying thegns. The new hugr tumbled in their wake, bewildered and raging, swiftly fading into darkness.

There were more shouts, clangs, and dying cries. More wraiths raced past Beowulf, cold breezes of death on his face. He heard men fall heavily, axes clattering. Then all fell silent.

It was a crawling calm, not quite silence; Beowulf knew he was not alone with the dead. Aye: there. And there again. Someone was listening just as he was, and creeping forward. A soft, deliberate, approaching tread, purposeful and drawing nearer . . . and nearer . . .

Beowulf held his axe slantwise before him to try to catch any attack, and drew back his sword to strike, waiting . . . and waiting . . .

The unseen one was advancing warily; could he—it—see? Beowulf brought his sword forward to join his axe, in a wall of battle-iron before him.

And then something hard and solid blundered into his axe, he heard the creak of armor that meant a weapon was being swung— and the King of the Geats sprang back a pace. The tip of a weapon just struck his axe, with a ringing clang—and Beowulf bounded forward, thrusting hard.

Into leather and meat beneath, his blade glancing up off bone to lodge deep, blood hissing forth.

A man screamed, right in Beowulf's face, and there was suddenly weight on his sword, his unseen victim sagging.

"Onela," the dying man sobbed. "I . . . ohhh . . . "

The weight slid off Beowulf's sword in a tumbling rush that left the King of the Geats choking in grief.

Onela was Orthnoth's lady. He'd just slain his oldest friend.

He leaned forward in the dark, reaching for Orthnoth . . . and finding him.

His old friend was sprawled in a twisted heap, warm and sticky with blood—blood that turned suddenly, shockingly icy.

Beowulf felt a wandering, caressing chill on his face, as if cold mist or smoke was rising up from Orthnoth. It was as bitter as storm-sleet, and his fingers now felt not warm and sticky but as cold as if he was fondling ice. Bone-deep cold, and growing colder.

He snatched his hand away for fear of losing his fingers, hissing in pain.

And that hiss was answered.

From out of the darkness nearby came another hiss, not his own. A hiss of surprise.

Something happened then.

Beowulf could feel more than hear, a creeping of the skin, an eerie, silent tingling in the tense blackness.

Slowly, as the feeling crawled up his arm, it began to glow. Not with blue fire, but with something weak and dim, ale-brown and purple. Up his arm it went, haltingly, as if searching for something, as the King of the Geats hefted his weapons in readiness and stared at it, wondering who—or what—would see it and come hacking and hewing out of the darkness for him. And what it would do to him, this fell and creeping magic . . .

There were other glows, now, in that darkness, kindling faintly here and there in the hall, rising like wisps of smoke from wet campfires. Rising from huddled Orthnoth, right in front of him, a thread as dull and dim as all the rest.

Beowulf could see the hall again; the dim glows were now numerous enough. Sprawled and silent thegns everywhere, hacked to death, and a ribbon of palely-glowing mist rising from each one, rising like a trained snake he'd once seen, swaying and undulating toward prey.

All of the glows were drifting across the hall, seeking the same goal, converging on one spot in the darkness beyond their feeble radiance. The same direction the hiss had come from.

Fell magic.

His own glow was crawling across his face and neck, on down across his shoulder, heading for his back. He might not have much time left.

Ealdred, draugr take you. I know not what is reaching out to take me, but draugr take you. And your royal bride, too.

† † †

The King of the Geats hefted his weapons again and grimly headed for where the questing streams of glow were drawing together. He stepped carefully around forever-staring Uthgar, who'd ask questions no more, his mouth slack above a throat that gaped wetly. A few strides farther lay the hacked, belly-gutted thing that had been Hrori.

Beowulf did not hasten. The tingling was worming its way down his back now. It seemed to grow stronger with each step he took into the deepening gloom. The threads of glowing light were streaming silently past him, to meet at . . . at something that looked like a pale spider. A spider as big as a man's fist, that—no, not a spider. It was a human hand, corpse-pale yet fleshed, holding up a stone that filled its palm. Something was stabbing at that stone out of the darkness, and at their meeting a glow was being born, a glow that grew brighter as the glowing threads from all over the hall drifted to meet it.

The stabbing thing was a long, sickly-pale crone's finger, its nail like a hawk's talon. The hand holding the stone belonged to the same crone, who was hidden by darkness or kept invisible by magic. All Beowulf could see was the hand, the stone, and the moving finger touching the stone.

The finger traced a glowing rune on the stone, an intricate sigil Beowulf had never seen before. Yet he did not have to know its name and what it meant to see that it crawled with magic—even before the stone vanished with a flash, and the hand dipped down into darkness to rise again with another stone, on which the finger was soon tracing a different rune.

Beowulf's skin was a-crawl with the tingling glow that was wandering over him, and he disliked the look of the second rune more than anything he'd ever seen. Yet would he do more harm than wisework, to plunge in and sword those hands, and break this magic? Could he touch those hands with battle-iron at all?

The second stone flashed and was gone, and a third was raised for scribing. Beowulf set his teeth, edged closer, and raised his sword.

Before he could strike anything, there was a flash that made his eyes see fire, and utter darkness fell again.

Snarling, Beowulf hacked and slashed at nothing, trotting forward as he sliced air again and again. His sword and axe found nothing solid, again and again, and he was panting in fury by the time he stopped and turned to peer all around.

. . . But in vain.

He was blind once more in unbroken darkness.

In disgust he grounded his blade on an unseen flagstone and leaned on it to catch his breath and try to think. The glow was gone from him, and its tingling with it. He could hear nothing but his own harsh breathing, and feel no storm winds. The darkness stank of fresh blood and death. It was a waiting, watchful darkness; Beowulf did not feel alone.

Nor was he.

Somewhere across the hall a tiny glow kindled, like the eye of some forest creature or moon-glint on the rings on a thegn's finger. As Beowulf leaned on his sword and watched, it grew. Tall and thin, growing both up and down at once, yet still dim.

Beowulf expected it to grow larger and brighter, and it obliged, quickening into a manlike outline. A glow he could see through, a wraith rather than a solid living man or draugr.

Soundlessly it strode toward him, raising sword and axe, growing brighter with each silent step.

It wore a hawk-feather king's helm like his own, it hefted weapons that might have been his in just the way he did, and it tossed its head as he did when striding to meet a foe.

Beowulf swallowed, and took up his sword in his hand once more. He was staring at a palely-glowing, translucent wraith of himself.

His own *vorur.*

A sure warning of death.

Dark sockets of eyes glaring at him, teeth clenched as were his own . . . another flash, and the phantom sword and axe were gone. The vorur now held but one weapon: the magnificent blue-glowing sword Beowulf had just coveted.

That blade was almost close enough to touch him, and moaning in soft longing. It wanted his life.

The wraith took another step forward, sword sweeping up, and Beowulf found himself fighting . . . himself.

The glowing sword cut down, trailing blue flames. The King of the Geats dodged, ducked—a wash of blue chill on his cheek—and with a snarl of triumph slashed the wraith across the back of the knee.

It was like slashing empty air, his blade touching nothing and passing through the phantom leg without seeming effect. Beowulf hurled himself forward, staggering, to escape the backstroke of the wraith's warblade.

He spun around in time to parry the blue sword, in a clash of hilts that left him numbed and shuddering, amid chill blue sparks. The vorur might be but ghostly air, but its beautiful blade was still solid enough.

Once, twice, and thrice their swords met, Beowulf's axe cleaving the wraith time and time again while they were locked together, slicings that only made the vorur grin. He tried to hurl the wraith back when they were locked together, but it was like pushing at air that had suddenly become solid stone . . . and then he slipped in slick thegn blood and was staggering aside, that moaning blade leaping at his throat again.

The King of the Geats struck it aside, roaring, and brought his axe up in a great slash that should have laid the vorur open from cods to chin—but instead passed through it harmlessly, chin and phantom helm and all, leaving Beowulf scrambling to parry the backswing of the flaming blue blade.

He managed it, somehow, the tip of his sword tumbling away in the ringing crash of the meeting blades, but slipped again—and the vorur's grin was gloating ice as its beautiful sword swung around, suddenly slow and graceful amid the pounding of Beowulf's heart, and sliced deep into his shoulder, as easily as if the armor it was cleaving wasn't there at all.

No pain but cold, bitter cold; a chill that raced to Beowulf's chest, clenched an icy fist around his heart—and squeezed.

Axe and sword falling from numbed hands, the King of the Geats fell into utter darkness at last, a cloak that welcomed him eagerly.

Somewhere behind him cold blue flames burned, and he fled from them in terror, down, down into the deep black cold.

† † †

Something was gnawing, nearby. Gnawing and growling, wet threatening snarls . . . and stone was hard and cold under the side of his face. He was alive.

Or was this Hel, and all its hounds were fighting over the chance to devour him?

Beowulf's hands were empty, or at least one was. He couldn't feel the other—the one the blue sword had slashed—at all. He was lying on bare stone with a chill winter breeze blowing over him, and a blue glow all around him.

Warily he opened one eye. The air in front of him was glowing blue twice as high as his head.

He was lying under the night sky, on bare stone, the dark branches of Argundrar reaching up all around him in a stark black twisted ring. Overhead, tattered clouds raced past like wraiths in a hurry to be somewhere warmer. Stars glimmered fleetingly through them as snarls rose in a sudden dispute right beside Beowulf. Where was his sword?

Trying to think of a curse, he rolled over. Wolves danced back and then stopped and stared at him, a ring of too many pitiless yellow eyes for him to meet and smilingly promise death to. There was his axe . . . and over there was his sword.

The axe was nearer, and Beowulf crawled to it. One leg pained him much; it had been bared by a sword-slash, to reveal a deep white scar just below his knee. A scar he'd never seen before.

There was no blood streaming from his cut shoulder. It, too, bore an old, dry white scar. It also hung heavy and numb, almost useless, until he managed to form its fingers into a fist and dashed that clenching against the stone beneath him a time or three.

Then he could scoop up his sword with it, notice that its tip was gone and dully remember seeing that loss, and heft sword and axe as he looked about.

He counted ten-and-four wolves devouring his dead thegns. They snarled in alarm and challenge when Beowulf staggered to his feet, but the glowing ring around him seemed to be keeping them back.

The ring of runes, their blue radiance rising halfway up his shins. Leaning grimly on his broken sword, he peered down at them. These runes he could read.

"If—"

He flinched, and stared all around. Whence had come that softly sinister voice?

A lady's voice, as soft and menacingly gentle as any young seer calmly speaking dooms in her trance. It had sounded close by his ear and a little above him, but he could see nothing there but the empty night air and a lonely white snowflake or two, wandering past. Shaking his head, Beowulf looked back at the rune.

It was gone.

The rest were still there, glowing their eerie blue, but the only one he'd read had vanished. The largest wolf padded to the gap where it had been, and stopped, facing Beowulf.

He stared into his eyes with a grim smile of promise until it looked away, and then let his eyes fall to the next rune, and the next, watching them wink out in swift, silent succession as that ghostly she-voice said them aloud.

"—you would wield the sword you covet, King of the Geats, and so become king of much more, seek the lady on the throne of skulls, and embrace her. Long is the way to Ginnungsgard, and fell its guardians, but the lady is fair."

That was all, and as the last rune winked out, the wolves snarled as one and rushed at Beowulf.

He met them with sword and axe, hacking and hewing grimly. His leg kept him from leaping to where he might set a tree at his back, or climb above their jaws . . . which meant he was doomed.

But oh, he would collect his own blood-price and make them buy his bones dearly!

"Hah!" he roared at them. "How many wolves is a King of the Geats worth? Hey? Hey?"

His axe caught a wolf under one foreleg and hurled it back atop its more timid fellows, as he slashed viciously behind him with his sword, blinding the largest wolf, who'd been trying to hamstring him. Beowulf spun around, bringing his axe down on the head of the next one, and kept on turning, to strike aside a leaping wolf and send it crashing to the stones.

Then they were all leaping at him, barking and growling, their jaws closing on arms and shoulders and dragging him down.

Beowulf fought to keep hold of his weapons, to thrust and hack with them still, but there could only be one end to this fray, and the wolves knew it as well as he did.

He was going down, buried under stinking wolves eager for his flesh, savaging him already wherever they could reach. "Grrrah!" he snarled in exasperation, as his sword was struck from his grasp and he clawed and elbowed in a frenzy, seeking to gouge out the eyes of the wolf who'd disarmed him. "Long indeed is my road to Ginnungsgard!"

That name echoed across the forest like a great skald-chant, deep and roaring and many-echoed. And all at once, the weight atop Beowulf was gone.

The wolves were fleeing in all directions. Wild-eyed, racing away with tongues hanging out and tails down. Even the sorely-wounded were limping or trying to crawl away from him.

Bewildered and bitten, Beowulf reeled bloodily to his feet, looking for his sword. "Ginnungsgard" was still rolling away through the dark forest as if it had been a giant's war-cry, and not a buried Beowulf's breathless snarl.

He had his sword in his hand again, and was grimly counting dead wolves and pondering how one would taste fire-roasted, when an echo came back to him through the trees in the same menacingly gentle lady's voice he'd heard before: "Ginnungsgard."

As that calm whisper spoke in Beowulf's ear, the clouds overhead faded away and moonlight fell bone-white and bright on Argundrar.

As the King of the Geats whirled to stare hard at the trees from whence the echo had come, they seemed to part. He found himself gazing on a far, lone keep, a black needle of turreted stone silhouetted against the moon.

Fell magic. Herding him the way wolves run stags to exhaustion in the snows.

Draugr take them all . . . every last snarling, biting wolf . . . and whatever witch was mocking him from afar, too.

If the draugr weren't too busy taking Ealdred and Mara, of course.

Beowulf shook his head and turned away—but was aware of a white light back the way he'd been looking. He turned again. The light was the moon, of course, a distant keep dark against it. When he closed his eyes, he could still see it.

Beowulf sighed, and turned his head away, but the light still shone in his head. Herded, indeed.

"I'm coming, witch," he told the night grimly, and started toward that distant stronghold. Limping deeper into Argundrar with every painful, stiffening stride. Wolves lifted their heads, far ahead in the tangled trees—and slunk away.

† † †

Sometimes he leaned on his sword like a crutch, and sometimes he flung it to stun or slay furred forest scurriers. Beowulf ate them raw, followed by handfuls of snow to slake his thirst. No creature approached him, and somehow there always seemed to be a clear path before him, running arrow-straight up wooded hills and down their far sides.

Straight onwards, from standing stone to standing stone, as one day became two, and two became three.

He'd gone around the Wolfwood betimes, in younger years. Surely it could not be this big! Was the path truly straight, as it seemed, or was he circling?

On a particularly high hill, the King of the Geats turned and looked back. Behind him, on distant ridges, he could see stones he'd passed already. So many sentinels like trolls gone to stone. In a line as straight as his outflung arm, pointing back to Geatland.

Which he'd likely never see again.

† † †

Unseen birds called in the lengthening morning, but there were no rustlings underfoot in the dead leaves. Nothing that could not fly dared come near this part of the Wolfwood.

Not even wolves.

Where the marching host of trees faltered and a great fist of bare rock began stood a great stone, set on end. From it a straight track ran down into the trees, as straight as an arrow's flight, and climbed a distant wooded slope over which the top of another standing stone could just be seen.

Something moved on that straight way.

Something ragged with half-healed bites, which reeled and growled like a hungry beast. By its reek, it was a man.

It came to where the forest ended and the rock began, looked at what lay ahead, and trudged on without pause.

Across clattering loose rock, and things more gray and brittle: bones. There were gnawed and split bones heaped everywhere, from where Beowulf walked—straight on, toward a standing stone in the green distance, beyond the shoulder of bare rock—up off to the side, to a dark hole in the great fist of rock; the mouth of a huge cave.

As the warrior's trudging shifted stones to clicking and clacking, something moved in the cave. Beowulf walked on.

That something came out of the cave. It was a giant, huge and filthy-bearded, clad in a robe of many rotting furs and hefting a great stone war hammer in hairy hands.

Three strides took it onto the track, barring the Geat's way. Where it grinned unpleasantly. "Be welcome, man-meal."

"Stand back and let me pass, or die," Beowulf said curtly.

"Ho ho! So cold a threat from the little half-dead man! So grim, so strong!" The giant guffawed, leaned forward, and spread his great arms wide. "Will you run, little rabbit?"

The wounded man's glare was sharper than his broken sword. "Why?"

The giant sneered, swung his war hammer back to his shoulder, and strode forward. "Should have cursed me when you had the chance, grim one! Too late! Too late!"

The hammer swung down at Beowulf like a dark, moving mountain.

Beowulf flung himself forward under the deadly swing, rolling unsteadily aside from the gigantic foot that stomped and then kicked at him, striking his axe and hurling him aside.

Overhead, the giant snarled in anger, grounded his hammer in a booming spray of stone shards, and then swung it aloft again.

At his next step, he'd bring it smashing down on the sprawled and feebly-cursing fool, and bring an end to this fray.

An axe and a sword bit deep into his ankle, and the giant found himself stumbling and hopping aside, roaring in dismay and pain. The heavy hammer overbalanced, its end struck the ground, bouncing, and—his wrist exploded in fire.

Then everything changed, and in sudden quiet the giant found himself blinking at the gore-spewing stump where his hand had been . . . and then down at the ground where his hand lay twitching in the rock-dust, still clutching the war hammer.

He groaned, lumbering back against his favorite sunning-rock. The killing blow would come in a moment.

His slayer was standing again, swaying a little. And then turning away, to resume his walk along the Way of Stones.

Bewildered, the giant blinked. "Grim one not slay Stone-eye?"

"Not," Beowulf replied, striding on.

"Grim one walks to death," Stone-eye called after him, sounding baffled. "Straight into the lands of Helhild."

Beowulf turned. "And who is Helhild?"

"The witch who kisses kings to death, and dances on their bones. 'Ware Ginnungsgard, where she dwells!"

Beowulf shrugged, turned again, and walked on.

† † †

Another day, and another, and still the standing stones marched. Walking the track, the keep stark against the moon in his dreams and whenever he closed his eyes, Beowulf crossed silent lands where most steadings and halls seemed deserted, the forest reclaiming fields around him.

The few folk he saw fled into the trees at his approach. He hailed them not, but went on. His straight way now lay along arrow-straight roads, through towns once rich and populous. Some of the standing stones marking the route bore runes that did not blaze with blue fire or disappear. Old and deep-graven runes that proclaimed proudly, "Traveler, you stand in Josastein," or, "This be Hearheld."

Beowulf had heard those names. Rich, proud realms that lay far indeed from Geatland and Orra, not between them. Conquered lands now, it seemed.

"Herded, I am," he told one stone quietly. "Witch, there will come a reckoning."

A raven flew out of the trees and shrieked at him mockingly as it alit atop the stone. Beowulf looked up at it, and added calmly, "There comes a reckoning for us all."

The raven eyed him sidelong, and then flapped away heavily, without another sound. Beowulf could not see where it went. He walked on.

In the next place, folk had fled so quickly that half-eaten food was still warm on their hearths and tables. The King of the Geats ate and drank what he needed, tossed coins from his purse onto the table, and stalked on.

† † †

There came a day when Beowulf stood atop a rise in the straight way and saw the keep he could not escape in his dreams, soaring tall and dark atop the next rise.

Between his height and his destination lay a reeking marsh of still black water and withered dark reeds, where no bird called . . . and no flies danced. Silent it was, like something dead.

"Hither come I," Beowulf told it, "silent, and like something dead. We are of a kind. Wherefore, I doubt not, you will try to slay me."

The straight way ran down into the waters and through them, ankle-deep under the waters like a drowned dyke. As Beowulf waded into the oily, cold black water, something bulged up from under it, near at hand.

And then another, on the other side of the dyke. And still another, and yet another, as he walked on, all of them rising up out of the waters, dripping and trailing a terrible stink, to stare at him with pale dead eyes.

Beowulf did not slow or pause, but stared ahead at his way— and glanced behind, too—to be sure nothing tentacled was reaching for his ankles.

And all around him, the severed heads of long-dead warriors, eyes rotting in their rusting helms, hung in the air just above the marsh and whispered to him.

"Turn back or die, warrior. Helhild suffers none to live."

"Think you to fight Helhild, and win? Fool, you are, and doomed fool!"

"Alone, warrior, you think to prevail? Death you'll find, if you go on!"

They gave him taunts and warnings in plenty as he strode on. Beowulf smiled once or twice. They reminded him of the crones of Geatland when he'd been young, always telling him he'd amount to nothing, could not hope to fill the boots of those now entombed, and did not deserve to even stride the same halls as the great warriors of yore.

"Tell me," he said to the last rising, dripping head, as the way he was following rose up out of the marsh again, "was Helhild your lover? How was she?"

The heads all sank without a sound. Save a few bubbles.

† † †

In front of Beowulf, the land rose steeply. Ginnungsgard loomed almost overhead.

Nothing green grew on the slope he now climbed; it was all sharp black rocks spotted here with sickly green-and-white lichen.

Loose stones stirred behind him. Beowulf whirled to face the attack he'd expected.

Draugr were rising ponderously from the marsh, corpse-pale and ugly, rusted helms askew and crumbling blades held menacingly. Empty sockets stared sightlessly at Beowulf, yet saw him. They were slow in their stridings, yet certain. Eel-eaten eyes, it seemed, were no loss to the walking dead.

They were all, of course, coming after him. Almost twoscore of them. No, more than twoscore now, lurching and dripping.

"I'll not see Geatland again," Beowulf murmured, turning back to the steeply-sloping way, to stride on. "Come, dead men. We'll see how many of you I can kill again."

† † †

They caught up to him only a few paces from the unguarded, yawning portals of the black stone keep. Three of them, who became four and five as he fought, hacking and clutching at the King of the Geats.

They stank of death, and their limbs were slow; Beowulf readily hewed his way free of them, pleased to see that when he severed a foot or an arm it stayed severed, and moved no longer.

He severed many, and went on.

They pursued him in a slow, shuffling procession, as he glanced back once at the open sky and hills rolling off into blue distance— and then turned and plunged into Ginnungsgard.

† † †

Dank it was, and seemingly deserted, though Beowulf kept sword and axe raised and ready as he went.

The cold stone halls echoed not as he walked, and were lit by a dim, eerie blue light that came from everywhere and yet nowhere.

Beowulf strode warily, the draugr following like tired dogs. When they got too close, and struck at him, he turned and hacked them down, brown and bony jaws bouncing in teeth-scattering ruin on the flagstones, skulls riven like the shells of eggs, more than one clawlike hand falling into a scattering chaos of fingerbones.

And he went on. Deeper and deeper, between pillars and through hall after hall, until it seemed to the King of the Geats that he'd come much farther than any keep—even the great many-bannered castles of the hot lands of the south, that skalds peopled with wingéd talking snakes and dusky-skinned dancing women—should stretch.

"Dark Magic," he murmured to himself—and stepped into the largest hall yet.

He was standing on glossy black marble, stretching away between two marching rows of stout stone pillars carved like writhing, tail-chasing clusters of dragons, to a stone like a tall black flame where atop a dais of seven steps stood a high seat, flanked by two pillars of real flame.

Or perhaps real flame, for those hungry, up-racing flickerings rose as tall as two thegns, and seemed to feed on nothing at all.

Now *this* was a throne-room.

The throne itself was yellow-white and curiously curved, and it was not unoccupied.

Beowulf whirled around then, took two catlike steps back to cut the legs out from under the nearest of the draugr, took another step to behead the one behind it—and knew what the throne was made of before he turned around again to behold it again.

It was fashioned entirely of human skulls, fused together. She who sat slumped upon it was unmoving—dead, or asleep, or frozen by magic.

Beowulf turned away to hew down more draugr, and saw that they were stopping at the doorway.

So he turned from them again to gaze properly at the woman on her throne. She looked alive, not rotting or withered, though she was chained in place by stout-seeming fetters of gleaming gold, at wrists and waist and ankles.

To him, she seemed a warm, welcoming white flame against this cold, grand hall of dark and dusty marble. The fairest beauty he'd ever seen, glowing softly with a radiance that seemed to well up out of her, she lit up the throne room.

Richly gowned in emerald green, long-limbed, with skin as white as new-fallen snow, she was lushly beautiful. Her long raven-hued hair spilled over bare shoulders that Beowulf swallowed at the sight of, his eyes drinking deep.

He'd been a warrior too long not to cast a swift, sudden glance behind him. The draugr were crowded together at the door, not advancing. Nay, they were kneeling.

To their queen.

Beowulf drew a deep, reluctant breath and started up the steps, trailing his axe behind him but keeping his sword up and ready.

She was achingly beautiful, even with the dust cloaking her in light gray. Her bosom moved not at all, and her eyes were closed. There was no sound of breath nor whiff of corruption. Herding magic.

Beowulf reached out and put the edge of his battered sword across her throat as delicately as if he'd been wielding silk, and growled, "Helhild?"

Her eyes snapped open—two amber flames boring into him— and his blade exploded in sparks and shrieking, clanging shards.

Beowulf snatched his numbed hand away, shaking it, and watched those slowly tumbling shards melt away into smoke.

Something tugged at his gaze, and he found himself staring again into the coiling flames of her eyes, as she looked up at him and breathed, "Come to me."

Though the chains held her wrists fast to the arms of the throne, the bodice of her gown parted, and was peeled back by unseen hands. Beowulf's swallow was almost a growl. Aye, she was more beautiful by far than any woman he had ever seen.

Yet in her leaping eyes he saw the hungry glare of the wolves and the rotting gazes of the dripping heads. And he hesitated.

Her eyes flashed anger like a strike of a lightning bolt, a bright and soundless conflagration that brought down utter darkness in an instant.

Out of it, as Beowulf felt hastily behind him with his axe for the first descending step, came racing something like an arrow, or a snake, or a falling star.

Something that glowed a familiar eerie blue. The sword that had hung in the hall.

As Beowulf stumbled down unseen steps, it came for him, flying point-first, as swift as any arrow, leaping through the air hungrily. It wanted his life. Beowulf fell the last few steps, rolled, swung his axe wildly around him to smite any unseen draugr, and ran. If he could get behind a pillar . . .

Moaning, the sword sprang after him. He whirled, lashing out desperately with his axe—and it struck up from under it, plucking him off his heels and dashing him against a pillar.

Blue fire flamed across the stone behind him, icy and alive. It had run him through, and pierced the stone behind him deeply. The King of the Geats struggled against it, bringing his axe up in leaden hands to chop at its guards to try to smash it back out of him. It was lodged solidly, and budged not at all—and Hel take him if he could lift that axe again!

The icy chill was passing, and in its wake came agony that left him gasping and shivering. This was his death, then, at last, alone in the cold dark.

Ghostly lips brushed his, heedless of the blood now welling out of them. That chill kiss seemed to drink both his pain and his strength, leaving him slumped dull and limp. He stared into empty darkness where there should have been a face, and drooled blood.

"Come to me, O King," Helhild's voice murmured.

Slowly, so pale and faint that he could barely see it, her shape formed in the air, face first and then descending.

She floated beside him as if standing, her lips glowing blue against the rose-red of his blood on them, and stretched out one slender wraith-arm to touch the sword.

Transfixed and weakening, Beowulf watched the rosy glow of his blood pass through the witch into the sword, which glowed brighter and moaned in hunger. Eyes of flame glowing in glee, she kissed him again.

"You will be my champion." Her whisper was a purr of triumph. "And wield this blade of Hel in battle for me, and conquer many lands. All the strength of heroes it has stolen for me shall be yours, as you swing it at my bidding, and you shall be my king. And thrall."

Her smile was cold and cruel.

And Beowulf, King of the Geats, thrust himself forward, letting fall his axe with a clang. With all the strength he had left, he drove his hands back against the pillar and shoved, straining and kicking against the carved stone.

"Struggle, doomed hero," the wraith murmured, swirling around him. "Struggle—and suffer."

Beowulf set his teeth, trembling, and thrust his head forward as if it was a ram to strike down the barred doors of keeps, growling like the bear he'd been named for.

And the sword tore free of the stone.

Staggering, panting in pain, he tugged it out of himself—dark emptying wetness tumbling in its wake—as Helhild swirled around him in shrieking anger.

Shaking his head to banish her noise, Beowulf settled his hands around its hilt.

His ears filled with a deafening roar; the roaring of many angry men, shouting faintly but as one. The spirits trapped in the sword were feeding him their fury, dark and hot and sharp, straightening him out of his trembling as their magic set about driving down the pain and healing him.

The sword's blue glow was as bright as a beacon now, Helhild seeming more solid as she darted back from him, hissing in fear and rage.

Her spectral fingertips drew sigils in the air, glowing runes that Beowulf sprang to slash out of existence just as swiftly as she could shape them.

Around and around each other they circled, Beowulf thrusting at the wraith. Ever she drew back out of reach and worked more runes, that he sliced to fading nothingness, as he sprang at her again.

And ever the sword glowed more brightly, its moan now a loud and angry chant, the throne-room as bright as if a blue sun shone on it. In its light, as they turned, Beowulf caught sight of the throne again. A shriveled thing of bones and long raven-dark hair still sat on it, slumped in chains.

And he broke off slicing at runes and hurled himself up the steps, Helhild's frantic shriek chasing him as he brought the laughing blade down on the throne, hacking at the bones there.

They whirled up into the air with a terrible wail, circling and seeking to come together as Beowulf hacked and chopped, hewing the skull against the black stone behind it.

The skull shattered.

Amber fire exploded within it, the sword in his hands exploded into blue roiling fire, and Beowulf, King of the Geats, fell over backward into it, darkness rushing in tinged with fading glows of blue and amber . . . darkness, always darkness, and the draugr . . .

Then there was only darkness.

And then, nothing at all.

† † †

The morning after the wedding was bright and still; a great, contented quiet reigned in all fair Briednir, the royal seat of Orra.

King Ealdred, who could not seem to stop smiling, was sitting on his throne, with his advisor, old Draedrolf, on his usual stool beside it, both their hands cupped around jacks that held not mead nor firewine, but warm broth that steamed up from between their hands when they weren't sipping.

"The queen . . . is well?" old Draedrolf asked carefully. The king's smile widened.

"Very well, and sleeps with a smile on her face," he made reply. "Yester, and the night that followed it, have been the happiest of my life. I am Orra, and three kings stood in this hall and gave me smiles and gifts." Then Ealdred's face clouded. "There should have been four. The greatest came not, for all his fair words."

Draedrolf held up a hand. "Lord King, Beowulf was coming hither, as was promised. Asolt of Gund saw him from afar, walking in the snow with a great company of his thegns, splendid in their armor. Bright-polished in honor of your happy union, not arrayed for battle."

"But what could have befallen them? The Wolfwood swallows hunters and woodcutters without pause, a man here and a man there—but a glittering company of thegns?" Ealdred's frown deepened. "I would speak with Asolt."

Draedrolf made a sign to the thegns who flanked the door. They hastened out and, knowing where to find him, straightaway found Asolt, a man always happy to greet the fresh sun of morning, and hungry besides after all the wedding drink. Roasts aplenty had been brought back nigh-untouched from the tables, to be warmed anew in Ealdred's kitchens.

Asolt came and told the king his truths. At the hearing of them Ealdred of Orra smote the arm of his chair and declared, "We shall seek the King of the Geats, and all the Geats he brought with him—for anything that can slay them is something I want not on my doorstep, and if no peril befell them I like even less the thought of them creeping about Orra, working mischief while I take pleasure with my queen! Draedrolf, do you muster the thegns of your house and kin to stay and guard my Mara and my hall! Asolt, to me! Will you swing sword with my thegns, and show us the way you took through the Wolfwood?"

"I will, and that eagerly," the Gundman made reply. "Let me fetch sword, helm, and all."

Ealdred dismissed Asolt with an eager nod, and the Gundman hurried off through a palace suddenly alive with bustle, as armed men and half-dressed men scurried up stairs and along halls, surly with last night's drink and muttering war-prayers.

† † †

Down they all went, afoot, to look for the King of the Geats. The boots of the king and all his thegns brought the folk of Orrar to their doors blinking in surprise as the royal war-band went down from fair Briednir, down through the streets of Orrar, and out the great gates to the shaws beyond.

A goodly hike through fair steadings brought them to Gutbridge; without pause they tramped across it into the waiting shadow of the Wolfwood.

Where they slowed, marching no longer, but going with caution.

Long they walked, keeping together in a great wide arrow of men—for those who stray off alone in Argundrar are not always seen again, and its gloom quite shut out the bright morning and its happiness with it—without finding more than gnawed and scattered bones of unfortunates who'd met their fates a season gone, or more.

Until, that is, they came to the deepest part of the wood, the place Ealdred's hunters called Haunt of Worse Than Wolves.

There stood a lone man in rich, bright armor, an axe slung on his back and a fair sword drawn in his hand. He was striding slowly, as if in a dream. The sword was unblooded, and the armor and man both looked unmarked, but the thegns with the foremost hunters recoiled from the twin flames of his eyes.

They drew back, and called for Asolt, who went forward. The King of Orra strode with him, sword drawn.

Both men recognized the lone warrior. It was Beowulf, King of the Geats, and his eyes were twin flames of madness, pain, and battle-fury.

"Ealdred?" he asked, his voice slow and hoarse. "Is it truly you? Or more of Helhild's deceit?"

Then his eyes fell upon Asolt, and he smiled, slow and wan. "She cannot have known you, Lord of Gund." He lifted his head, and his eyes lost their fire. "I am back out of nightmare. Her magic is broken."

"Beowulf," Ealdred asked gently, "what befell you?"

The King of the Geats sheathed his sword, and stalked forward.

Many thegns drew their swords, but the King of Orra waved at them to put back their blades and let him come.

Beowulf spread his arms and embraced Ealdred, as the others crowded in close around them.

"I make you poor greeting, king, and come late to your happiness," the Geat said wearily. "I am sorry for that. Have your ears time for a tale far stranger than I could spin from fancy?"

Ealdred grinned, and hugged Beowulf heartily. "They do," he said.

"Then walk with me," Beowulf said. "This way."

† † †

And so they all walked, on into the deep and endless gloom of the Wolfwood, through trees as black as coals and as gnarled and huge as whales storm-broken on rocks. Thegns strode narrow-eyed, watchful for treachery and beasts, their swords glittering ready, as the King of the Geats told a strange tale of Ginnungs-gard and Helhild.

The men of Orra began with silent scoffing, lips a-curl, but as the Geat calmly spoke on, they became as pale as bone, and muttered charms against terrors that had been whispered to them in their cradles.

Then they came to a place where trees grew not, and beneath much-churned moss there were cracked and heaved flagstones underfoot. There, amid clouds of flies, a great company of men in bright armor lay sprawled with swords and daggers in their hands, as if fallen in battle.

There was not a mark on any of them. And they were all dead.

"The fairest blades of Geatdom," Beowulf said grimly. "This was the feasting-hall. Here we first fought her."

Something gleamed where the dead thegns were heaped highest. Something golden.

Gently the men of Orra lifted the fallen and laid them aside, and gasped at what they found beneath.

The tumbled shards of a shattered stone seat black with age, and amid them a great heap of gold and gems. That mound of riches was as long as three men lying boot to helm, and as far across as two sprawled thegns.

It was more than all Briednir held, and King Ealdred's mouth fell open. "What is this?"

"The wealth of Hearheld, Josastein, Skolas, and Tharfrey," Beowulf said with a grim smile, waving a hand at it. "Hail, Ealdred, King of Orra. I am come late, but bring you a goodly wedding gift."

"If the witch Helhild is truly no more, she who haunts all our dreams from when our nurses first warn of her, then this is the smallest part of your gift to me," Ealdred said slowly.

Beowulf's smile widened into sun-brightness. For a moment he swayed, as if he would fall. Then he drew his sword, snake-swift, and leaned on it.

"She is no more," he said wearily. "And now I must go. I crave home, and a lack of fell magic. Will you walk with me, Asolt? All my thegns dead; the walk will be longer, alone."

Ealdred put a hand on Beowulf's arm. "But what will you do?"

"Go back to my people, and sire more thegns," Beowulf told him bitterly, and turned away.

After a few steps he turned back to the Orrar and added gently, "I must tell the kin of these my swordsworn that they died well, in mighty battle, so the hero-songs can be sung. King of Orra, will you burn them with honor, that the wolves not have them?"

"Beowulf," Ealdred said hoarsely, "we will. It shall be done before this night. Look for the smoke behind you as you go—and may you fare safely back to Geatland."

"My thanks," Beowulf said grimly. "I will take my leave now, for the way is long, and walks seem longer to those who walk alone. I was one of many, but will return home just . . . Beowulf."

The two kings nodded to each other, and then the Geat turned and strode off through the trees.

After a moment, Asolt of Gund nodded to Ealdred, and then hurried after Beowulf.

Such a man deserved more than loneliness.

Beowulf never looked back, but Asolt did once. King Ealdred was standing there with all his thegns around him, all staring after Beowulf, and then down at the heap of riches, as if they half expected it to vanish.

But all the coins and gems stayed right where they were. Gleaming.

† † †

No more storms came, but the way seemed long indeed. Asolt made fires at night, and killed things that he roasted over the flames for them both. They heard wolves once or twice, but nothing menaced them—though every night brought a few wisps of dark shadow that chilled as they slid past, seeming to glare at Beowulf.

The King of the Geats heeded them not, and spoke not a word to Asolt, all the way.

Until they came to Geatland, and could see the fair hall that was Beowulf's. Then the grim king turned and clapped the Gundman on the shoulder and said, "Have my thanks, Lord of Gund. I'll not forget this kindness. A journey out of death is one best traveled not alone."

BEOWULF AND THE
MASTER OF HIS CRITICS
Conclusion

°✝°

"These stories are all quite entertaining in a pedestrian sort of way," the Master asserted, "but really they are of no use to me. "Pedestrian."

"Entertaining, yes . . . but not the sort of thing one would study at Oxford . . . or even Cambridge for that matter."

"But don't you realize you are the Beowulf authority? Surely you were staking a claim to such a position with your lecture . . . and sources have even indicated that you were in the process of your own translation of the text."

"What of it, if such a thing is true?"

"Then perhaps my associates can be of some assistance. We have need for such an authority on this tale."

The Oxford magister was beginning to lose his patience.

"I don't see how I can help you. Judging from these tales, as you call them, you are more in need of a Fleet Street editor than a classics scholar. True, there does seem to be a market for such entertainment . . . *Beowulf*, however, was a poem, an epic poem. You might recall that if indeed you had paid any attention to the talk I gave that you claim to have a familiarity with."

"Maybe the stories need a better translation, perhaps by someone such as yourself . . . and we would be willing to make it worth your while"

"Who is this 'we'?"

The man from Cambridge was too late to bite his tongue.

Well, it was all or nothing.

"A certain group of Germanic scholars and benefactors interested in the cultural—"

"Bah!" the Oxford man interrupted.

"Bah?"

"Indeed."

The man from Cambridge was puzzled. Could his advance intelligence have been wrong?

"Forgive me," he implored. "I had heard that you were enamored of Germanic culture."

"Of years past, yes."

"And the Germanic people and their virtues."

"Ah," said the Master. "Is that what this is about? Well now I realize what this is all about. Indeed, I have applauded the Germanic culture with a certain bit of zeal and on occasion I have made reference to certain virtues that seem to be strong among the German people"

"Virtues are to be admired."

"Sometimes," the Master replied, setting down his pipe as if to indicate that the meeting was coming to a close. "The virtues, generic, I was referring to were their patriotism and their obedience, qualities that can be admired but as with great works of literature must be placed in the proper context. No different than the heroic exploits of a larger-than-life warrior doing battle with monsters."

The man from Cambridge realized that he had failed, but gave it one last Apostle try.

"Politics aside, there is a great deal of interest in the Beowulf materials . . . not just these retold fragments but other more intriguing matters as well. I assure you the recompense for your expertise will be quite satisfactory and the work will also be quite enlightening . . . All you would have to do would be to come back to London with me—"

"I have no desire to go traipsing about . . . and besides, I have moved on from Beowulf."

"Moved on?"

"Yes. Beowulf had his Middle Earth, and I shall now have mine. Allen & Unwin have contacted me about a manuscript I've been working on and they are interested in accepting it for publication."

"A serious work of scholarship?"

"A children's book. Now, good day."

He recalled the first time he was shown the mummified arm, the claws blackened by age, the feral skin leathered and tan. Truly monstrous. Whether it was really real was for other judges. The benefactors had an interst in such matters of the occult . . . that and a weakness for Oxford scholars.

Burgess guessed he would have to have better luck with the BBC position . . . and in the long run who really cared about such long-forgotten matters as the Barbarossa? And years hence who would ever remember a Beowulf scholar, pah, children's book author by the name of J. R. R. Tolkien?

Besides, he had masters to serve, and a cause to further . . . and most of all, he had gone desperately long without a drink, and as he recalled, there was a pub betwixt here and the bus stop.

† † †

(Editor's note: There is no evidence that the paths of Guy Burgess of Cambridge and J. R. R. Tolkien of Oxford ever crossed. Prior to joining the BBC in late 1936, Burgess had been assigned to make inroads with various German groups. Nineteen-thirty-six was also the year of Tolkien's Beowulf lecture and the acceptance at Unwin of *The Hobbit*. Nonetheless, stranger paths have crossed and Tolkien's interest in the Germanic tradition might have made him a subject of interest for the various research projects of the Reich, the evil empire of the east that would soon cast its shadows over all Europe.)

A Partial, Annotated Bibliography of the Beowulf Canon Through Today

✣

John Kemble, 1837. *A Translation of the Anglo-Saxon Poem of "Beowulf."*

Benjamin Thorpe, 1855. Close literal translation into English.

Thomas Arnold, 1876. English translation into literal prose.

Henry W. Lumsden, 1881. *Beowulf: An Old English Poem,* done in ballad meter.

James M. Garnett, 1882. *Beowulf: an Anglo-Saxon Poem, and the Fight at Finnsburg.*

John Earle, 1892. *The Deeds of Beowulf: An English Epic of the Eighth Century.*

John Lesslie Hall, 1892. *Beowulf: An Anglo-Saxon Epic Poem, Translated from the Heyne-Socin Text.*

William Morris and Alfred J. Wyatt, 1895. *The Tale of Beowulf, Sometime King of the Weder Geats.*

John R. Clark Hall, 1901.

Chauncey Brewster Tinker, 1902.

Francis B. Gummere, 1909. (One of the more popular public domain verse translations)

Robert K. Gordon, 1923. (Currently available as *Beowulf Unabridged*)

E. Talbot Donaldson, 1966. (Reprinted in *The Norton Anthology* and used as the seminal college text on the subject for many years)

Kevin Crossley-Holland, 1968. *Beowulf: A New Translation.*

Michael Alexander, 1973. *Beowulf: A Verse Translation.*

Howell D. Chickering, Jr., 1977. *Beowulf: A Dual-Language Edition.*

Albert W. Haley, Jr., 1978. *Beowulf.*

Michael Swanton, 1978. *Beowulf: Edited with an Introduction, Notes and New Prose Translation.*

Stanley B. Greenfield, 1982. *A Readable Beowulf: The Old English Epic Newly Translated.*

Ernest J. Kirtland, 1983. *Beowulf.*

Ruth P. M. Lehmann, 1988. *Beowulf: An Imitative Translation.*

Frederick Rebsamen, 1991. *Beowulf: A Verse Translation.*

Seamus Heaney, 1999. *Beowulf.* To the editor's knowledge, this is the first Beowulf translation to make the *New York Times* bestseller list. (It has also replaced the Donaldson in the first volume of *The Norton Anthology of English Literature* from the year 2000.)

R. M. Luizza, 2000. *Beowulf: A New Verse Translation.*

There are also allegedly full translations of *Beowulf* done by J. R. R. Tolkien and another by Randy Lee Eickoff (who previously translated the Ulster Cycle). The Tolkien translation is evidently tied up in an estate squabble and the Eickoff has yet to appear in print.

(Editor's Note: Numerous poets and authors of renown have translated sections of the poem or included sections and/or allusions to it in their work, including Alfred, Lord Tennyson; Henry Wadsworth Longfellow; R. W. Chambers; Richard Wilbur; Kingsley Amis; W. H. Auden; and Jorge Luis Borges. I would also be remiss if I did not include a mention of the poetic contribution by the esteemed author of *Bored of the Rings*, Henry Beard, the short poem "Grendel's Dog" from the collection *Poetry for Cats.*)

BEOWULF IN OTHER MODES
Spin-off Novels:

W. H. Canaway, 1958. *The Ring-Givers* (London: Michael Joseph, 1958). A novel where the monsters become figments of the protagonist's imagination. It incorporates material from eddic poetry and *Hrolf's Saga* to fill out the sixth-century story. In the words of the *Sunday Express*, "An adult novel of blood and action—a kind of Anglo-Saxon *Shane*."

John Gardner, 1971. *Grendel* (New York: Knopf). A first-person narrative by the monster Grendel himself that manages to convey both a sympathetic and philosophical take on the tale . . . at least as seen from the monster's point of view. This is probably the most lauded adaptation of the story, by a professional medievalist and master modern novelist.

Michael Crichton, 1976. *The Eaters of the Dead: The Manuscript of Ibn Fadlan, Relating His Experiences with the Northmen in A.D. 922* (New York: Knopf). Brings together the Arab Ibn Fadlan's *Risala* and the Beowulf story as a pseudo-first-person narrative of thrilling adventure wrapped in mock scholarship complete with fake footnotes. The grendels, a whole race of them, come across as a lost tribe savage Neanderthals (which makes for some witty observations on the part of the Arab narrator who saw his Northern warrior companions as "savage" at least as compared to those he was used to dealing with. (See *The 13th Warrior* under Films at the end of this list.)

June Oldham, 1979. *The Raven Waits*. (London: Abelard-Schuman, Ltd). A novel from the point of view of the *Beowulf* bard/poet witnessing the events he would later cast into an epic.

Larry Niven, Jerry Pournelle, and Steven Barnes, 1987. *The Legacy of Heorot* (New York: Simon and Schuster). *Beowulf* recast as a science fiction novel of interplanetary colonization where the monster that "the grendels" appear as is a natural response to humans disturbing ecological balance on the planet Tau Ceti Four. Beowulf is cast as security chief Cadmann Weyland who deals with the threat amidst numerous bloody encounters (The sequel is *Beowulf's Children*, 1995). (Note: Simon Green also used the Grendel moniker on a creature construct/monster in his *Deathstalker* novels.)

Poul Anderson, 1988. *Hrolf Kraki's Saga* (New York: Baen). A retelling of the saga as a modern fantasy novel of the northern mythos complete with the Beowulf themes and motifs.

Tom Holt, 1988. *Who's Afraid of Beowulf?* (London: Macmillan). Parody novel of

Viking mythos who intrude upon our modern world, including appearances by Arvarodd (Arrow-Odd) and Hrolf Kraki, and, of course, Beowulf. (Later republished as *Expecting Beowulf*, in 2002, as a closer tie-in to Holt's biggest success *Expecting Someone Taller*.)

Parke Godwin, 1995. *The Tower of Beowulf* (New York: Morrow). Fantasy novel in which Grendel's mother is Loki's ugly daughter by a giantess, whom he turns into a loathly lady—a magical female capable of appearing beautiful. In her lovely aspect she seduces "Shild" and gives birth to his son Grendel. Godwin has recast several other "mythos" in this historical romance genre including the Arthurian story as *Firelord*, St. Patrick as *The Last Rainbow*, and Robin Hood as *Sherwood* . . . so it was only a matter of time for him to get around to Beowulf.

Frank Schaeffer, 1996. *Whose Song Is Sung* (New York: Tor). The novel is subtitled "A Narrative of the Travels of Musculus Herodes Formosus, Known as Musculus the Dwarf, through Barbarian Territories, Including an Account of His Sojourn with the Northmen, and a True Description of the Demise of a Monster Known as the grundbur at the Hands of the Hero, Beowulf, and certain other Related Incidents, which elsewhere have been Misrepresented." The subtitle says it all and the execution is entertainingly exceptional. (Note: this is not the same Frank Schaeffer who wrote *Shane*.)

OTHER MEDIA AND ART
Music:

Roger Bourland, "Beowulf, A Pageant," 1979.

Kenneth Cole, "Beowulf, A Rock Musical," 1980.

MARILLION, "Grendel," 1996 (seventeen-minute-long hard rock song).

Films:

Grendel, Grendel, Grendel (90 min), 1982. Animated film with screenplay by Bruce Sweaton based on Gardner's *Grendel* of 1971. Produced by Satori Films,

Australia. Geats and Danes speak in outback Aussie, the monsters in posh Brit. Faithful to Gardner's source material, the monster provides the voice-over narration. Grendel's voice: Peter Ustinov, Beowulf's voice: Keith Mitchell.

The 13th Warrior (102 min), 1999. Based on Crichton's 1976 novel *The Eaters of the Dead*, this film sat on the shelf for over a year during the post-*Jurassic Park* Crichton film boom as they tried to come up with a different title. Directed by John McTiernan with a Crichton screenplay, the adaptation faithfully combines the historical AD 922 journey of the Arab Ibn Fadlan (Antonio Banderas) with the Beowulf–Grendel storyline with a token bow to pseudo-historical accuracy and mock scholarship.

Beowulf (93 min), 2000. A futuristic post-holocaust fantasy setting with Christopher Lambert as Beowulf, a half-demon spawn who must suppress his affinity for evil by battling its manifestations, in this case Grendel. Graham Barker directed this interesting amalgam of *Mad Max*, *Predator*, and *Highlander* with dynamic martial arts bouts reminiscent of *Mortal Kombat*, and an interesting take on Grendel's parentage that allows for several steamy seduction scenes.

Beowulf & Grendel (2005). Canadian-produced version of the tale directed by Sturla Gunnarsson with an accent on adventure and violence (The film's tagline was "Heads will roll!"). Rumor has it that it was rushed through production to beat the Zemeckis film. The title characters were played by Gerard Butler and Ingvar Eggert Sigurosson heading a joint Canadian–Icelandic cast.

Beowulf (2007). Robert Zemeckis helmed production with a script by Neil Gaiman and Richard and Roger Avary utilizing motion capture computer-generated animation (that Zemeckis had previously used in his film version of *The Polar Express*). An all-star pantheon of talents provided the voices and personality profiles of the main characters, including Ray Winstone as Beowulf, Anthony Hopkins as King Hrothgar, John Malkovich as Unferth, Crispin Glover as Grendel, and Angelina Jolie as Grendel's mother.

(It has also been duly noted that the Beverly Cross screenplay for Ray Harryhausen's Perseus epic *Clash of the Titans* utilizes a structure borrowed from the

Beowulf tale whereby the hero confronts a trilogy of challenges—a demon-spawn named Calibos in the place of Grendel, a Medusa in the place of Grendel's mother (though the mother of Calibos is indeed the instigator of the monstrous threat to the city that Perseus has sworn to protect), and the Kraken in the place of the dragon.)

(It might also be mentioned that the plot to *The Brotherhood of the Wolf* also resembles parts of the Beowulf tale . . . but that film was supposed to have been based on a true story.)

Television:

Star Trek Voyager (1995). Episode entitled "Heroes and Demons" uses the Beowulf storyline and setting as the basis for a holodeck program-gone-astray episode.

Xena, Warrior Princess (2001). A three-episode arc (Titles: "The Rheingold," "The Ring," and "Return of the Valkyrie") that merged the Wagnerian Ring cycle with the Beowulf–Grendel mythos with a touch of Tolkien thrown in for good measure. Here Grendel is Grindl, the child of a monstrously transformed Grinhilda, mistress of Odin, fallen under the omnipotent thrall of das Rheingold. Beowulf also appears as an emissary of Odin's and a temporary warrior sidekick for the warrior princess.

Comics:

Michael Uslan. *Beowulf: Dragon-Slayer* (New York: DC Comics 1975–76). Comic book serial that may have originally been intended as a possible launch for a new monthly comic book series. The first is a "Conan-esque" retelling of the battle with Grendel. The five sequels have Beowulf and his busty sidekick Nan-zee (a sexy female substitute for Wiglaf) engaging in further adventures straying from the original mythos, including battle, with a minotaur, Dracula, and aliens.

Jerry Bingham. *Beowulf* (Evanston: First Comics, 1984). Lavishly illustrated graphic novel adaptation of the tale, whereby the narrative is told via voice-over (as Hal Foster did with his classic *Prince Valiant* comic strip) with the accent on Conan-esque scenes of action. Other titles in this limited series included *Conan the Reaver* and *Kull—The Vale of the Shadow.*

Gareth Hinds. *Beowulf* (published in three issues and as a single compilation volume) (Cambridge: TheComic.Com, 1999). Fairly faithful graphic illustration/adaptation of the 1910 Francis B. Gummerre verse translation.

Brian Augustyn. *Beowulf: Gods and Monsters* (Toronto: Speakeasy Comics, 2005). The latest incarnation of the mythos with a dose of *Highlander* immortality thrown in as the legendary warrior, sword at side, continues his battle against evil forces into the future.

Acknowledgments

Special thanks to Frank Weimann, Philip Turner, and Victoria Weimann for their assistance on this project.

Contributors

✚

Lynn Abbey, ex-New Yorker, ex-Michigander, and ex-Okla-homan, moved to Florida in 1997 which she says is nice, but she misses the snow. Her first novel, *Daughter of the Bright Moon*, was published in 1978. Since then she's published more than two dozen novels, mainly fantasies, the most recent of which is *Rifkind's Challenge*, a sequel to her first novel. She is also respon-sible for the resurrection of the *Thieves' World* series, now pub-lished by Tor. She says she writes fantasies because when her imagination gets going, it's full of magic, intrigue, and the colors of a stained-glass window. If science fiction is the fiction of possible futures, then fantasy is the fiction of possible histories.

Wolfgang Baur lives in Seattle with his wife, his daughter, and their ludicrous dog, a Tibetan Spaniel. He writes primarily for magazines and for the Web, on topics from ghouls to gambling to the 1001 Arabian Nights. Baur first wrestled with Beowulf in high school (Baur lost), when reading John Gardner's *Grendel*. Wolf-gang Baur started his game career at the heart of the role-playing game industry at TSR in Lake Geneva. He started as the assistant editor at *Dungeon* magazine, and by the time he left he was the editor of *Dragon* magazine and had been involved with freelance design and editing for Planescape, Al-Qadim, and almost every other setting of the early to mid-'90s role-playing scene. He is also a big fan of the wide-ranging work of Anonymous.

Born in 1959 in what is now Toronto, **Ed Greenwood** is an avid fantasy and science fiction writer, collector, and reader, whose main claim to fame is his creation of The Forgotten Realms(r) (arguably the largest and most detailed fantasy world setting ever). He is an award-winning game designer, a best-selling fantasy author, and a well-read scholar of the literature of the fantastic.

Jeff Grubb is the best-selling author of fifteen novels and over thirty short stories, many of them set in the universes he helped create with others. He is also an award-winning game designer. This short story is set in the oldest shared universe he has been a part of to date. He lives in Seattle with his wife and two cats.

Brian M. Thomsen is the author of over thirty short stories and articles and two fantasy novels, as well as such nonfiction works as *Ireland's Most Wanted*, *The Awful Truths*, and *Man of Two Worlds*. He has also edited *Shadows of Blue & Gray—The Civil War Writings of Ambrose Bierce*, *Commanding Voices of Blue & Gray*, the critically acclaimed *The American Fantasy Tradition*, and *The Man in the Arena—Selected Writings of Theodore Roosevelt*, as well as co-edited with Eric Haney *Beyond Shock and Awe* and with Bill Fawcett *You Did What?!!* He grew up in Rockaway Beach, attended Regis High School in New York City, and now resides in Brooklyn with his loving wife Donna and the two extremely talented cats Sparky and Minx.